The Tortoises

Also by Veza Canetti
Available from New Directions

YELLOW STREET

VEZA CANETTI

The Tortoises

Translated from the German by
IAN MITCHELL

New Directions

Design by Semadar Megged
First published clothbound in 2001
Manufactured in the United States of America.
New Directions Books are printed on acid-free paper.
Published simultaneously in Canada by Penguin Books Canada Limited.

Library of Congress Cataloging-in-Publication Data:

Canetti, Veza, 1897–1963.
[Schildkröten. English]
The tortoises / Veza Canetti ; translated from the German by Ian Mitchell.
   p. cm.
ISBN 0-8112-1468-0 (alk. paper)
I. Mitchell, Ian.   II. Title.

PT2605.A588 S3513   2001
833'.912—dc21   2001037026

New Directions Books are published for James Laughlin
by New Directions Publishing Corporation
80 Eighth Avenue, New York 10011

CONTENTS

PART ONE

I.	The Cross	3
II.	A Mushroom, But Not a Palatable One	36
III.	Conspiracy in the Garden	44
IV.	The Banquet	66
V.	About Furniture	89
VI.	An Airplane Takes Off	103
VII.	Moving Out	116

PART TWO

VIII.	Moving In	123
VIIIa.		140
IX.	Yom Kippur, the Day of Atonement	148
X.	The Innocents	161
XI.	The Great Fire	168
XII.	The Airplane Crashes	179
XIII.	Mistaken Identity	194
XIV.	November	199
XV.	The Hospital of the Sorrows	211
XVI.	How Werner Traveled	224

Postscript 233

Veza Canetti: A Chronicle of Her Life 237

The Tortoises

Part One

1. THE CROSS

Eva, going up the hill, kept her head down. She fixed her gaze firmly on the earth, as if she were searching the ground. She was walking very slowly.

To right and left of the avenue, broad parks with lush trees stretched out in the sunshine. In the parks stood the villas.

Eva breathed in the fragrance of the roses with no real pleasure. She was exhausted, and once, she stopped.

As she moved on, her face lifted, without her volition, to the sky, as if striving upwards with longing. New features showed in that face, a new sorrow cut hard lines across it, cutting through the soft shadows. It must have been a beautiful face. When she lowered her head once again, her dark hair fell across it.

The path leveled out and now wild shrubs jutted out of the earth. They grew in profusion over a lattice gate, hiding it from sight. Eva laid her hand on the gate. Fatigue paralyzed her will. She stood, incapable of pushing the gate open. Suddenly, it easily gave way to her light touch and swung wide open.

The unexpected yielding of the gate relieved her of any need for effort. She was standing, it seemed instinctively, in the garden.

Then she flinched violently. From the balcony, there hung down, broad and long, a flag, clinging to the wall all the way down to the ground, mercilessly spreading out its red color. It trembled and blazed in the breeze, dilating to gigantic proportions, and then, abruptly, it shriveled away again.

Now a man appeared, who had been standing on the balcony, but hidden from view. He spread his arms and, overshadowed by the flag, he made a sinister picture. His eyes seemed embedded in hollow cheeks. He tugged irritably at the rope and pulled the flag out to its full breadth. Once more it rose, swollen and bru-

3

tal. Satisfied, he now looked down at it, his face narrowing even more as he lowered it. The flag looked like blood. Like blood that flows, that oozes, that dries and is freshened up again. He gave it a vigorous flourish. It swept in a blazing wave across the ground.

Eva tried to hurry past, but the flag billowed out as far as the sloping drive of the house, sweeping over it, blocking her way; she was unable to retreat, became entangled, and tumbled to the ground.

Anyone lying on the ground is admitting defeat. One has nothing more to bear, if one is lying prone. No pride is left, and there is no load to carry either. One is relieved of any burdens.

She directed her gaze upwards and saw the man smiling. The way Death smiles. He was looking at her, with hollow eyes. She stood up, disentangled herself from the flag and hurried into the house.

The house had an entrance hall in subdued colors. The walls were rather scratched and dented, but meticulously clean. Two pillars supported the second floor; everything looked a little sleepy and bewitched.

As if still chased by the red billows, Eva sought refuge in her own apartment. Quietly, she opened the door to one room which lay apart from the long row of rooms on the south side. Like a monastery cell, gleaming bookshelves ran along the walls. The wall on its south side opened on to the balcony with the flag.

The man reading at the finely polished table in the middle of the room was engrossed in a book. Nevertheless, as the door swung on its hinges, he turned and smiled.

A person's smile can reveal much about his character, his goodness, his profundity, his receptiveness to all that life is. Or it may expose and unmask him. In this instance, however, nothing of that sort was to be feared. There is a kind of smile, the unveiling of which overpowers the beholder.

Eva recovered her composure when she saw his smile, and quickly closing the door, she tiptoed out on to the balcony.

The hero with the banner had disappeared. Possibly he could have climbed down it. In fact, there he was, standing in the garden, contentedly inspecting the flag which had now been tamed to its full width and obeyed him. With a cruel smile, he strode out of the garden, turned once more and finally strolled off down the hill.

The man reading in his library seemed completely engrossed once again and could not have noticed the incident. It seemed as if he were immersing himself intentionally in another mind.

How, she thought, do you go about telling him, as if it were a piece of good news or something perfectly natural and straightforward? How do you manage to change their language in such a way that it might be heard here? The language of those men with a death's-head as the symbol of their power.

She stepped back into the room from the balcony and touched him lightly on the shoulder. She tried to smile; it cut into her face, leaving only the shadows. Concerned, he stood up and led her out on to the balcony. Without a word, he gestured towards the flag.

"Is it this flag that is alarming you?"

Her face wore that look which he loved so, because it restrained with so much strength all that it needed to express so forcefully.

"Let me tell you a story. About our biggest winegrower down in the village. On no account would he attach a flag to his house, so they bring one and nail it to his balcony themselves. The next day, of course, it has disappeared. They put up another one, which is in tatters on the third day, as if it had been slashed by a thousand pairs of scissors. Again they drag another flag along, and this one stays put. It glows red, people walk past and laugh, the whole village parades by, everyone brings a friend from the neighboring village, everybody has fun with it. Because overnight, you see, the flag's colors have run together into one single plain surface. The swastika has disappeared, the whole thing is red all over, showing no white ground, no black brand.

"A fourth flag is brought along, firmly fixed along each edge, and the black cross is burned into it. The next day, there is a cross there, but not the swastika. A brown crucifix with the Saviour is hanging in the middle—Christ bleeding to death and coloring the flag with His blood. Since that time, the winegrower no longer has a flag, but the cross instead. And he will keep the cross."

He was stepping back into the study when she suddenly called to him and pointed to the balcony:

"The flag has shriveled up again!"

She followed him into the silent vaulted room, spacious and endowed with dignity by the rows of books. She could hardly bring herself to say it:

"Our winegrower's wife spoke to me today. She says the sky presaged it all. First it was garish red, in the depths of the night, and that was the omen. Then the comet appeared, and that's a sign of disaster. Now she's praying that an earthquake won't come as well; if an earthquake comes, that means war."

"The earthquake has come, Eva."

She stared at him like some lost creature. Like something no longer built on anything but hope. Like someone trying to walk on the sea. She was unable to express it.

"You haven't told me, Eva, what was decided down there."

She felt as if she were speaking casually, as if her expression was firm and calm. She was unaware that even her lips had blanched: "You have to leave the country, Kain."

He turned his head to the side and looked out over the landscape. Only the slight pulsing of his throat betrayed him. Those were the ranges of hills and meadows that belonged to him, and the trees up there, lining the horizon, pointing towards the sky. This was the house, as if designed for him, a house that irritated the bourgeois and delighted the artist because it was so rambling in its construction, so lavish, with absurd hideaway corners. With towers above the roof-line and below it, with spiral staircases even in the rooms. The garden as big as the whole country. A ridiculous garden. Everything here overgrown and running rampant. To think that wild proliferation can be beautiful, even the weeds that children pull out down there. They look as small as bugs and as large as turnips. The Venus, there, casting a black shadow, she is alive—or where would she get a shadow from? Suppose someone carries you off from here in your sleep, catches you unaware, or sets you upon the back of a bird, so that, lost in dreams and amazement, you forget what you have to leave behind. Suppose someone lands an airplane in front of the house and you climb in and fly off, straight to the island of happiness. . . .

"We will have to leave the country, and retreat, exhausted, not in triumph. There will be struggle, and fear, mortal fear. If only it does not take too long, so that faces do not change too."

She averted her gaze quickly. How, just how, can she come out and say it—the faces have already changed! Here they are experiencing how evil feelings can be awakened, how the fist holds them down or lets them go, simply according to the fist's own whim.

"What are you so frightened of today, what is it, really?" He bent affectionately towards her.

It was the ringing of the bell that startled her so violently. Every ring, here and all the time. The ringing at the door, not the church bells. The ringing at the door.

"But the bell hasn't rung, not the doorbell. The small church bell has tolled, and in the church tower the baker's wife has been pulling the bell-rope. That's how peaceful things are up here. There's nothing of death and violence."

"The German officer frightens me, the one who has just moved in. With that blonde woman. I walk past that woman and

I only come up to her shoulder. It weighs me down, I slink past with my head lowered. It's as if to show his contempt that he has brought that woman with him, that German woman who looks as if she has been fetched from the woods and dragged here by her pigtails. Forcibly."

"Yes," he says. "That's exactly the way she looks, proud but as if she had been carried off by force. And far too beautiful to engender hatred."

"And are you able to believe that nothing of it will stick to her? Nothing of the new laws? You're out of touch, Kain. Every day, new laws rain down on us, laws against people with black hair. In the end, it will have its effect on her, too."

He gazed at her, who, after all, had never been capable of kindling hatred. And even this woman, with her strength of character, had become insecure.

"If you like that woman, your Dürer figure, then she will like you too, it's always a reciprocal thing. Beautiful women like to throw their arms round each other's necks."

"But they have their ears filled with the speeches of their leaders; if they go along with them, soon there will be no room left in the big cemetery. The Jewish community is going to have to buy a large extension to it. . . ."

"But the people are not going to let themselves be fooled."

"That's what you think," she said. "You can think that way because, inside, you are at peace. Because you are not affected by these glances. Because your features happen to be Slavic and your eyes light in color. But as for me—people suddenly hate me, so much so that I hate myself," she admitted with vehemence. She walks past a German woman and wishes she could sink to her knees and cry out, accusing heaven and earth. One is black, and all around is blackness. And like a gloomy, sinister shadow, one slinks like a slave past the painful glances.

"Who would look maliciously at you, Eva!"

"It may well be that I can feel it and cannot prove it. But feel it I certainly do! And how that can break one's pride! I am afraid—the children in the street, throwing stones at me, that's what I am afraid of, stupid as it may sound."

"Come now, Eva!" He stroked her hair. "What you fear is something quite different. Is it something you have experienced, has someone threatened you, written something in a letter, told you something?—I don't know what. If only you could put it into words, it's such a torment when you repress it!"

"That man. . . ," she stammered, going pale at her own words. "That frightful man . . . who has draped the flag across the balcony . . . like an evil omen . . . now he's standing in the avenue . . . there he is, standing there!"

Apprehensively, she points to the avenue through the garden.

"Well, why look down, then? Keep your head up and look upwards! Climb the towers and look out at the countryside! You haven't been up to the tower for a long time, and besides I have prepared a surprise for you. I've brought it down now, otherwise it will pine away, your surprise."

He opened a box. In it lay a tortoise, on a bed of grass. He had rescued it from humiliation. The new masters are not satisfied with hanging up their flags, the swastika is springing up everywhere till people are sick and tired of it.

"Down in the village, the wood-carver is selling in his stall, as souvenirs of this happiest city in all Central Europe, tortoises branded with a swastika, burned for all time into their shells. This one has been saved. To think that the swastika was to live on in the animal even after the idea that had implanted it there had already begun to decay. The Chinese say that the tortoise lives to a very old age; they consider it an oracular animal. They heat the shell until it glows and read their future in its patterns."

"And how are we supposed to feed it?"

"With a handful of grass."

"How helpless it is. Now it has fallen over and can't right itself. Lying on its back it would be bound to starve, no matter how modest its needs. Let's take it into the sun, to the swallows," said Eva.

With the tortoise carefully bedded down, they went up the spiral staircase to one of the rooms in the tower. Hidden behind a concealed door, there was a little loggia. The swallows had found everything peaceful and comfortable here and had built a nest in the window-frame. Now the tortoise would have its home along with them.

Eva set the box down in the sun. Then she picked up the animal on the flat of her hand, in order to admire its head. Suddenly startled, she hastily put it back. Was even the sun itself blinded, that it should bring this to light! Was it a portent? A Chinese oracle? There it was, quite distinct to her, the detested symbol.

"Can you see something?" she asked, full of trepidation.

He leaned over the enigmatic creature, amazement in his eyes. Into the network of markings on the shell, nature had woven a fantastic figure, a swastika. Dark and barely discernible against the background. Not visible to every eye.

"A rock on St. Helena anticipated the head of Napoleon, even before he appeared there. Every traveler sees it that way, Eva, although only since Napoleon was imprisoned there. It is we who give form to the formless."

"But Napoleon died there." In horror, she stared at the little animal, lying there in the sun like a terrible secret. "We had better go. Up here, we can't hear if the doorbell rings." She covered up the box with a woollen cloth, to muffle the power of the magic spell.

"In that case, it would almost be better if we stayed up here."

Slowly, they went down the stairs. In the spacious room, the spell was broken.

"Won't the swallows torment it?"

"It's only large birds that do that. Vultures like to swoop down on tortoises."

"But then it would hide away in its shell."

"That doesn't do any good. The vulture grabs it in its claws and carries it high into the air. Then it lets it drop, to smash to pieces on a rock. So it can scoop out the tender flesh at its leisure."

"That's sinister. Every large bird of prey is sinister. Because it has nothing human about it, apart from one thing—its predatory grasp. It's like a symbol."

"One behind which Zeus himself hides when he goes out in search of prey. But why are you so frightened by your own thoughts, Eva, what is it about them that so terrifies you?"

"My God, no . . . it's something else . . . the doorbell is ringing."

The condemned man, facing his execution, behaves in curious ways. It can happen that he walks erect to the scaffold to meet his death, this is not infrequent with political criminals; those heroes die with the declaration of their beliefs on their lips. The common dastardly murderer breaks down like a coward. Indeed, many a murderer has been seen to behave so wretchedly that one had to ask oneself where they summoned up the miserable courage for their crimes. They have to be carried to the place of execution and dispatched, unconscious, into another world. Of course, there are also others who have trod that terrible path in apathy, so devoid of emotion that one then wondered whether they knew what was going on, did they have no heart in their body, not even for themselves? When, however, a fanatic treads the final path, sometimes it is as if some god were protecting him against the ability to envisage what is about to happen to him.

Fully conscious, and with a deathly chill upon you, you make your way to the door when the bell rings. You open it and stand in their way, because their way is strewn with corpses.

The bell rang, rang a second time.

What if it signified the end, that ringing? What if a man

dressed in black were standing outside, with the death's-head on his pommel and his cap? What if this is the last response? If the man is already outside and demands entry?

Icy-cold, Eva opened the door.

In the doorway stood a young girl.

She is blonde and her hair tumbles over her face. Her tall figure overpowers her sailor-suit. It is almost as if no dress were there at all, so proudly does her body assert itself. Her strong shoulders sweep broadly out. The girl is self-assured, yet she hesitates on the threshold. She looks at Eva inquiringly and enters only when the latter smiles. She goes on, still hesitantly, through the second door and into the spacious room, the one with the broad balcony. He is sitting far away, very far away, she moves towards him, and has much to conceal: the fact that her hands are trembling, that she is blushing! If only she were not so young; a mature person knows how to compose herself. This way, everything is written on one's face, and a man like this is especially able to read it.

Kain holds out his hand to her and is happy to see her.

The room is transformed.

Is it the young girl who has dispelled the shadows? Her body seems to drive them out and to take the burden of these two people on to herself without being aware of it. Because Eva, too, behind her, Eva is laughing.

"It's a good thing that I live next door," declares Hilde, and it is not clear whether she means good for her, or good for her older friends whom she has come to visit. She sits down on the edge of the divan.

Eva thinks, how tall she is, she sits as if hovering, with that radiant body, as if she were as light as a feather.

"It is indeed a pleasure that you live next door, Fräulein Hilde. Did you mean something more by that, or was it simply a general remark?" He smiled.

"Actually, I do have something to tell you!" She is still

breathless, still diffident, but she is also relishing the notion that she will succeed in arousing this man's interest. He has turned his hand to all sorts of things, has listened to lectures, has acquired large amounts of learning, he thinks ahead, and what he doesn't know, he works out for himself. Undoubtedly that is the way with all writers, they have that vision which can see into your head, as if your eyes were made of glass. It hypnotizes you, you can feel it, right into your heart.

"It must certainly be something interesting, if Hilde pays us a surprise visit," says Eva kindly. "And she's so hot and bothered, her cheeks all flushed like a child's. And forever squinting down into the avenue. What's going on there that is so crucial?"

But then, sitting there is precisely the specimen—the very type of person that is supposed to terrify Eva. How stupid that theory is! What is there about this girl that is different and accentuated, what characterizes her as not "Aryan"? Not even the lack of regular proportions about the features, something commonly found among the townswomen here and, in this girl's case, attractive.

"It'll be the flag on our balcony. But I did not hang it there myself, I can assure you."

"I know that." Hilde blinks, contented and inscrutable, like a cat in the sunshine. "And I know something else besides; I know who did put it up! I know the man!"

Kain sits down in the armchair, prepared for anything.

"What would you say if I were to get you out of Austria in an airplane? If only I had learned to fly—I could do with that now! What would you both say to that, Eva?"

"That it's good to be so young. Then one enjoys life, and onlookers who share your enjoyment can distinguish enthusiasm from wishes and possibilities."

"Now you're not taking me seriously, and you're going to be ashamed of that in a moment. What an experience I've just had!"

The bow on her blouse is flapping around and is as red as her mouth. Her neck juts well out of the fold of her collar.

"I shall do it! I shall get you both out! You'll be amazed! The whole city will be amazed! We'll rise up over the country and leave it behind with contempt. From high above. We'll spit down on it!"

And now Hilde tells her tale. For this distrust is paralyzing. One loses belief in oneself if one hesitates too long.

Hilde has had an interesting experience. With a man who looks like a bare branch in winter. He is standing in the avenue fixing a flag to the aspen tree, stretching it across the breadth of the allée and tying it to the telegraph pole. Anyone who approaches not wearing a swastika is stopped.

Frau Wlk wishes to pass. She is a cleaning-woman and cleans the house in which Hilde sits at this very moment. She originally comes from a village not far from Prague and is not wearing a swastika. Thin and careworn, she stands there, and one feels the man cannot have anything against her. But she has a sense of humor. She opens her jacket, and across her chest she is wearing a huge picture of the Führer, a swastika, a harvest posy, a cornflower and an imitation Party badge. She is barked at for keeping her convictions hidden, instead of displaying them openly.

Behind her, the landlady comes toddling up, the landlady of this selfsame house in which Frau Wlk does the cleaning and in which Hilde is now a guest. She, too, is not wearing a badge, but she is treated mildly. For her National Socialist sympathies are well known. A rich man does not carry money about his person.

Now, with heart and soul, she is for the new order, the race. Now, it is the Führer who is worshipped, and not the man on the cross. That is what this flag means. The Führer has decreed: men and women are Aryan. They are trusting. They believe in him and bow down before him. They refrain from all individual thoughts, renounce all independent authority. They place themselves under the power of the Führer. He will take care of them. Better than Jesus Christ.

In order to defend his sovereignty, the Führer has set in place his satellites. They lie in wait in the streets and squares. And make sure that everyone submits.

Fortunately, Hilde is blonde. And for that reason, the man by the flag forgets his mission and strikes up a conversation with her. Hilde stops, because this is an SA man of high rank, he assures her of that. And also that he will create order and will take firm action. Whoever offers obedience has nothing to fear. But why is she not wearing a swastika?

Because she is a Jew, says Hilde.

The man is dumbfounded. The flag droops from the telegraph pole and weeps. Isn't there some mistake? Wasn't she abducted as a child? Is it not that her mother is Aryan and, forced into marriage by the banker, has then taken her revenge with the gardener's boy? Mixed up the banker with the gardener's boy? For he must be a banker, her Papa, that's obvious from the string of pearls at her throat and the fine stockings.

No, nothing of that is true. Papa is a scholar. Her grandmother was tall and fair, like Hilde herself, but she came from the ghetto. Mama, yes, Mama is dark and already inclining to stoutness, Hilde admits, but other people are even fatter.

The man is moved by such frankness. It is a mark of the representatives of his party that they protect the weak. He offers her his protection. Is she not afraid of going on further? He will accompany her. She thanks him, but she is not afraid. She lives here, just up there in the next villa, and it's her villa, Papa's villa.

That's the villa without a flag, he says pensively. He is sorry but he cannot do her the honor of planting one there, precisely because of that grandmother from the ghetto. For only people of Aryan descent are members of the master race. The others are slaves and will be put in their place, they will have to serve the Teutons, there are no two ways about that, the Teutons who are about to rise up and become masters of the world. Of course, if a girl is beautiful, then she is a beautiful slave. And things always go well for a beautiful slave. And she may ask a favor of him: he is waiting.

She has one to ask right away, she says. Posters have been put up on all the buildings saying that we are bad, don't deserve to be living here, we are base and nasty and should go away. There is nothing left for us but to leave the country. There are a lot of problems about that; no one is permitted to take any of their possessions with them, and no foreign country is willing to let beggars in. To put it bluntly, you can't get a visa. She would go to any expense, and would like to get out. She is telling him this because she can see the pilot's insignia on his uniform. She would dearly love to fly out of the country. It would be a mere trifle for him to take her across the border.

He laughs. It's not as simple as that. There is strict security in place. Especially at the airfield. Everyone is interrogated separately and stopped and searched. Even Aryans have to put up with being checked, for there are traitors who do not want to fulfill their duties here. Even if, in her case, one would like to forget . . . But there is another way. She should buy herself an airplane. That would work.

She claps her hands in joy. But then he's forgetting another thing. Who would sell it to her?

He has to think about that. Of course, it's difficult. It's almost impossible. But not for him. He can buy it for her—she need not even come into it. She has to remain silent. All she has to do is to keep quiet, at all costs. Otherwise, everything will change and will turn against her with the utmost severity. Any suspicion would fall on her, he himself is above that. An SA man does not take bribes.

He will think it over and meet her tomorrow. And let her know. To meet any eventuality she should bring the down payment with her. Naturally, this involves a figure which is more than a mere gratuity. She is buying an airplane, not a horse.

When Hilde had reached this point in her story, she was interrupted. And indeed, both her listeners began speaking at the same time, each horrified for a different reason. Kain prophesied an unhappy end to this deal. He described to her how the man would take her money and then lock her up to prevent her from letting a word of this get out. (He was exaggerating, in order to frighten her.)

She doesn't want the airplane for herself, she says, her feelings hurt. Nor does she want it for her parents. It is for her friends here, so that Eva does not always get a fright every time the doorbell rings. So that they can climb in and, in a few hours, land on the island. And she looked at Kain with eyes that would have thrown a harder man into confusion.

But Eva will not be moved. People are being humiliated, in these times and in this city. But one does not give in to it. One does not meet with an SA man, one does not permit him such presumption. She will not countenance this rendezvous!

"If that man is standing down there," Kain then blurted out, bringing the story to a complete stop, "and Werner happens to come up here! Werner, who does not take kindly to being stopped. Who believes in nothing. And will never believe that he has been totally deprived of all rights. That he is a foreigner, an *untermensch*, a thief, an exploiter, a molester of children—worse than all that since he is 'non-Aryan.' Even though he was in fact the first to be dismissed from his institute because his nose crooks just a tiny bit downwards. He still cannot believe that there really is such a thing as this Führer."

Kain was very worried about Werner, his brother. Whom he so resembled outwardly, and yet did not resemble, because his own nose turned upwards, fortunately for Kain, against whom the new order knew so much, namely that he was a writer, independent in his work and not "Aryan."

Eva responded, her mind elsewhere. Werner wouldn't be coming, since he never came anyway. There was nothing to interest him up here. No new stones to discover. And apart from that he saw no reason to come up here. Brotherly love, perhaps? Or maybe because the older brother might feel he should be worried about the younger one, in times like these? No, Werner wasn't like that.

"No new stones?" Now Hilde was taking an interest.

Werner is a geologist, she is told. Rocks mean everything to him, and for that reason he has no intention of leaving. That's the secret. He has a visa and won't leave. With every fiber of his being, he is bound to this land. He is welded to this place.

"He's like a tortoise," Kain explains. "It clings to cliffs and blends in with the rock. It has a hard life, if it falls on its back. It is bound to starve, it cannot right itself. Its shell is its house, and, at the same time, its death. Werner's house is his homeland."

"And this tortoise is your brother?"

Kain himself was startled by his own comparison.

"I'd so terribly love to get to know him."

"He's a confirmed bachelor," replied Eva. "His rocks mean everything to him, rocks that he brings home and labels with loving care."

Hilde was hurt. She wasn't planning to marry him, was she?

If she is offended at this early stage, before she has even seen him, what will happen when she does, thought Kain. Werner is contrary and gruff. Yet anyone with vision must be amazed by his pure, clear eyes, which tell his whole story so frankly. Not that that is of any importance to him. He doesn't care what other people think. Nor does he conceal anything. He has nothing but his uprightness, and that he has no need to conceal.

"I watched him recently, standing at his shelves. Carefully, he touched a stone, stroked it tenderly, picked it up, smiled, and his beautiful eyes became quite bright. But all of a sudden he recoiled. He was remembering that it no longer belonged to him, and he replaced it as if it were a glowing coal. He no longer has any rights in his own country. He won't even let me have a proper look at his collection."

"Because you're only a woman."

"He sounds to me more like a fat, prickly cactus. To think you have a brother like that!"

"I've always felt so deeply sorry for the wolf in Schönbrunn. He dashes back and forth in his little cage, until he is exhausted, then he drinks and, refreshed, goes on rushing about, in a state of gloomy agitation. That's how it is with my brother. He has imprisoned himself, in his room with the little stones. He prowls up and down and his honest face is lined with care. It is a pain he cannot comprehend, not its origin, or its cause, or the sense of it."

Hilde wanted to hear again about what he looked like.

"His eyes," Eva said, "are clear and blue. He wears his hair ridiculously close-cropped, like a poodle in summer. So he does not have to waste time grooming it. He is broadly-built, lively in his movements and with a fresh complexion. Because he spends a lot of time in the mountains carrying out his excavations. As he works, he is touchingly devoted and looks at his veined rocks through his magnifying glass. He looks very like Kain, or I should say Kain resembles him, since Werner is much the elder of the two."

Eva, who had just been talking so calmly, now went deathly pale. She began to tremble and sat as if paralyzed. Then she stood up and walked like an automaton to the door, but she no longer seemed to be herself.

And now she was thinking how good it would be, this airplane. So that it would not always be ringing, that bell ringing at the hall door. So that one did not have to tremble, in constant mortal fear. How good it would be to fly away, at any price, and to leave the country.

Sitting there in the room, the two shared the same thoughts. Hilde, aware of her position, put them into words.

How would it be if she were to taxi the plane up to the house and he would climb in? The new masters would stand down below, looking on peacefully! Is this a possibility in this city? But then one wouldn't have to leave the country. Because how bitter it is, having to leave the country.

To leave the country.

These words and this new decree are the order of the day in this city in Central Europe, which once was known as the happiest of cities. The ordinary man in the street hears them. He forgoes his simple happiness and, his face blanched with fear, makes ready for migration. These words startle the doctor, and the doctor sinks his head in shame. For he has healed more wounds than there are cobblestones in the streets. And the doctor decides to go. The lawyer hears these words, he sees himself doomed. The ordinary man may well begin again from nothing in a foreign country, the doctor may build a new hospital, but the lawyer enters a foreign country taking with him laws that are no longer valid here. None of his learning counts as learning there, no one listens to him. He is a man devalued.

These words are heard by the painter, who has chosen this landscape. His eye blends together the gentle colors of this corner of the earth, his pictures tell the story of this city. The painter packs up his palette and decides to migrate. And it is a difficult decision.

It is the poet who is hardest hit of all. The language is his soul, the characters he creates are his body. He can draw breath only where his language is alive, and where he no longer understands and is not understood his life is extinguished. Perhaps that is why these words hurt the poet so badly, even though the decision has already been ripening within him for a long time. Even though he compels everything within him towards parting. Even though he regards it as a happy stroke of fate if migration to a foreign land succeeds, if a new world opens up for him, if he gains admission and is not turned away at the threshold. If his good name smoothes the way for him into a new homeland. Because, one thing he knows: he will not easily set out on his journey. He will give in, exhausted, there will be struggles ahead, mortal terrors. Terror now reigns in the heart of Europe, where the inhabitants used to be known as "the charming folk." Whose houses were history itself. Whose womenfolk sang Schubert songs. Terror wears a brown uniform and the swastika. It intensifies itself into a black uniform with death's-heads on it. It reaches its apogee in a Führer who has nothing human about him other than his inhumanity.

The brown uniform, known as the SA, arrives in broad daylight or at dead of night, and rings the bell. Everyone is terrified by this ringing. For everyone has offered up a prayer at some time or other, has paid homage to a duke, has thought a thought and known a Jew.

If the simple man speaks his thoughts, he is damned. Yes, here even he who does not speak is damned. The believer is damned because he believes in God. The freethinker because he will not allow himself to be restrained. The artist because he yearns for the wide open spaces, the politician because he seeks a solution, and the Jew is nailed to the cross because he is descended from Christ. And all of them are dragged from their houses to the accompaniment of shrill cries, and taken away, put into camps and humiliated until their souls cannot go on and their bodies die.

At the sound of these cries, the Czechs are stricken by fear, because they love their homeland. The Czechs live here as indispensable craftsmen. The men tailor the best suits and stitch together the best shoes. The women cook the best meals and make an excellent job of cleaning the house.

Thank heaven, at this ringing of the bell, Eva's fear is groundless, for outside stood Frau Wlk, the cleaning woman. First, she works upstairs, in the landlady's apartment. She cleans the whole apartment, the hall, the pillars, the stairs, she sweeps the top floor, she washes her things, which are all pretty well-worn, she makes the broth for the old dog, she works herself to death, all for the landlady.

When she is finished upstairs, she dusts off the books down below in Dr. Kain's study. She cleans the notebooks in which he writes his books, the countless sheets of paper on the desk, she does not throw out a single scrap of paper, because through every word he writes it is sanctified.

Last of all, she scrubs the kitchen in the large apartment, and by this time she is very tired. Her movements have now become slow and distracted. And she talks. She talks and her expression does not change. She does not carry her face under her arm, like Death. She does not distort it, like hatred. She does not tear it apart, like lies, she does not pull it to pieces, like calumny. She puts on her true face, she speaks today exactly as she did yesterday.

In this city, in which everyone has become a shadow.

And so Eva finds something to busy herself with in the kitchen, in order to listen to her as she tells her tales. Nor does it do any harm to give her a little help, she really is tired. The hand on the clock runs on, the work comes to a halt. She isn't cleaning, but time flies. Hours have passed, many hours, for a kitchen that remains all wet, the crockery is dripping, the stove is streaming, the floor is awash, her feeble hands have left nothing but puddles.

But what a good storyteller is Frau Wlk.

Eva looks at her expectantly. It is all so important, what her mood is, what topic concerns her today, so important for an exile. So important, when thoughts are being prescribed. For Frau Wlk will not tolerate being told. She rails about brown and black, about the leader and the misled. And is especially agitated today. For there is a man down there, in the apartment house where she lives, skinny as a broomstick, with a face like a death's-head, some fellow from the Party, an SA or whatever it's called, just yesterday he hung a flag on the house. Even though there's nothing but Czechs living there. Now he's standing in the avenue shouting at people. His name is Pilz—Mushroom! Toadstool, Mould, Fly Fungus, Frau Wlk goes through all the variations. He lives down there where she lives, he's a brownshirt, a bigwig, because he has a low number. Having a low number means he was one of the very first to be in the National Socialist Party. He was, as it were, among the founding members. That makes him worth as much as a benefactor who has paid the most money towards building the hospital. He's worth nothing, she corrects herself, becoming angry at her own words. He harasses the Czechs who live down there and on election day he set himself up in the polling station and kept an eye on how everyone voted.

It seemed that this low number exudes a fascinating effect. Because Frau Wlk was complaining. Even the landlady, here in this house, who is so kind, for whom she cleans the house, even she has been taken in. She who, after all, goes to church every Sunday. Who puts her last penny into the collection box to pay for a new wax figure of the Holy Virgin. Here in this house, the right atmosphere reigns to corrupt the landlady. The Mushroom came up and immediately won her over. And, simply because he has promised her South Tyrol, the landlady, who is so persnickety, is letting him move in here.

"For heaven's sake, Frau Wlk, that man is going to move in here?"

"She is attached to South Tyrol because she has her sister there and she was born there."

"He's moving into this house?"

"By the time I've got from one end of it to the other, my feet are killing me. All those doors! Anyone could easily hide here if the police come. They could run in one door and out by another. That's very handy in times like these."

"What apartment is he getting, this Pilz?"

"Now, just when are you leaving, Frau Doktor? It's a scandal, I mean, the Herr Doktor wouldn't harm a fly—and they're chasing a man like that away. But he really must leave, they're beating people to a pulp."

"One thing I can assure you, Frau Wlk. The Herr Doktor would never allow anyone to beat him."

"He ought to leave before the Mushroom moves in."

"But which apartment is he going to get?"

"Just look at Fräulein Hilde! Standing in the garden with the Herr Doktor, she is. He's a big man, and strong. And now he's got that horrible frog in his hand again."

"That's a tortoise, Frau Wlk."

"He has such a kind heart, even that beast moves him to pity. He's sorry that people make combs out of the animal. I'm not sorry for it; now, a dog, yes, I'm sorry for it, but a creature like that doesn't have a soul. Now he's showing the frog to the children. The children like it, though."

"What apartment is he to get?"

"Who's getting an apartment?"

Frau Wlk can be contrary at times. Or does she just not understand how vital this question is! How terrifying it is! How urgently it must be answered, answered at all costs! So, let's try a roundabout way. Does he have hollow cheeks and a grubby skin? Yes, indeed, she declares and says she wouldn't like to be in that man's skin, not even if he were a brownshirt ten times over.

How rich Fräulein Hilde is! As a child, she had long golden curls. And used to come down to her house to play with her boy rather than go to school. So much so that they would often be out looking for her in a panic all over the village, and she would be sitting happily in her parlor, on the bare floor, next to her lad. Now the boy is doing labor service in Pomerania, and Hilde is big and strong, almost taller than the Herr Doktor.

Now he's going upstairs to his room and Hilde is going away.

How she looks at him! He really must leave, and not try to stick it out like his brother, Herr Werner. *He* won't go; he says this is his homeland here. He's a good man, too, only no one is allowed to dust his "stones." He shaves his head so badly, his hair looks like grass.

"Of course, the Mushroom looks quite different," Eva tries again. "He's so thin and very tall."

So, does she know him, then? Frau Wlk asks, suddenly attentive. And touches on this horror at last! This cruel specter! For there can be no doubt about it, this SA man with the low number, one of the original campaigners for his party, he haunts the area. He has spread a flag across the balcony here, that flag that keeps shriveling up. It was he who hung the flag across the allée and has been stopping people out for a walk. And he stuck the flag up, down there where the Czechs live, that horrible man.

The fear becomes too great. Eva leaves Frau Wlk and goes in search of the landlady. She has to ask her whether the man is moving in, when he is moving in and into which apartment. It is all no longer bearable.

She looks for the old lady and cannot find her. Not up in her apartment, not in any of the turrets, not in the hall. She hurries through the garden and there at last she sees the landlady—and knows that she will not ask her anything.

In fact, she is standing under Eva's balcony and staring up, enraptured. She is looking at the flag, spread wide and long over the balcony. Tied with ropes, so that it will stay fixed.

What a lot it means to the landlady, this flag! The *Anschluss* of little Austria to the great German Empire. The annexation of this land they mercilessly dismembered twenty years ago. Now it's great again and powerful and one empire, along with the German provinces. Everywhere, people speak the good, honest German language, not like back then, in that Babel of all sorts of gibberish, with those Czechs, Poles and Hungarians. At a stroke, its borders reach to the sea. And now comes the greatest happiness of all: South Tyrol will be reunited with Austria. The most beautiful part of the country, and her homeland.

The nymphs on the drive are rejoicing, the Venus in the garden is dancing, the faun is smiling: everything is happy because South Tyrol is coming back. She has also been praying for this every Sunday in church, and this land is worth all her prayers. And most of all, this house. Her house. Impatiently, she tugs on the old dog's leash, because he is no longer content to stand and admire the house. She scolds him. She also rails a little at two small boys, the children of the new lodger, the officer from the Reich, because they are scattering earth all over her drive. And running in the flower-bed. And tearing lumps out of her hedges.

No one looking at her strong, small peasant's face could guess that she has any notion of the beauty of the rooms, of the grounds, of the grille round one of the concealed windows, of the gate to the drive, of the wild bushes. But she has more than a mere notion. She has experienced, has watched, as every corner of it was designed and constructed, as one stone was laid upon another, until the whole thing grew and became huge and massive. She has watched, lost in adoration. For the venerable, up-standing man who had this house built, he was her father.

Reverently, the landlady gazes up at her house before finally picking up her heavy watering can and filling it to the brim with water. She drags it over to the smaller path, to the almond tree. Puffing and panting, she puts it down and takes rapid, healthy breaths.

On the stone bench, she spies a stooped figure. The head is bowed, as if deeply troubled. How misfortune gnaws into people. Only six months ago this was still a woman in full bloom.

The landlady leaves her watering can standing there, and goes over to the stone bench. This is a fine woman, and she is sorry for her. But, it's better that some small bunch suffers than the whole German people.

"There's something I wanted to say to you."

"Please, landlady, sit down."

"It's hot, and these lads are making a mess of my garden."

"Are those the new lodgers' boys?"

"Yes, the officer from the Reich."

"But they are sweet."

"Rascals, they are." The landlady sighs and her chin trembles. And Eva is aware that it is not trembling because the boys are being naughty.

"I've something I must tell you," she mutters. "I've been to the party offices twice already—I'm obliged to—there's nothing I can do—I've told them I don't want to."

"What is it they're forcing you to do, then?"

"To give you notice."

That's the answer, Eva thought. That's it. That man is moving in. He's moving into my apartment. Into my apartment.

"That doesn't matter at all, we're leaving, and very soon."

"I'm so glad."

"All we are waiting for is our visa. So, when do we have to—move out?"

"In a month, as of today."

"In a month we'll be in London."

"I didn't want to hear of the Herr Doktor being given notice. But there's nothing that can be done. One other thing I wanted to say. There are often people coming here, from the party, in their brown uniforms, I always send them away."

"I know."

"Couldn't the Herr Doktor go up into the attic room, into the little loggia—just while they're in the house—no one will find him there—in any case they only come because they're going round inspecting all the houses. I mean, it is rather suspicious if I keep saying he isn't here."

"You're quite right, only—he has no intention of hiding."

"It's an injustice. They're not acting lawfully at all, they're young fellows taking more liberties than is right and proper."

27

"I've been meaning, for a long time now, to thank you—landlady—but it's so difficult . . ."

"The next thing is, these people will be on *my* back if I keep sending them away."

The landlady says this and then flinches in alarm. For there they are again, another two in brown uniforms standing by the gate. And any moment now they'll come in again—and ask that question again.

The woman next to her notices nothing. She is sitting with her head propped in her hands, as if in the depths of despair.

"Perhaps that's just as well," thinks the landlady, standing up and almost tripping over her watering can. With her tiny steps, she hurries past St. Florian and offers up a little prayer to him, although whether it will do any good is questionable, since St. Florian only watches over fire. She toddles on past the ever-smiling, eternally beautiful Venus, who is alien to her and could sometimes annoy a person, but then, it is a work of art. She goes up the steps and through the large hall and rings the bell. She has to talk to the man himself and make him see reason.

The door is opened and the landlady stands there, struck dumb with fright—all of a sudden she cannot say it. She cannot tell the honorable gentleman before her that he should go into hiding. That he should run up the spiral staircase and conceal himself in his own home simply because two youths are down there going about their miserable nonsense.

She would like to ask him something, she says. But she herself does not know what she is to ask him.

Courteously, he shows her into his study. Here, everything is so solemn, just as it always was in her father's day. A good atmosphere reigns here.

"Upstairs, in the attic room," she says, and does not know how to go on. Now she has to commit a sin, she is going to have to lie, and this affects her deeply. Even though she knows that there are such things as virtuous lies.

"Are you perhaps needing to go up there?" Courteously, he leads the way and opens the door to the attic. She trots after him and glances in helplessly.

The concealed door is half-open, affording a clear view into the little loggia. In the window recess, the swallows have built their nest and found security and quiet. She gazes at the graceful little birds with something bordering on reverence. She cannot get enough of them.

It's about the concealed door that she has come to ask. Is it never closed and never opened? The house is large and she is getting on in years.

She is quite old now, he thinks. What kind of wild notion is this? And how long she takes to understand him.

She does indeed need a long time. In the meantime, the boys in brown have already been ringing her bell, the one here, and for every apartment in the house. Now they're already on their way back through the garden towards the gate.

The landlady trips lightly down the spiral staircase. Then she looks round again, turning her honest face towards him.

"I wanted to ask you something, Herr Doktor, just between us. Do you believe that South Tyrol will now be annexed? People with evil tongues would like to ruin the idea for us."

"Tyrol will be annexed, quite certainly, but not just immediately."

"I've been waiting for it twenty years now. I suppose I'll just have to wait another few months."

He watches her as she goes and then looks out over the landscape. In the avenue, some louts in brown uniforms are making a noise. They are here to destroy all the delicate things that man has been able to devise. Restlessness overcomes him. "And I would like to rescue it all. And I am unable to save myself."

He went down into the garden.

All those brownshirts in the avenue! He goes out into the garden like someone who no longer lives here. Who is a stranger and has no right to be here. For the very first time, he felt insecure in this house, even though the woman to whom it belongs had only just now behaved kindly towards him, with a look almost as if she were protecting him. Normally she is very clearheaded and not at all softhearted. He had promised her South Tyrol, he was sorry for her. My God, how insignificant are her cares, and his have no place in this garden. He had to walk away, even if into the midst of the brown rabble. For if you don't walk, you cave in. But above all, don't lose your composure. Difficult to keep it when you are rushing downhill, striding towards the village.

On the left is the small police station. The door stands open. In the tiny room, the policeman is sitting almost at the threshold, his pencil behind his ear. On the right is the parish priest's house, a delicate building with a crown over the entrance. In front of it stands the wood-carver's stall, the one who now burns swastikas into his madonnas. Well, he had rescued the tortoises from him, quite a shock, he had bought a whole basketful of them. A black flag with silver lightning flashes on it casts gloom over the neighboring building, probably the undertaker's; no, he has his premises a bit farther on; the black flag next to the priest's house belongs to the guardians of the new order, the *Sturm-Staffel*.

Another flag attracts his attention. This one is in the process of being dragged across the square. It is hoisted and darkens the sky. A cluster of youths in brown shirts is at work. Orders are being given by a gaunt man with sparse hair and no eyes. That is to say, deep hollows are to be seen where eyes ordinarily are. His skin is as grubby as the insipid color of his party. The painter who first mixed this color has truly failed his exams.

Kain hurried on along the broad main road towards town. How beautiful the soil was, broken up by the plow and warm, how beautiful the bark of the oak trees, how beautiful the brown autumn foliage, but the brown of that man in uniform—that looked dipped in hemlock. Walking on past one of them doesn't help, for there stands another one, and over there they are forming a cordon, they're stopping a pedestrian and asking whether he is wearing a cross. Yes, he's wearing it, but concealed within him. That's the man they are looking for, they're seeking out slaves on the street and herding them together.

Kain walks on through, he's not carrying a flag, not wearing an image of the Führer, or a harvest posy, or a cornflower, no party badge, no swastika, he's wearing none of these, his coat is flapping, his hair fluttering, and no one comes up to him. And anyway, how could this energetic man with his bright complexion belong among the slaves.

But he stops of his own accord, for everything here reminds him of witch-burnings, of the plague, of Christians living in the catacombs—they had to, they hid, they fled, and now they are here, those Christians, they have been discovered—no, those aren't the Christians, they are the Jews. Strange how like the persecuted in the catacombs they look. They are standing in lines, although not stiffly to attention, they are stooped, maybe they are not even old, a stream of people gathers, no Christians they, they want to see this. It has begun already. The man in hemlock brown is putting on a performance, he raises the curtain, we're playing the Middle Ages here. Look upon these pallid people, hopping, first on one leg, then on the other. They swing their arms, their eyes closed, no, their eyes are blind, or can these eyes see?

We are in the twentieth century and are witnessing a strange hunt. Headhunters pursuing savages? No, we are among Germans.

And then it happens. It happens that one of these pallid faces becomes mobile. One of them draws back his lips. Pale and wan, he smiles. He looks at the others in the row, one after another, they take notice and smile. The first one bursts out laughing. They are all laughing. Is their laughter shrill?

The onlookers mutter and disperse. The man in the hemlock uniform goes red in the face. Why doesn't he have a whip with him!

The old ones let their arms drop, they are no longer dancing, no longer hopping, suddenly they are standing there alone, forgotten. They have deprived the audience of the desired effect.

For a long while they stand there, at a loss, their fingers intertwined.

Kain hurries away. In a room, a spacious room with quiet tables, with waiters serving, kindness can be bought. The newspaper, though frowned upon, is brought, the waiter slips it to the client; the endless routine stuff is all very well for ordinary people, but not for a bespectacled gentleman, doubtless a professor at the university; they are regular customers here.

Kain opens up the English newspaper, huge and broad, drinking in the civilized language; he becomes engrossed in the lenient words of a judge, then turns to the admonitory appeal of a poet, that those in torment should not be forgotten, calling for vengeance for the ignominy now setting its stamp on the twentieth century, people once again being nailed to the cross and Barrabas holding sway!

Kain is no longer sitting in the coffeehouse, but on a ship. It is gliding smoothly forwards; he can see the sea, can smell the sea, it is heading for England, how light are his spirits.

Then he senses the shadows falling on him. They are emanating from cold eyes.

A lady has picked him out. She is finely dressed and heavily powdered. She turns her gaunt face towards her neighbor, they whisper. She has recognized him and she will not let go. She beckons to the waiter. The waiter looks over to Kain and ponders. He scrutinizes him and cannot remember. There have been many writers and many pictures in the newspapers. He does not take long to consider, for a silver coin falls on to the table, the bogus university professor, who has sneaked in here with his fair hair, is already gone, and one cannot just get up and run after him. The lady may be mistaken, the gentleman is unsure, picturing someone who runs off without paying his bill; this man is not one of those, a fifty-pfennig tip is still half a mark.

Kain is having a bad day today. He is already on his way home, he is already in his village when a man jumps out at him. Who is it? One knows so many, one knows so few, and fears them all. It's someone who has attended his lectures, an admirer, no, certainly not, he is wearing a swastika. He is wearing a swastika and says, "I am an ardent admirer of yours, and for that reason I advise you—You must leave! You must flee!"

He does take flight. Up the hill, past the undertaker's, past the black flags, the group lined up, the police office, he flees before the blows, back into the cage, the gate opens at the lightest touch, so that he almost stumbles and falls. He can see the balcony, the flag draped mockingly over it, he can see the drive up to the house, open and free, he can see Hilde standing in the neighboring garden, expectant and rather forlorn, he hurries past her, rushes upstairs and, drawing a deep breath of relief, opens the door to the room where books reign.

And here, in Andreas Kain's study, bent over a stone, sits Werner, his brother. Werner is here, and is staring, boundless astonishment in his blue eyes at—no, it isn't a stone, it is the tortoise at which he is gazing so raptly, which has sought out the sunny patch on the carpet, and which immediately shrinks into its shell if things are not to its liking. Werner is to its liking; it turns its clever, tiny eyes to him, although somewhat warily. But then Kain approaches and, with almost god-like haughtiness, it hides its head, it is no longer in the mood today.

Because the tortoise has turned ungracious, Werner takes note of his younger brother. But not in a friendly way. He reddens and looks him straight in the eye.

"Sit down, brother, I need to talk to you. Just briefly, I have to get back. Mark my words, once and for all. I am not interested in what they call the new order here. Let them bring in their racial identity tags, they will pass no laws over my soul. No regulation and no alphabet will separate me from my homeland, whether it calls itself 'A' or 'S' or 'SA,' that is all one to me. I shall not leave my home, so put out of your head any idea of putting that out of *my* head. Do not send any strangers to me to make me offers, I shall not leave this land. No offence meant, but that is final. This tortoise has more common sense than all of us, it drags its home around with it, on its back. A superb creature."

"Dear Werner, it doesn't often happen that I am exhausted. But today I have experienced so much during a single walk that it has been enough to unsettle me deeply . . ."

"Especially with such a feeble constitution as poets possess. I walked the whole way up and nothing upset me. Except, perhaps, the loose stones up here," said Werner grimly.

"I am conscious of my weakness and I try my best to smooth the way and spare my feelings. And so it is to my credit that I can respond to you even though today you have started off in a tone which is not customary between us. I just came from a hunt. I was chased, I was chased, and I sought refuge up here and now I am being hounded further.

"It is remarkable, and, for me, it always has been, just how little you understand, how little you feel for others. How, while the world is coming apart at the seams, you can come up here just to assure me yet again, monotonously, of the same thing over and over. While I, exhausted, am incredulous that there can be such a thing as any hope of getting out of here alive, I can, with the last ounce of my strength, assure you of this: if I leave, then it is with you, Werner. Do not take it out on the tortoise and let it drop on to the table—on that highly polished surface any movement is bound to be torture for it."

"A likeable characteristic," declared Werner, placing the tortoise up on the palm of his hand again. He bowed his egg-shaped head over it and his gaze was so clear that his younger brother was moved as he watched.

'If you were a nobody, then you could remain in the city, scot-free. But as things are, you have rendered this city out-standing services, and that is dangerous. You walk around, as it were, without a stain—not so much as a mote of dust clings to you—and that is bad. You give the lie to those in high positions in this country. You are a silent reminder, even if you have no wish to be. They have no use for you, and they will cruelly drive you out if you do not go of your own free will. You represent the truth, a beautiful truth, and that is why you have to leave. And no matter how bad your temper becomes, I shall not cease to press you. Because I too find leaving difficult, I too am a nui-sance here, I too am no longer invited among right-minded peo-ple, true, in a kindly way, and for my own good, that is obvious to me, and I have even had to put my signature on a guarantee that I will leave the country. However, Werner, I cannot leave if you remain behind, so get that into your head, and show some consideration for me."

These last words from Kain were addressed to an empty room. For Werner had rushed out abruptly and had absent-mindedly taken the tortoise with him. In the garden, he noticed it in his hand and dropped it in the grass. The tortoise stuck its head out, looked around, it liked it here on the ground and it began to move, it started to walk and then disappeared.

II. A MUSHROOM. BUT NOT A PALATABLE ONE

The children are standing beneath the balcony. They are standing in a circle and are smiling. In the middle is a man in traditional Alpine costume. His legs are done up in white stockings. How hollow his cheeks are.

His fist is hollow too. The children are bending over it and are happy. His fist is scrawny. But how charming: he's holding a sparrow in his hand.

A little girl with red hair is standing well apart from the others. The thin skin is stretched tight over her thin limbs. The little girl, too, is smiling, or rather she has only spread her lips, while her eyes are fixed earnestly on the open fist with the little bird.

"A sparrow," the man in the Alpine outfit is telling them, "is not really so useful. Think of the beautiful red cherries, it bites into them, it is this greedy bird that has bitten the brown scars into them."

The red-haired girl becomes very serious. She is no longer capable of even making a pretense of twisting her mouth in a smile.

"Nevertheless, we let it live," the man in the Alpine costume is saying. "Man is magnanimous. But not when it is sick. A sick sparrow is like a cripple. A parasite. A parasite: that's the same thing as a scrounger. So, now you know what a parasite is."

The man took the little head between two fingers and broke the bird's neck. Eva turned her head away. The children cried out. The red-haired girl collapsed and had foam around her mouth.

"A sick sparrow is like a cripple," he repeated. He examined the broken neck and threw the tiny corpse into the grass. It fell under the lilac bush. The children edged towards it. They glanced sidelong at the man. But by this time he was directing his gaze towards the gate. Packing cases were now being carried through the garden.

The children were glad when he left them and went towards the path that led up to the drive to the house. They placed the sparrow on a green leaf and then into a box. With their hands, they dug a hole in the earth and laid the sparrow in it. They bedded it in scraps of silk and filled in the grave. They drew a circle and planted it with leaves. Into the leaves they stuck blue flowers. In the middle came a heart. They were happy once again, the children; only the red-haired girl sat against the wall and sobbed.

The man, by the drive, counted his crates. Everything was correct. They were very heavy, and it took a great deal of effort to bring them into the hall.

Now the landlady comes up to him. He whispers, she points to the balcony. It is good that Eva has made herself so small, she cannot be seen as she peeps out, pressed close into the corner.

South Tyrol? A beautiful little corner of the world. The Tyroleans, a loyal little people, true. But a small bunch. The Sudetenland is big and rich. Millions are languishing there. First of all, the Sudetenland will be liberated, then the Tyrol, that's a promise. He raises his eyelids in false reassurance and glances down on the little woman. That may well be just the way the spy looked who betrayed her hero Andreas Hofer.

What on earth can be in the crates? Certainly not glassware, they are too heavy for that. It takes four men to carry one crate. So long as they don't mix them up, for Doktor Kain's crates of books are standing in the hall. They are to be collected soon.

Where are these packing-cases to be taken? Is that not her doorbell? Yes, it's ringing. The man in the Alpine costume is standing at the door, and he has rung it.

He looks like Death.

He apologizes. May he come in? Just a minor matter. You see, there are crates being delivered, and there is plenty of space, for example here in the pink room. It was standing empty, it was too garishly painted. How did he know all this and what did he want? He wanted the apartment. He was the new tenant and he had had a good look round. There was plenty of room for the crates. But it would not be advisable to open them, their contents were not for ladies' eyes.

"Not snakes, I hope," Eva blurted out.

He gave a thin laugh. No, not that. Not exactly snakes. But one should not fool around with fire, what was in them was powder, gunpowder, ammunition. How easily ladies are alarmed. Come, come, he was not going to blow up the house, nor, for that matter, the Reichstag. He was about to go on an expedition, for honor's sake and for the sheer joy of brave deeds. He was actually a pilot and, more particularly, a painter. First he had painted the skies, then he flew up into the skies, and now he was setting foot where things seemed to him most dangerous.

"Have you led any expeditions before?"

More than that. He has taken part in the foundation of a party. His party. Until a greater man than he set the whole thing in motion. The one who is now at the head. The Führer. Who dedicates his days and nights to his people. Who is fulfilling a mission. He has been sent to save his people.

"But not by God," she cannot stop herself saying it.

"Him we don't need. Him we have within us. Everything German, which has been snatched away from the land of its origin, is now being gathered back together, and Germans will be set as masters over the other nations. People will *have* to believe that!"

"Why did you kill the poor sparrow?"

"It was a parasite on the state economy. Invalids belong under the earth. We need space to live, *Lebensraum*."

Someone ought to cut the skin under his tongue. He speaks as if it were glued.

"It was sweet, the sparrow's little head."

"An invalid," he says sadly.

"How could you do that?"

"You've no idea what I can do! In the war, I put the Russians up against a wall. No one else had the courage, so I fired."

"But why shoot them?"

"There was no food for them there, not even enough for us."

"And that's why you fired!"

"Orders were to shoot down the lot of them! Take no prisoners."

"Why did you do it?"

"That's what is called subordination."

"You could surely have let them run away!"

"We mustn't let our hearts run away with us. I'm saving that for peacetime."

"Can you draw a line somewhere? I mean later. When the war is over."

"War is war, and in peacetime the bold hunter stalks his way close to the wild deer. I once painted a picture, a stag that had been shot by a hunter. The hunter is bending over the noble quarry, as if in a state of euphoria. A beautiful thing, hunting!"

"I thought it was an expedition you were going on."

"I wanted to ask whether I can put the crates in here. In the pink room, which you are not using."

"How do you know all about the pink room?"

"We know everything. I have one further request. I am, as it were, homeless. Could I move in right away, today? Nothing grand, just in the attic room upstairs."

"You know the attic as well?"

"Of course. I know everything, and can do anything."

"Then you also know that we shall be leaving soon."

"But your visa will not be here as soon as all that."

"How can you say that?"

"I can even say that I shall be ensconced over you for some little while."

"But now there's one thing I'm sure you don't know. That in fact I live across there. Next to the study. Because it is sunny there."

"But against that, I know that behind that door stands a packing-case."

"There's a packing-case there? Who brought that in?"

"I did. I opened the door myself. With my knife."

"But that's . . . with your knife?"

"I'm not going to stand politely ringing the bell, not with *my* Party number. You find that hard to believe, because of my *lederhosen* and my Alpine shirt. But that's now civilian dress for us national comrades. But the number is genuine, you'll have to take my word for that."

"In my own apartment, you show me that low number—that's really not very nice of you."

"Surely you're not going to be afraid of me? The weak are protected in the new Reich. I'm an enormous idealist. I fight for an idea which is going to spread all over the world. I was one of the first, and that's why I have the low number. That was a hard struggle in those days! But a lot has been achieved. *We* know very well whether someone has fought and suffered, or whether he has stuck a freshly-minted Party badge in his lapel. Like the tenant farmer down there. With his cow. He is going to have to give up his cow. He has made the cow sick and won't hand it over. We are fighting for a great ideal."

"Against a tiny minority."

"Against a few minorities, my dear little lady, as you will soon see."

"You want to take over the Czechs, too, just like the Austrians."

"We'll take them over."

"But they aren't Germanic, are they?"

"We have to cleanse their land for them, of the . . . I can't say that to you, I wouldn't want to offend you. Not you."

But now something dangerous occurred. Through the open door to the corridor, the blonde head of a girl could be seen, and gradually, with every step she took, the whole figure appeared. The girl had come running in haste. When she entered, she stopped, taken aback, in front of the man with the pilot's insignia.

Eva looked at her, mute with terror.

"If I am not mistaken," said the SA man to the blonde girl, "this is not our first meeting."

"I, too, think . . . we have met . . . I . . ."

"In fact I know quite definitely."

"Yes, now I remember too."

"The young lady had an appointment with me; she forgot about it. I waited an hour for you. I haven't forgotten that."

"I . . . my parents wouldn't let me get away," stammered Hilde.

"So. Your parents were the obstacle. Yes, in that case, of course, I am powerless. That's the villa next door, the one without a flag. I know. Your esteemed parents believe I am wasting my time. Or that I'm in the mood for jokes. To be laughed at."

"You are quite right, I no longer pay any heed to them, I just go ahead and do what I feel is right, I . . . are you angry at me too?"

"I won't hold it against you. I'm happy not to have anything more to do with the whole matter."

"A pity. I haven't abandoned the plan yet," Hilde rashly let slip.

"At that age, one has a new plan every day. I don't know what this is all about, but this girl's plans are always very quickly forgotten, Herr . . . ," said Eva.

"Baldur Pilz."

"Herr Pilz. Please don't take her seriously. There's no doubt, she wants to become a pilot. She's had that idea going round in her head for a long time now. And I'm sure she also wanted you to give her flying lessons the moment she spotted your airman's insignia."

"Are you going to have a bad opinion of me now?"

"That all depends."

"Actually, Herr Pilz is moving in here."

"Yes, I'll be taking over this flat."

"That's marvelous!" exclaimed Hilde. "You'll be able to protect us."

He laughed. His eyes receded ever deeper when he laughed. And then he said, in a matter-of-fact way, "With us, no one is in need of protection. Whoever has a clear conscience can sleep peacefully. Here, everything is done fairly and legally now that we are creating order."

"Those Germans who are now coming into the country in droves, they make people afraid. They're not as nice as the Austrians. A German has also moved into the house here. I'm terribly afraid of him whenever I come over here."

"We are now all Germans, Fräulein, I mean, we—Aryans."

"Herr Pilz, here is the key for upstairs, for your attic room. The bed has been freshly made up. I'll lock this door to the corridor down here."

"Thank you most kindly. I'll be going now."

"I hope we'll meet again," said Hilde, reaching out awkwardly in her excitement to take his scraggy fingers. Hers were warm and alive. He met her eyes with the same look as before in the avenue, when he had suggested their rendezvous. Then he went off up to the attic. Eva stared after him, with a fear that made her pale face narrow, like a knife-blade.

This was Hilde's doing. It had been set up by her right from the start. And wretchedly continued by her, Eva. For she had forbidden the rendezvous. That that one, of all men, had to move in here! How could she have foreseen that everything would take such a diabolical course! So consciously diabolical and complicated! How dangerous to carry on with the game, since where was the girl to get the large amount of money needed by this campaigner for his ideas? And he won't allow himself to be made a fool of a second time!

"An unfortunate encounter," Eva said, looking as if she were about to be flayed alive.

Hilde laughed conceitedly. How mistaken Eva was again! How she exaggerated! Incredible how some people have the knack of distorting everything favorable and fortunate in their lives. The man is a stroke of luck. They had, as it were, hidden their gold in the thief's own chamber. The thief goes looking for it everywhere but in his own room. Even more in this case, for here the hangman will make sure they won't be hanged. This man would certainly not tolerate others poaching on his preserve! And he won't be easily talked round—she should know, she has known him longer.

"You were also afraid of that officer from the Reich, Eva, the one who lives here now. Isn't that right?"

"Yes, he's living here now."

"And he has a wife who looks like a Madonna by Dürer."

"Yes, that's what she looks like."

"They've two little boys. They're actually charming."

"The children are sweet."

"Nothing has happened to you, even though he is living here."

"Nothing has happened to us, but I can tell you this: I fear every ring of the bell, every meeting, every whispered word, every letter and every message, every face and every back, I fear the people who are now living in this house, that German officer and all those that have still to move in. But there's nothing and no one I am more afraid of than this SA man, Pilz."

Again, the children were standing in a circle, this time in the garden at the back. Again, the man was standing among them, this time in his brown uniform. But this time the children were not smiling, they were looking up at him apprehensively. Nor was the red-haired girl close to them, but quite a distance away. She kept her arms crossed behind her back, and round her neck she was wearing a chain with a star on it.

There was someone else standing to one side, the landlady. She was holding on to her dog by its collar. The dog raised its head towards her and looked at her with sad eyes.

But it was no good. Horst, the biggest boy, bounded over to her and tried to tug the dog away from her. His little face was flushed with eagerness. The dog was stronger. And in any case, the landlady was still holding on to its leash.

The man came to his aid. He strode up to the dog and dragged it into his circle.

"The dog," he said to the children, "is a really faithful animal. It barks at beggars and catches thieves. It protects its master and mourns over his grave. Indeed, it has even happened that a dog has starved to death by his master's grave, refusing to touch any food. And then there's Saint Bernard's dog which searches for bodies in the snow. Often it will find a person still alive and will save him. You have to know how to handle a dog, that's for sure. It is mankind's great benefactor. But not when it is old. When it's old, it is a parasite. What a parasite is, you already know. A parasite is a scrounger."

Now the shocking thing happened. The children had to hold the dog while the man took aim. The landlady covered her eyes.

The tenant farmer stepped out of his shed and grinned help-lessly. The cow in the barn bellowed, perhaps it could smell blood.

Only when the dog's eyes glazed over did the children realize what had happened. But they didn't dig a grave and put the ani-mal in, they went over to join the red-haired girl. Her smile was almost gloating.

"You're no Hitler Youths, you," shouted the man. "What kind of stuff are you made of! None of you would be allowed to join the movement, I can assure you of that."

He gave the farmer a signal, and he buried the dog.

The man went into the house. She could hear the scuffing of his feet as he came along the corridor and knocked on the door

"Good morning, little lady! Busy in the kitchen this early? I've already been going about my business too. I've shot the old dog. The beast was ailing."

"I worry that now the landlady will suffer, the dog was all she had."

"It was a parasite on the state economy. In life, everything must have a meaning and a purpose. And be usable. There is a branch of science, it is called economics, invented by the Ger-mans. It teaches that everything must be utilized to good pur-pose. Anything that is not useful belongs in the grave."

"That must be why the number of deaths is increasing so noticeably."

"You have no idea how true your words are. Anyone who dies an easy death belongs in that place to which he has descended so easily. Anyone who dies is not worthy of living. In that way the world is cleansed."

"And the old dog had already gone to the dogs."

"You catch on very well. Pity, that you are . . . Success comes only to the strong."

"But there are also frail people who achieve fine things. Per-haps precisely because they are fragile. For example, the German painter, Menzel, whom I am sure you, as a colleague, must appreciate."

"You have gone into things very thoroughly. Will your husband be writing about all this in the newspapers abroad?"

"In the periodical, *Press Forward*? It doesn't exist. Besides, he doesn't write for newspapers. He writes novels. You are always evading the issue."

"Me? Well, well, imagine that!"

"Now then, you still owe me an explanation about this nationalist painter. Especially since he did etchings of Frederick the Great, didn't he?"

"Ah yes, the great Frederick, that's a different matter, he is a predecessor of our Führer."

"Do you consider him to be so erudite?"

"No, Frederick the Great was not so important. Our Führer is a really great man."

"I meant it the other way around, but no matter. And of course, you also admire Machiavelli."

"Now that was a shrewd man!"

"Machiavelli was humble and fearful, always concerned about his own head."

"The things you're interested in! A German housewife concerns herself with the housekeeping and the children."

"Sometimes there is an advantage in not being a German housewife."

"I wouldn't like to be in the shoes of anyone of inferior race. They will all become extinct, every last one of them. The Führer is going to weed out and eradicate all lesser races and nations. If only he had more time!"

"Why on earth is he bothering his head about the small nations? If he annexes them, he is endangering the Germanic race."

"Sometimes, where a nation is concerned, its kerosene is of more interest than its race. The Führer knows what he wants, and it's no one's business to question him. He wields the whip and brings them all to their knees."

"As the Czar used to do, with the lash, but with the whip, you have to have a horse."

"You're always ready with an answer for everything! Incredible what a little woman like you has in her!"

"I wanted to ask you whether you wouldn't like to bring your wife here. We have an extra bed for her, here in this paneled room. It really is very nice, just have a look for yourself."

"How do you know I have a wife?"

"Because everything you do honors the wishes of your Führer, and besides, you're wearing a wedding ring."

"Oh dear, oh dear, I should have put it in my pocket. Now you know my secret. But as for my wife, I have no use for her here, I am of an artistic nature and I have to have a break sometimes. Anyway, there is no room for her here."

"She could have this wood-paneled room."

"A nice little room."

"It looks like a coffin."

"But why so gloomy? That doesn't suit you at all. Just look at the view; you can see three mountains at once, and there, behind the monastery, there's a pond. Do you know it?"

"Over there?"

"I could show it to you. Not just now, I have to get back to work. Requisitioning. But I'm free this evening, and I'll come and collect you. No one will disturb us, since my wife is not allowed up here and as for your husband, we'll lock the gentleman in, just for a few hours, so that he does not get in the way."

He left her no time to respond. He saluted with a loud "Heil!"

She followed slowly behind him. As he trotted his way down the hill, she waited until he was out of sight. Then she went over to the edge of the garden and waved up to the next-door villa.

There, Hilde was sitting with her head buried in her hands.

She was wearing a sailor's blouse, her hair falling over her face. Her eyes sparkled in the sun, and she looked like a cat, taking its ease in the warmth. When she caught sight of Eva, she came bounding across the crunching gravel towards her.

"Come over, Hilde, I've got to talk to you."

This was a border that was easy to cross. One jump over the hedge and Hilde was across.

"That man Pilz has just stomped past. How are you coping with him?"

"Not at all. You have to help me, Hilde."

"Eva! I'd never have thought you would lose your nerve!"

"You must come over to us this evening, and you're not to leave my side for an instant. I'm exhausted. Do sit down."

"It's lovely, this garden. Just like Paradise. With apple trees one is not allowed to touch, just like Paradise. This stone bench with its lion's paws, what a pleasure to sink down on it. Venus is dancing, even in such difficult times, and St. Florian is there to charm fire; that's why your house never catches on fire. The flag on the balcony has shrivelled up yet again. How that must annoy that Pilz. The children over there by the pile of sand are all so sweet, even little Horst. He comes over to me every day, raises his hand in the new salute that has been dinned into them and confidently asks for chocolate, and gets it. Then he runs off, overjoyed, and as he goes he raises his hand again and calls 'Heil!' And he hasn't the faintest notion of the blasphemy he is committing."

Eva gazes past her, as if she were a total stranger telling her something completely remote and meaningless. This juggling with hot coals was something she detested. She was not in the mood, it didn't appeal to her, simply didn't appeal. Putting on a pleasant front for an SA man! When all he does is talk, and steal. A man who merely puts on an act and is out for gain, and nothing but gain. It takes a lot even just to have to listen to him. That's the hardest thing in this life. To have to conceal one's own character. No longer to be able to see, to hear, to think. To have to dissolve into nothingness, like a Buddhist monk, to be nothing, to want nothing, all this merely in order to escape. To fly away at last. To go up in a puff of air.

Every means would be justified, Eva reflects. Even this attempt with the airplane. Perhaps he will sell them one after all. Perhaps he will demand an outrageous sum but will nevertheless provide a genuine airplane in return. For one journey, just for one journey. Perhaps they might be able to pacify him with money, with this purchase, and then, perhaps, they can leave!

Now she looked at Hilde, as if she had only this moment arrived. And Hilde's happy, fresh face looks just like it always does. And now Hilde puts her arms round her neck. And spontaneously starts to express all the things Eva has just been thinking. And develops her plan.

She will persuade her parents; Papa is rich. And the money has to remain here anyway. Papa will be perfectly happy. They can all get aboard. Hilde already has the airplane and kind-heartedly takes along everyone who wants to come. For joy, she falls on her old friend's neck. They have to make an impression on the man. They are buying something from him which he has. Any means is justified.

Hilde is letting her imagination run away with her. Immediately she has an idea for this evening. How they are going to thwart the proposed stroll without endangering Kain. For that must always be the main thing. They will not endanger him, they will simply make use of him. They are going to arrange a picnic. They will wear out the SA man with bombes glacées and caviar. By the time he goes home, everything will be fixed and he is bound to feel honored. He will be powerless in the face of so much hospitality, his mouth will water and they will mix the water with wine. They will also invite Werner, the close-cropped, cranky brother, and make it a proper banquet.

There was no point in that.

"Why not, if it's for his brother's sake?"

"He'll just look at you in amazement and won't understand. He knows no fear."

Hilde fidgeted uneasily on the stone bench and was surprised that it was not hard, perhaps the lion's paws beneath were yielding a little, perhaps the bench had been made softer by use, it was certainly old enough, its edges rounded off by age. Just why didn't Eva like this Werner, for in fact she did not like him. That was something you couldn't ask about. There are so many puzzles, so many secrets you can't ask her about.

Was it because Hilde's expression suddenly became serious and pensive that Eva flinched? The plan was reprehensible. It put the girl in an awkward position, and all of them with her. The man is on the prowl after gain. The way he had looked at Hilde's string of pearls! For a moment, she believed he thought he could buy the girl off cheaply. The way he buys airplanes is the way he buys anything, he simply takes things.

There was another thing to be considered, too: the girl didn't have the money. She would have to ask her parents for it. Her parents would forbid the deal. Then she is in a trap. For anything that proves a failure for that stubborn devil would be a failure for all of them, would prove their undoing. Especially if they were the instigators. No matter how you looked at it, Kain was right, it is dangerous.

Kain will at this moment be moving about among crates and ammunition that an idiot on the loose employs as the fancy takes him. Books are being removed, ammunition brought in. Imagination is on the retreat, she thought darkly, and the cannons roll up. And all the way up to the Kahlenberg, they are surrounding the vineyards, they bar the way. A murderer orders us about in our own house, and can, with impunity, say things like "And as for your husband, we'll simply lock the gentleman in for a few hours."

Her face went pale and Hilde noticed how she was digging her fingers into each other, boring her nails into her own flesh.

"This evening everything will work out just fine!" she exclaims eagerly, as if she were just waking and seeing a person grieving in this beautiful world, in this heavenly garden.

Blonde people, Eva reflects morbidly, can never be unhappy. They are bright, and they see the world brightly. Has it perhaps to do with the color of their eyes? It is impossible for a girl with such radiant blue eyes to be able to see the world darkly, even through a smoke-tinted glass. Such people are incapable of seeing, in every SS man, a gravedigger. In each swastika a rune of gruesome significance. Of itself, a brown eye colors the world brown. Here, this intense young creature builds castles in the air, as we all do, but hers do not collapse on her. The sky remains blue and who would not greet her with a smile, this charming Hilde who meets life fearlessly! Only hope and trust radiate from her. And she gets what she expects. Should one not simply let her have her head? In the end, she will succeed in everything. Why should this happy creature not relieve her of some of her burden? Especially since that is her wish!

Tentatively, Eva tells her she has not considered how impossible it is to withdraw large sums of money. That is not allowed these days. The National Socialist Party takes care of that. It lays down how much of one's capital one may withdraw. One must account fully for it.

That's true, but in her large household there are payments upon payments being made. Daily, bills are arriving, and they have to be settled on the spot. Take her brother's expenditures alone, he has certainly not been stinting himself. He is good-hearted, but lax, a great worry to his parents. People he has fêted on champagne now avert their eyes from him. At the moment, he is in no mood for nightlife. Now the hangover has set in, in the form of the bills which must be presented to the police superintendent so that they can be paid. They also show his parents in an embarrassing light. Sums like these could meet the cost of an airplane. Twelve thousand, the man demanded that time, as he was putting up his flag in the avenue. Three times it fell down, the wind blowing across the avenue, billowing the flag out until it got out of control.

They are now living in straitened circumstances, it is true, having only a certain amount allocated for household expenses, and yet that still swallows more than enough, an airplane could come on top of that, they would pay it off by installments, and she, Hilde, has jewelry, and what else are these bits of glass good for anyway? Before they are stolen during a "house search," she'd rather sell them. Money is no problem for her.

There is something else troubling her. The secret surrounding these two brothers. This Werner, who never came up here. Eva doesn't like him, you can sense that, and now she has let it slip out—not that she had intended saying that—but sometimes things just come out without her meaning them to.

Eva kisses her flushed cheek. It's only on lively children and blossoming young girls that these signs of a heightened heartbeat show. It was a delight to touch Hilde.

Eva does like Werner, oh yes indeed, but there are things about him that annoy her. His quirky moods are embarrassing, his intolerance borders on hard-heartedness. He just will not understand, not even himself. He puts himself down too. He is fossilized. Frailty, which makes many a person attractive, is something he detests. He scolds Kain for the very character traits that in fact distinguish him. His enthusiasms, his sensitivity, his over-generosity with both himself and his possessions. His "seafarer's life," as he calls it, because he moves about on unsteady foundations, like a sailor. Yet the instability of the poet is in fact his wisdom, for nothing has any permanence, and how forcefully that is being brought home to everyone these days and in this city. This city in which, like none other, one recognizes that the artist alone is still capable of rescuing human dignity.

How marvelous, thought Hilde, are problems like these. How select and profound. When I think of what it's like at home. There, the problem is the roast. Whether it's properly cooked, or crispy, or tough, or fresh. Mama goes on at length about what she will wear in the evening, Mama, who is no longer as young as she was, and so stout. That brother of hers is always ready to lend a helping hand and not uneducated, yet so shallow! The way he is so preoccupied with his tie or the latest premiere. Not just at the moment, just now melancholy and local gossip dominate his thoughts. And that's even worse.—And here, this paradise! Such an exalted level of the spirit and of suffering! Visitors here, and Mama's guests! Here it is a poet who sets the tone. They will put up a monument to him when he is dead. While he is alive, they chase him from the country.

But Eva was still talking. "What I have to cope with here is no small matter. Having to avoid angering that semi-human from whom my cleaning woman averts her eyes, and yet to maintain my dignity. It is a humiliation, it's a sacrifice, but Kain has made a greater one for me."

"I know."

"You know nothing of it."

"For your sake, he has not fled across the border. You know, I can see a few things that don't quite meet the eye. Why, in fact, didn't you leave with him, instead of still having to struggle on here?"

"He has got it into his head that escaping over the mountains, and the terrors of being pursued, would be too much for me."

"Does he think you are so spoiled? Why is that? Can't you persuade him?"

"It's too late now. Now it really is dangerous. The borders are closely guarded."

"And that brother of his, that Werner, naturally he encourages him to stay here, out of selfishness, because he himself doesn't want to leave."

"No, Werner's not doing that. I've given you completely the wrong picture of him."

"I can't stand him—he's so coarse-grained."

"I really must tell you, though, how badly I once behaved towards him, and how he is not at all coarse. Once, he put Kain in danger, and I took that very much amiss at the time."

"I would have, too . . . anyone would have held it against him."

"Kain was almost arrested because of him."

"What? Really arrested? And because of him?"

"No doubt, Werner's attitude is certainly brave, but it's a sad kind of courage, in this city where what's right is held in contempt and every honest word is seen as a crime."

"And he spoke out honestly? How? About the Führer and his pogroms?"

"We were out for the evening in a country inn. Kain had taken him along to take his mind off things. In the early days just after the putsch, that was still possible—the laws against dogs and Jews hadn't yet been passed."

"You mean the laws *in favor of* dogs and against Jews."

"Well, we come into the inn, it's packed full, Kain and I find two seats at the head of a long table while Werner sits down at the foot of it and doesn't mind in the least that on either side about a dozen strangers are seated between us. He drinks his wine and listens to the jolly music without looking to right or left. He has a large earthenware jug in front of him, and that helps to reconcile him to life. Exactly how a conversation was struck up with the others at the table, I still can't say today. What is certain is that we suddenly hear him shouting, 'There is no pure race, you ignoramus!' The result of this is that two men, who later turn out to be SA men in 'civvies,' start making fun of him. They begin reeling off his racial characteristics. His small stature, his large nose, his ears, then they add his close-cropped hair, his nice brown hair which he shaves only for the sake of convenience. As they come round to his egg-shaped head, the one who is speaking receives a jugful of wine right in the face. That was Werner's way of washing out his mouth."

"And very brave, too."

"And foolish. For the two men stand up, reveal themselves as SA men and arrest Werner. Just as they start cursing at him, Kain jumps to his feet. He hurries towards them, stands beside his protégé, and says, 'If you are arresting this gentleman because you don't like his race, then you'll have to arrest me too, please. I'm his brother.'"

"Wonderful!"

"And now comes the embarrassing bit. At this, the two brownshirts start laughing fit to burst. And it is not only them laughing, and not just those at the long table, but the whole room is laughing. They are laughing because Werner, burly and ordinary as he looks, cannot possibly, according to their opinions and theories, be Kain's brother. It's a joke, a marvellous joke, and all the while the younger brother is close to tears, it pains him so much to see the elder one being mocked in this way. That's an essential trait of his character: to the best of his knowledge, the world consists of nothing but sensitive people constantly being wounded and insulted, while he himself is unstinting in his efforts to make up for these insults. In most cases, I look on and listen with a smile while he defends one of those 'wounded,' who usually realizes he is being insulted only once Kain starts talking. So now, in the inn, the same thing happens. Kain speaks up for his brother, addressing the whole company, and by this time Werner has made off and is waving frantically to him through the window, urging him to come outside. At last, with me pushing him along, he follows him and, as we go on our way, he tries to think up all sorts of words of affection in order to console his elder brother. Werner looks at him, his clear eyes filled with astonishment, and declares, 'How ridiculous they are with their race theories. It's all coming out again. We are very much brothers indeed!'

"'You should leave fools to deal with their own mistakes,' I tell Kain instead of giving any kind of response to this. 'And you shouldn't put yourself in danger for their sake.' And Werner raises his head and reflects, and he is utterly amazed at me, at himself and his brother, and replies, 'Actually, she's right. Yes, she's right.' Even after this disarming response, I still refuse to relent and go on quarreling with Kain, who is not listening to me, but still 'consoling' his brother, because, as he sees it, he has been deeply hurt and is trying to hide it."

"I know a secret about him, too. That business about the trade in tortoises."

"How he bought the tortoise to prevent it having to bear a swastika?"

"How he bought the basketful of tortoises so that they don't have to be branded with the swastika. He bought the whole basket and even had the wood-carver take it to the winegrower's place. All the customers there had a great time letting the wobbly little animals wander about the inn. And then he tries to hand them out among the customers so that everyone can take one home and take good care of it, but then they all back out because they don't want the trouble of looking after them."

"And yet they only eat grass and sleep half the year round."

"At that, Kain announces that he'll stand anyone who takes one a quarter-liter of wine. Then they were all willing and quite crazy about the tortoises. Kain laughed his head off. When he laughs, he wins people round at once. I was just arriving as everyone was trying to grab a 'pet.' The winegrower played a trick on them and stated that, for a quarter-liter of wine per head, he would take care of the whole basketful. And in fact he actually did take the money for their keep, I know, because I was standing nearby waiting to order wine for us."

"That's why Kain always stops in there whenever he is in the village."

"Of course. The whole garden is swarming with tortoises.

Don't give me away, because he asked me not to say a word about it to you. I'd like to ask you something, Eva, do you think that Kain . . . are you both so nice to me just out of the goodness of your hearts?"

This question brought Eva alarmingly back to the present. They were caught between the devil and the deep sea. The devil is that SA man here in the house, and if they run away from him, they run into a sea of brownshirts, blackshirts, enemies. Perhaps Hilde really can help them; she seems to know how to handle that man.

Oh, Hilde can promise her that. She is looking forward to this game, just as Eve in the Garden of Eden had fun with the apple. She will not give the man a moment's peace. She will keep him busy and lead him up the garden path. She is not going to say how she will do it, but she'll manage. It can't take forever for those visas to arrive. Even supposing they don't manage it with the . . . She leaves it unsaid.

But suppose it does take forever! Every day is an eternity, indeed, every hour. Every hour here, exposed to the whims of such people, stirred up to the point of hysteria. One fool creates many fools, that's one thing the Führer, Adolf Hitler, has proved. Kain has had to sign a paper that he will shortly leave the country. No horrible old ballad can measure up to this terror. You must meet the deadline for your exit permit, even though you don't have an entry permit. Not for anywhere.

"Kain will pay back that bargain," Hilde says in an enormously grown-up tone. "Once he is in England, he will write a play in which the modern Shylock is portrayed. The Shylock in brown."

Once he is in England. Will we ever reach it, Eva wonders. What will it be like when we are at the border? That minute, when we cross it. That feeling! How we shall seize each other by the hand, how Kain's eyes will suddenly light up. How he will laugh—he can laugh so heartily! How he will hold back that bellow, like an animal's, how he will restrain himself from greeting his newfound liberty with a shout. How she will be unable to quiet his rejoicing—and he will rejoice! When they ride across the bridge at Kehl, for they are going to take the route through France. And spend a few days in Paris. That moment when they cross the border will be the happiest moment of her life. She dreams of it every night and dares not dream of it during the day. Yet, in the night, too, yes, at night, too, she fears, in her dreams, that the journey will be interrupted, they will be stopped, the train will turn back. Because it is too beautiful, too burningly beautiful! And it will happen. These peaceful gardens are giving her their promise, these mountains which you can see from a long way off. That's the start of the Alps, how beautiful this city is, you can see the Alps from their garden. This young girl is giving her promise, she belongs to them, she is coming too, she will come. How could eyes like these be disappointed! Only once they are in France will they have time for reflection, time to contemplate themselves and to know once more who they are. To be proud again. In England, they will collect themselves. There, people are serious and one can find one's true self.

How she longs here for the English character, which is so scoffed at. Because these are people who never lose control. They are a people isolated from the rest of the world on an island. Her heart becomes light; these people are as if chosen. They whisper rather than talk. They bestow smiles rather than praise. Civility is ingrained in them and is a part of their beauty. The women walk as if on soft carpets, they hold their heads proudly, but there is graciousness in their eyes. It is difficult *here* to imagine that a country exists where they want to dig flower-beds, and not graves. Especially difficult to hope that one might get there. Faced as one is with this Pilz, this fungus who mildews the very walls. Everyone in the house has changed, the house itself has changed.

"These new tenants are very much to be feared, that officer

from the Reich. He looks like a hangman. The wife is so blonde that I prefer to cross to the other side of the street. The children are sweet and come running up to me, but I have to avoid them."

"You'll soon be a case for a psychiatrist, Eva. Whenever you see 'blonde,' it does something to you. The Germans are not always brutal, some are even quite nice, really."

"But the nice ones remain in the Reich. To be honest, however, they are not so deceitful as our cozy Austrians. Not like that Pilz."

"So why have you let this Pilz move into your apartment? After all, you don't have to vacate it yet, do you?"

"I can't help smiling—I didn't let him move in, he just did. He forced the apartment open with his knife and installed a packing-case in the pink room. And then told me all about it himself."

"A bad joke. Where has he put his wife?"

"That woman could be my salvation. But how can I find her? Where is she? He's hiding her deliberately. You must help me, Hilde."

"Of course. I'd love to. I'll send our servant with a basket full of things. Bombs for the Mushroom. From Papa's cellars. And if Kain touches on dangerous topics, I shall interrupt. But now I have to go home, I have a dancing lesson. There are all sorts of things to be done, you see. I have a marvelous plan for getting a visa quickly so that I can follow soon after you both—in case, that is, we can't all . . . you know what I mean. And for that, I have to learn how to dance well. The ballet mistress at the Opera has a hand in it all, and I have my feet. I shall get a proper contract, an engagement as a solo dancer, abroad. I've even got a dance audition, although I've never set foot on a stage. Now I must run."

Despite her being so tall, her steps were light and soft as she hurried away.

The garden was so beautiful. Without a border it merges into the steep vineyards. Without a border . . .

What a view! Those little sons of the German officer are really just too sweet. They are tumbling in a knot on the grass and roll towards Eva. Then two figures are standing in front of her like garden gnomes. Honey-brown children's eyes gazing at her, they pluck at her skirt and run away. Run down the slope, stumble and fall, then they sit up and suddenly stop laughing. Fat tears roll down their chubby cheeks.

All around, there is no one to be seen. And even if there were anyone in sight, Eva would not be able to call them. Who would listen to her?

The two boys are sitting in the stinging nettles, unable to stand up, and Eva is not allowed to help them to their feet.

For these are the children of the dreadful man from the Reich.

The little boys try to get out, and in groping around, their little hands take a real grip on the fiery leaves. They look reproachfully at Eva, so disappointed, so bewildered because she is leaving them in the lurch, in the middle of this fire.

And now Eva gets to her feet.

"You're two naughty little cherubs," she says and carries the two casualties on to the cool lawn. "And such little darlings," she whispers, kissing their soft brows. These sweet brows, so round and delightful as only children's can be.

They are laughing once again, tumbling around on the grass, then they start rolling and land back in the nettles.

"You are terribly naughty. And you don't listen to what you're told! You have to understand. Those leaves are not your friends. You have to stay here on the lawn. No, you're not to go back in there again."

They laugh in delight and thrash about. They will not be restrained, and already they are rolling themselves into a ball again.

Then two strong hands seize the two cherubs from behind.

A young woman holds the two boys in the air and sets them down on their feet, powerfully and with finality.

It's the wife of the German, of the enemy from the Reich.

"Thank you very much for allowing the children to play in your garden. May they come back tomorrow?" She raises the two gnomes' plump little hands in salute.

Eva blushes. Doesn't this woman know, then?

"I don't like this part of the world at all," says the young woman, as if that were an answer. She says it so hastily that it seems the words were scalding her mouth.

And then, with a long, clear stare, she heads for the house, a child on each arm.

That is something all the painters have missed—that the real Madonna bears two children in her arms.

"How blissful!"

"You're here in the garden, Kain?"

"For some time now."

"Eavesdropping on me."

"I very much enjoy it."

"Were you listening in on my conversation with Hilde?"

"Of course."

"What were we talking about?"

"About why the Mona Lisa smiles. She doesn't know, and you know, but you wouldn't tell her."

"And I'm not going to tell you either."

"Go on, Eva, tell me, please."

"That's my secret, and I can only sell it to you."

"For the finest apple off this tree."

"Kain, don't forget that the garden no longer belongs to us. Don't touch it."

"What did Hilde want?"

"Didn't you speak to her?"

"She darted past me as she was leaving."

"She wanted a book from you. I wouldn't allow you to be disturbed."

"And what did the German woman want?"

"Did you see the polar-bear cubs?"

"The whole idyll."

"So, where were you?"

"Behind the willow tree, in the deck chair. You know, Eva, just because the whole world is standing on its head you shouldn't get all topsy-turvy. You mustn't get agitated because a German housewife talks to you."

"But she said, 'I don't like this part of the world.'"

"That's brave of her."

"I would have loved to reply by paraphrasing the words in the Bible: 'I have lost the world and my soul has been sorely troubled . . .' but ever since she said she didn't like this part of the world, I have started to like the world again."

"Here in this heavenly garden, yes."

"From which we have been cast out, Kain."

"And about which I am already feeling nostalgic."

"Which has no borders. No borders."

"All the way to the edge of the Alps."

"The Alps are also a part of your garden, Kain."

"Of my garden."

"How wonderful it will be to travel over the Alps."

"Yes, that will be wonderful."

"Now, it all seems much easier to me."

"Here in the garden."

"Isn't it too hot for you, you've gone quite pink. You look like an angel blowing his trumpet, Kain."

"Thank you. I'll sit down on the grass, then."

"About the German woman. There's nothing to fear from that direction. And I'll soon get the better of that Pilz."

"Is he that clown who . . . ?"

"Who's living in our house. I shall have to introduce the two of you, there's no way of avoiding that."

"He introduced himself, most obsequiously, yesterday evening."

"But he wants more."

"What, then?"

"He wants us to treat him like an artist."

"Like a trapeze artist."

"More like a hunger artist. He talks like a professional faster, monotonous and hollow."

"And what does he want of me?"

"Hilde has invited him to tea this evening."

"You don't know what you're saying, Eva."

"You mustn't make things so difficult for me."

"Let me come straight to the point: I refuse to sit down at the same table with him. And that is final!"

"You didn't always speak to me like that."

"Only this year have I talked like this—is that surprising?"

"How long have we known each other, Kain?"

"For an eternity."

"Is that too long for you?"

"I believe I have always known you, Eva."

"But not vice versa. That's why the first years were so beautiful. Your strangeness was so beautiful."

"But you say that as if weary of my yearning for beauty."

"Is there not a higher longing behind that, Kain? One that cannot be fulfilled?"

"I had no idea you understood that."

"How I must have failed you. And you think you have an intelligent wife."

"And a wife of complete understanding."

"For your purchases, Kain. Do you remember the tenant farmer here on the estate having difficulties?"

"After that bad fruit harvest."

"And you bought his cow for him."

"So that all the children in the house could have fresh milk. Eva, for shame, you find out about everything. A little more discretion, please."

"As soon as that cow appeared in the pasture, I knew it was yours, even without it being branded, like so many tortoises."

"The children have fresh milk now, and the man has been helped."

"Not *all* the children. When he got the cow, he didn't ask to see its baptismal certificate. But now, when he sells milk, it's only to the blonde children."

"Because he is afraid. He has been intimidated. Everyone is like that now, like a gardener always dependent on the weather. He has to watch the sun anxiously—is it going to give generously and provide him with food this year, or will he starve to death? I'll tell you about something else, something topical, a much better story. Last month, after that terrible outbreak of violence, all three waiting rooms at the station were full of prisoners about to be shipped off to the concentration camp. But confusion arose, and, as they were boarding, one whole waiting room of frightened people got on the wrong train and, instead of going to Dachau, they went straight abroad."

"That's marvelous!"

"I have another story. There was a girl, a Christian, whose sweetheart was locked up. She decides to rescue him and, because she is very beautiful, she manages to charm the policeman in the prison with her talk. She gets into the tiny cell where her lover is squatting on the floor with eleven others. He is happy to see her, but refuses to leave unless she also rescues his friends first. So she carefully leads them, one after the other, along a secret passageway into the open air, twelve times altogether, until they are all saved."

"How wonderful! How did you hear of this?"

"Made it up."

"Made it up, Kain? You invented both stories? You're cruel."

"Was that very bad of me?"

"Of course."

"You know, sometimes I have to tell you stories like that, otherwise I can't bear it."

"You're right, Kain."

"You tell yourself about all of them escaping, from prison, from house and home, from the city, from the country, getting out . . ."

"If you carry on being as clever as you've always been, you will soon get out, too."

"If you go on being wise, Eva. You were wise."

"So, to sum up, you are in my debt."

"Deeply in your debt."

"And you acknowledge that debt."

"Fully and completely."

"And you want to pay it off."

"Willingly, if I can."

"Then you'll sit down at dinner with us this evening. I beg you."

"The way you talk—does so much depend on it?"

"With your help, we want to get that Pilz with his back to the wall, where he belongs. Did you know he is always making passes at Hilde?"

"Typical! Hilde will be able to fend him off."

"She is afraid, for her parents' sake, on account of the houses they own."

"And tell me, is he also making advances to you?"

"He's always wanting to go for a walk in the moonlight with us, and to divert him, Hilde has invited him to dinner."

"And what has that to do with me?"

"You will set the right tone."

"I can promise you that much, Eva. If I come, I shall certainly set the right tone!"

IV. THE BANQUET

It felt as if they were sitting in a ditch in the small wood-paneled room, since the rectangular table took up almost the whole space. It was bending under the fine dishes. In the middle, a tureen, with its lid still on. An open can stood in a bowl of hot water, and was now emptied into a deep dish. A slimy gray mush flowed out, an offence to the eye. This mush was intended for the guest, who immediately spooned it up with relish. He examined the label on the can, with its astonishing information: "Turtle Soup." The guest had never tasted the like, but he found it delicious, even invigorating, flowing as it did like new blood through his veins. He was amazed that his hosts should pass up this delicacy, but Hilde, who was seated at the long side of the table, to his left, declared that there was a reason for this. You might say, this was food for the dragon. So that it would spare the inhabitants of the city. At this, the guest could not help laughing, even though he did not understand what she meant. And so he asked for a more detailed explanation.

"It's like this, Neighbor Pilz," said Hilde. "You are the dragon, and we are the tortoises. Can I say more, when we are sitting here in this fine house? Here, *bon ton* rules, that is to say, courtesy, or, actually, the lie. Our host, who is laughing now, but will stop very soon, insists on addressing you as 'Herr Ingenieur,' even though twice already I have given him a kick under the table, because you are in fact not an engineer at all. Is this simply our host being polite? It has to do with his tendency towards extravagance."

"I do however deserve the title, Fräulein Hilde, I know my machine inside out. A certificate issued by some old fogies at a university is not crucial."

"But for me, a title matters very much. I love Captains passionately. The very sound of it: 'Commander'! Though actually, I have never seen one in real life."

"That's why you love them," said Eva.

"Aha. So that explains why you always wear those sailor's blouses. May I introduce myself? Captain of the largest airship. It has not yet been named, but I shall see to it that it shall be named after you."

"For heaven's sake, what are you thinking of! Then it would be a non-Aryan airship!"

"You are very sweet. But I with my simple mind still don't understand the thing about the tortoises."

"The Japanese, Herr Ingenieur, see in them the symbol of inner happiness. So surely it is a good omen for our banquet to serve it here."

"Why inner happiness?" sighed Eva.

"Because they grow to such an old age. Because they are so slow-moving. It's impossible to wipe them out, despite constantly hunting them."

"Enviably old. The tortoise is already old when it comes into the world. And I am so offensively young. I have to listen to that all day."

"You know, Hilde, what Casanova calls youth: a delightful failing, which improves with the passing years."

"Yes, the Herr Doktor is quite right there, you are indeed a delightful failing. And because of this delightful failing I must apologize to the lady and gentleman for wearing my uniform here. That is a matter for the conscience of the young lady, that delightful failing on my left. My neighbor, you might say, in both the narrower and the wider sense. At table, because she is sitting next to me, and in the house, because I now live here and she lives next door, in the villa."

The host, however, did not understand the point about the uniform.

"Well, the young lady has a passion for uniforms. It's the same with all young girls, which accounts for the military man's luck with the fair sex. The Fräulein here expressed the wish to sit at dinner with an SA-man; if not a naval commander, then nothing less than a brownshirt would do. She finds it exciting, which is easy to understand. Although it infringes the rules of etiquette, I mean, towards my hosts, it is still only polite to fulfill the young lady's wish, as I am sure you will understand."

"Yes, that is my wish. To sit at dinner with a brownshirt is like the haunted castle in the Prater. Exciting and thrilling. One is terribly frightened, yet everything is made of wood."

"So I am sitting here in the place of a wooden ghost?"

"Not in the least! And to prove it, let me offer you some of this goose-liver pâté. It has certainly not been prepared for carved images. Have you any idea how complicated preparing this is? You should hear our cook on the subject. First, beef is boiled, then the liquid is boiled down—over a long time, for a really tasty pâté, of course—and next the finely-chopped liver is added, with salt and spices, and stirred slowly."

The guest immediately fell in love with the pâté. He asked for pumpernickel, something he had had to go without over a long period.

Why was he denied it for so long?

"I was forced to live in Munich, Herr Doktor."

"Who forced you?" Hilde wanted to know.

"My political stance. I was in the Austrian Legion."

"So *that's* why you have the low number!" she exclaimed.

"How do you know about that?"

"Word gets around," she smiled mysteriously.

"The Herr Ingenieur already had his Party low number when he fled," the host corrected her.

"Was your escape dangerous?" the girl persisted.

"Escape is always hazardous," Eva said, and found it advisable to turn the conversation towards the wonderful view through the window.

"But I'm interested in how my neighbor Pilz likes the view inside the room," Hilde thwarted this calming suggestion.

This led to a compliment on the part of the guest which barely remained within the bounds of good taste.

"I enjoy the view inside the room a great deal more than the panorama outside. Nature does not interest me, but here in this room the muses reign, one blonde and one dark in the pink glow from the light . . ."

"I didn't mean that—for instance, Eva finds that this room looks like a coffin. It reminds our host of a railroad compartment, while I myself compare it to a candy box. What do you say, dear guest?"

This gave rise to a *faux pas*. And from that moment on, the conversation became disjointed, sinking below the previous level until it ran disastrously out of control.

What happened was that the guest replied—a straight answer to a straight question, he said—that, as far as he was concerned, the room—*honi soit qui mal y pense*—was set up like a booth for private assignations.

This response earned Hilde a sharp glance from the master of the house. There followed a pause in the conversation, and during this pause the girl lost her last shreds of respect for the guest, and the head of the house steeled himself. The lady of the house, however, who knew that look of her husband's only too well, and feared it, was filled with anxiety. This anxiety prevented Hilde from defiantly throwing down the gauntlet. It reminded her of her obligation to achieve victory by cunning.

She became the perfect little hostess, offered round the platter with cold cuts, passed the caviar, lifted the lid off the tureen to let the aroma of sausages waft into everyone's nostrils, drew attention to herself and the various dishes, saying that they came from her Papa's kitchen and cellar, and the wine (she filled the glasses) was a French one.

At that word, the guest became as attentive as a cat when it spies a bird.

"Your Frenchmen are pretty scared of us."

"Of course they're afraid," acknowledged Hilde—sounding as if she were dealing with someone who had escaped from a lunatic asylum—and laid some salmon on his plate.

"Is the salmon from dear Papa's cellar too?"

"No, salmon don't swim around in the cellar."

"Salmon swim in water, pretty young lady, and your Herr Papa is swimming in money."

"And I'm swimming in bliss when you call me pretty young lady."

There followed a pause, which Eva hastily filled; she expressed the thought that swimming through the air—flying—must be bliss.

"From up there, can you see that the earth is round?" asked Hilde. "I really mean it. I'm sure you must fly so very high that you can see that the earth is round!"

He expressed his most sincere thanks for such a lofty opinion. And in response to her invitation, he told them how he had come to take up flying.

His friends, now colleagues, had brought it about. They felt that painting wasn't much of an art, but flying was real artistry.

"That's one of the newer definitions," the head of the house interjected.

"One day, I go along with them to the airfield, where we're sitting around a long table, drinking. Then I get them to explain the aircraft to me, as a colleague has just landed. And then, whoops, I climb in and suddenly make the plane take off. They are all startled and rush towards me, but too late. I was tipsy, which explains my bravado. My friends down below are thinking

I'm going to crash at any moment and the plane will be smashed and I'll be squashed to a pulp. I fly a fair distance, flawlessly, and then comes the return home. And the moment for reflection, for during the landing, oh, dear, then I really did have my work cut out for me. The plane wobbled about a lot, my goodness, yes, before it was all over happily. But finally I touch down perfectly and roll up in triumph. There was no more laughing at me after that. It's a wonderful feeling, flying. You feel like a king."

"Like a dictator," corrected Kain.

"That's too simplistic a view. Ruling a Reich is no easy matter. The Führer has worries."

"The Field Marshal has worries, too," said Hilde. "The Austrians aren't to his liking, they are too artistically inclined for him. Nor, by the way, is he to their taste. He is too martial for them." And anyway, the guest was not helping himself. What, after all, was the point of all the food on the table?

"If I put all that away, I'll never become a jockey."

Hilde cried out. He wanted to be a jockey too!

That was only a joke, he said.

In these matters, said Hilde, he was not to be taken seriously. Flying was not enough of a sensation, expeditions not dangerous enough, so perhaps horse-racing would be the sport for him?

"Then, I'd prefer big-game hunting in Africa."

"Because hunting here is not dangerous enough for the Herr Ingenieur." This interjection came from the host.

But the one at whom it was directed seemed not to appreciate the bitterness in this. He replied calmly that hunting rabbits indeed did not appeal to him at all. He caught rabbits with his hands.

Kain's interjection went to Hilde's head. It provoked her to greater boldness. She poured wine for herself, drank it straight down, topped off the guest's glass. The wine was strong, she was feeling merry, her wishes were turning into plans. Without beating around the bush, she came straight out and asked the guest whether he would take her across the border in an airplane.

"If you buy one for yourself," he answered brusquely, "it will be no problem."

She had been wanting that for ages.

And had been taking ages to think it over, too, he retorted.

And how would she get it out? Across the border? This plane?

"I'd fly you across the border and set you down."

"You'd really do that? Nice. Very nice. Papa must buy me an airplane."

This turn in the conversation was not to the host's liking. Startled, Eva glanced across at Kain, who was frowning and looking pointedly at Hilde and then, turning towards the guest, said:

"I would advise you not to put too much weight on the enthusiasm of my young friend here, Papas don't buy airplanes quite so easily. She has always wanted to be a pilot, and she hasn't achieved that."

"Come, now! Papa would buy me anything! As a child, I wanted him to buy me the Kahlenberg. . . ."

"And he did buy you the Kahlenberg, Hilde."

"He bought me a meadow round the foot of the Kahlenberg . . . you are always treating me with such irony. Now it's been closed off and guns are standing on it. Eva, feel my cheek, how hot I am."

"And all disheveled! But with blonde hair, that doesn't matter. So you wanted to be a pilot."

"They rejected me, because of the baptismal certificate in fact, because I don't have one. That's not my fault. How cool your hand is, you always smell so nice and it's lovely here in your house. I feel so good, as if I already had the plane."

"For that, you have only to come to me."

"And for that, you're going to get a large piece of hazelnut-cream cake; our cook was making it back in the days of Emperor

Franz Josef. Why do you want to lead this expedition? Aren't you afraid of the natives?"

"Me? I know no fear. No one is going to sneak up on me from the rear, you can rest assured. My men are all behind me, guns at the ready."

"What if they cause trouble in front of you? What will you do then, Herr Pilz?"

"Fire, Frau Doktor, shoot them down. Don't take such fright, I'm not shooting yet, and certainly not at you."

"So that's why you've had these crates of ammunition brought here, now I understand! Papa couldn't work out why you would need ammunition up here at our place."

"What are you talking about? Herr Pilz has his ammunition for hunting."

"So is hunting out in the country dangerous enough for him, Eva?"

"This is no rabbit-hunt. Out there, there are very different kinds of danger, and that's exactly what attracts me, danger. And that's why I'm sitting here with you, because I enjoy danger."

"I hope Hilde is the greatest danger for you, Herr Pilz."

"And you'll let all the people live, you'll only shoot somebody when they cause trouble, and then you'll get an even higher rank if you shoot a lot of them."

"Yes, perhaps. So, am I supposed to wait until somebody kills me? We'd look pretty silly if we were always hanging about for the others to open fire first."

"You've no more wine in your glass, here's some, let's drink together. Down the hatch! My Papa would also like to meet you. Will you visit us too?"

"Why not? If that would please you. I like to give pleasure to everyone."

"But only as a sideline, Herr Ingenieur," said the host.

"Oof! The wine went down the wrong pipe. Please excuse me, neighbor."

"Hilde, I don't like you always drinking it straight down."

"Eva, let Hilde drink."

"You see? I'm allowed to drink! I'm brave enough for anything when I drink; I'm even daring enough to ask for us to be on a first-name basis and address each other as *du*, Kain—I really would love to call you Andreas, it suits you so much better. Can we drink to close friendship?"

"Not today, Hilde."

"You sit there so relaxed, not eating or drinking, saying nothing and simply scoffing the whole time and now you turn me down flat. I'd so love to address you as Andreas."

"You may call me Andreas."

"But Hilde wants to drink to close friendship with you."

"Hilde is too much of a stranger to me today. I'd rather wait until I recognize her again."

"That was a rebuff. It upsets me terribly . . . but it's not altogether my fault . . . you must realize that . . . a poet knows everything . . . to tell the truth, I'm disappointed you don't know that . . . let's you and I raise our glasses, Herr Legionary!"

"With pleasure. Here's to the former Austrian Legion!"

"If you were with the Legion, then you must be someone who throws bombs! Are you in fact the man who threw the bomb at Krems? How exciting! We're sitting here at the same table as the bomber of Krems! Surely you weren't the one who threw those bombs! So you *have* killed people?"

"Well, that usually happens when bombs are thrown, little lady."

"Do please tell us, was it you, at Krems?"

"Hilde, you are asking rather too many questions."

"Let Hilde ask what she wants, Eva."

"But Herr Pilz must be proud of his bombs! That's why he has risen so high! That's the way it is when they hand out ranks, isn't it? Drain your glass, otherwise I'll think you are some shabby cheap drunk!"

"Don't do as she asks, Herr Pilz, that wine is strong."

"Let the Herr Ingenieur drink, Eva."

"Herr Doktor, you have my interests at heart, haven't you? Cheers, to the lady and gentleman. You wanted to ask me something, Fräulein Hilde. Do what you wish with me, ask me as much as you want."

"You are so terribly nice to me, and I'm being so terribly nice to you."

"Are you still quite sure of what you're doing, Hilde?"

"Quite sure. If you like, I'll pile up all the plates and carry them out, Andreas."

"Fine. I'll put you to the test."

"Oh, lovely, what are you going to do?"

"When we are all finished, you can take the plates away."

"Is that all? How disappointing! If it's no more than that. . . . Is that your last word on the matter? Is that the way a poet talks? What about the fluffy clouds? I'll have to conjure them up for myself . . . why are you laughing? . . . I can see a slight mist already, and I can see you double, two poets. I'm frightened enough of one and I'll have to hold on to you, Neighbor Pilz. Please, stretch out your arm towards me. May I?"

"Of course, with pleasure. Hold on tightly; there's enough strength there. Take a good grip."

"My fingers are digging into the swastika. Now I'm going to ask you something else—don't faint, but another bomb is on its way, and it's this: you can't possibly have killed anyone with a bomb, otherwise you'd be a *Gauleiter* by now! Why are you laughing, Andreas?"

At this point, Eva wanted to know whether he had been on an expedition before. Didn't he dislike such long journeys?

Herr Pilz had been in Africa. The sun burned hot there, and

monkeys leapt about all over the place, he said. He didn't like it, because the people there, the natives, were so cruel. When a person was dying, they would carry him into the forest and leave him there to expire. Once he was driving with some friends when they saw a swarm of vultures at a certain spot. They got out and approached. There lay a man, white and emaciated he was, the vultures were feeding on his body and he was still giving out his death rattle. His left leg had already been gnawed clean, like a skeleton's. What they did there was to abandon people in the throes of death, probably in order to avoid any trouble with the corpse. That was the kind of barbarians they were in Africa.

"I've had a gruesome experience too," said Kain animatedly. "But it wasn't in Africa. What do they call the docks again, over in Leopoldstadt? There I saw a woman running, her hair flying loose, with red, very blotchy cheeks and wildly staring eyes. On her outstretched palms in front of her she was carrying a small parcel. In the parcel were . . . "

"Were her diamonds, Herr Doktor."

"In the parcel were her son's ashes, which had just been sent to her. She went all along the street shouting 'Heil!' She was crazy."

"I can tell you in strict confidence, and you could have told her this if you had known, that those were not her son's ashes at all."

"What's that? You mean her son is still alive?"

"Nothing of the sort. But they don't have the time to pay attention to what ashes they send to whom. They send off one lot with the others and don't give a damn about who gets what. Ashes are ashes."

"Please change the subject. Just look at Eva."

"But, Frau Doktor, why so sensitive? Nothing is going to happen to you. No one can harm any of you, you can rely on me for that."

"Now there you are, see how nice Herr Pilz is. You know, I

can tell you between ourselves that I don't believe a single word of what you are saying. You haven't thrown any bombs or plundered any homes or burned anyone's hands with acid. . . . "

"Those are excessive measures."

"It's very nice of you to admit that. But why do the police allow it?"

"If you want to force your way into a house, you have to throw meat to the dog in the yard. The Christians, too, were thrown to the lions, and now, well, now a few Jews are being thrown to them."

"Is that so? Is that what they do to the dogs? Is that what burglars do? They throw meat down?"

"The meat they throw to the dogs, Herr Ingenieur, is poisoned."

"Poisoned? In the French Revolution heads rolled like potatoes out of a sack. With us, everything proceeds peacefully apart from the odd excess."

"What do you mean, Andreas, about the poisoned meat?"

"You'll come to understand that later, Hilde."

"Now you've spurned her again. Now don't faint; wouldn't you like to hold on to me again? Please, I'd like that, Hildy."

"Thank you, Pilzy. I'm glad, too, that you have your uniform on. Beneath it you're wearing a woollen undershirt, and yet people always think you're all so tough. It's all a fraud, then. Or are you wearing the woollen undershirt because you're so skinny?"

"Eva, if Hilde doesn't behave, then I'm going to have to leave."

"Now he's really angry with me. . . . "

"Hilde, take the dishes out now, and when you come back, you will behave yourself and sit down properly and talk civilly again."

"I'm supposed to talk civilly to this monster, to this scarlet mushroom. I get a red face even looking at him. Now you're angry too, Pilzy, aren't you?"

"Not at all, Hildy. Let it all out. If I don't like it, I'll stop you."

"Then help me carry this tray out, because in fact I'm seeing two trays, and if I lose my grip, everything will fly all over the place, and I wouldn't dare have that happen in front of these two stuffy people here."

"Let's do it then. You take hold of this side here—wait till I've opened the door. There, I've got it. Let's go, Hildy . . ."

"You certainly served up a very clever banquet, Eva."

"And you, Kain, what tales you do spin!"

"Unfortunately, he doesn't notice a thing. You have to keep dropping the broadest hints."

"Hilde's doing more than enough of that."

"Hilde isn't being altogether honest, she's crafty."

"She is doing it for your sake, Kain."

"For her age, she is almost too crafty, to my mind."

"And for all the wine she drank, she is amazingly in control of herself. You can't tell her she may drink and then expect her to carry on talking soberly. Every sentence she utters makes me tremble."

"The words you tremble at delight me, and those that you like annoy me."

"What's the purpose, Kain, of talking with that parrot in human terms? He just cannot understand you. He only talks in hollow phrases he has learnt and can grasp only empty phrases."

"The purpose, Eva, is this: that I should not be ashamed of myself."

"Don't say another word. . . ."

"Eva, we're back! Frau Wlk has left you all the dirty dishes from lunchtime!"

"That was me. Frau Wlk isn't coming any more."

"Hildy wanted me to wash dishes out there. You're laughing, Herr Doktor."

"That brings us back to our topic: what your Führer, I believe, calls 'clearing the decks,'" said Kain.

"What do you mean, Herr Doktor?"

"Well, you are driving people to suicide in their thousands."

"Every revolution has its sacrifices. Just think of the way everything was in the World War, and after the war the odd bunch of people here and there is of no account. You keep forgetting that a revolution has taken place."

"Can it be called a revolution, Herr Ingenieur, seriously, or was it a sneak attack?"

"Sneak attack? Don't make me laugh! It was well thought out. You're barking up the wrong tree if you believe that."

"Will you share this apple with me? Will you, Pilzy?"

"I shall share with you whatever you wish. The Führer is merely grinding out the rust; if anyone proves difficult, then a way out will be found for him, you can rest assured of that, Herr Doktor. The Jews have their way of doing things. The ones that take their own lives, well, they're no great loss anyway. Who's going to go kill himself? The Führer is only cleansing their ranks, he's a benefactor to the whole of Judaism."

"Bite a bit off. My, the way he's looking at me, how nasty, and you've gone quite red, like deadly nightshade, no, like that red mushroom! And your uniform is like that . . . the way you're looking at me, Pilzy—you'd like to strike me dead on the spot."

"Where are you going, Eva?"

"To the window, Kain."

"To take a look at the mountains in the moonlight?"

"No, at the earth."

"Eva has a brother-in-law, he's called Werner and he's always peering into the earth. That's what makes her so fond of the earth."

"But I'm looking in the ground for something else."

"What are you searching for?"

"I'm looking for past people, Kain."

"Why do you want them to have become earth?"

"The earth is fruitful, peaceful and good—humans metamorphosed into such a form would be a comfort for me."

"My brother would tell you that humans crumble to dust, such fine dust, so minute, that nothing remains, nothing."

"I know, Kain."

"So you will have to keep a tight hold on your soul."

"It's in the process of dying out."

"Now, there I'd rather believe the words of a greater man: 'Nor can the eons erase the trace of my days on earth.'"

"The traces of his days on earth—now is when they will be erased, Kain."

"Not at all, Eva, so long as there are people who stand at the window and gaze into the earth."

"And how long will they remain?"

"But what's the matter with you today? Why on earth are you sad? It's far from the end of the world, the sun will last for a good while and there's no comet to be seen. Have a cigarette. That'll do you good."

"I thought, Pilzy, the Führer was the new comet in the heavens."

"Yes, the Führer, that's true."

"When a comet appears, it means war is coming."

"The Führer doesn't want a war."

"I know, I know, Pilzy, God is his witness, but why does he always invoke God, since after all he doesn't like people who go to church?"

"Because they let themselves be persuaded by the high priests."

"But they are the servants of God."

"They are the Pope's sidekicks, and he is always trying to interfere in politics. With him the Führer is already angry enough.

When the bible-thumpers meddle with politics, all hell's let loose."

"That reminds me of Napoleon's phrase which Madame de Staël parried so well. Unfortunately, it loses something in the translation."

"Now you're reminding us of Napoleon, Pilzy."

"Napoleon said to her: 'I cannot stand it when women meddle in politics.' Whereupon Madame de Staël replied: 'Sire, if someone chops off your head, surely you ought at least to know why.'"

"Very good. He was a great man, that Napoleon. But the Führer is greater, he conquers all countries bloodlessly. And what a man he is! So uncomplicated, so modest! He lives off nuts."

"Without bloodshed your Führer will not conquer all countries, Herr Ingenieur, that . . ."

"Neighbor Pilz! Pass me over the pastries. From the little table over there. What delicate plates you have, Eva, with works of art on them. Is that Venus?"

"Oh, look at this! Now that's funny! She's just stepping into a steam bath!"

"What are you talking about? She's not, she's flying off up to heaven. I can see a cloud there."

"No, Hilde, that's heaven descending towards her. That's Jupiter who is embracing her. It's Io."

"That's nothing but pure pornography, I'll have to confiscate it immediately."

"You could have admired this pornography in the art museum, Hilde."

"Now, around midnight, after four glasses of wine, you have to give me a lecture. Pilz didn't recognize Io either, and he's a painter, like the Führer. Do you know the Führer personally, Pilzy?"

"I'll say I do! He has spoken to me personally, and shaken my hand."

"I know a Jewish woman he shook hands with too. She filed past him with a group of people on an excursion."

"As Napoleon did with those suffering from the plague. But he couldn't have been aware of it,' said Kain.

"Otherwise he wouldn't have shaken her by the hand. Our Führer is very particular about that sort of thing."

"What do you mean, particular? He shakes hands with so many people. In that respect, the Pope is more refined, you have to kiss his ring. Would you like to kiss the Pope's ring, Mr. Pilzy?"

"If I ever got close to him, I'd do the Führer a favor!"

"Now I've had enough! If you keep being so horrible, I'm not going to speak to you any more."

"Come now, Fräulein Hilde, you're not going to cry, are you? What are you crying for?"

"Because you're so cruel! It would be better if you were to go and burst open the concentration camp! I'd never have thought you could be like that. . . ."

"But that's just what I have done! Now you see how nice I am. I have freed a prisoner!"

"Do you hear that, Hilde? Will you also have a cup of tea, Herr Pilz?"

"Now at last you've taken to me! All through the evening, you haven't paid me the slightest attention. Oh yes, people are grateful to me. I fetched him straight out of prison. They all shook my hand, his mother-in-law can't even speak German right—they're from Poland—and all of them stood around me thanking me. His wife, her mother, her brother, her sister-in-law. 'Thank you, thank you,' they kept on saying."

"You just tore down the walls and rescued the man from Dachau?"

"He wasn't in Dachau, he was in the Lizzie. That's the prison on the Elisabeth Promenade."

Herr Pilz had known the man for years—an admirer of his

art. The man bought paintings from him, a hunting scene too. It showed a stag that had been shot, a sixteen-pointer, with the happy hunter bending over the beast. When the man was arrested, Herr Pilz went to see his wife. This time, Herr Pilz told her, he was going to buy something from her. Namely, the cinema. But she wasn't allowed to sell it, she had no power of attorney from her husband, she replied, extremely apprehensive. And started crying. He felt sorry for the woman, and thought to himself: get him out yourself. So he went to the prison in order to release him. And how difficult that was! There was some fellow there who didn't want to let him in. Herr Pilz showed him his party number and, in a flash, there was the . . . Israelite . . . standing before him. The joy of the man! He didn't even read the power of attorney, he signed and there he was, free! Herr Pilz then walked him part of the way home, a good-natured fellow, by the way, though small and fat with enormous nostrils, like a negro.

Hilde thought it was a pity she wasn't going to be staying on in the city. She loved going to the cinema.

So when was she leaving?

"Not for ages yet." She was going to miss this room, the pictures on the walls, the carved wooden figure, the balcony over there, even with the flag on it, which shrivels up every day anyway. "And I'll miss these two, and if I come across them abroad, they'll be strangers."

"You'll follow us soon, Hilde." Eva kissed her hot little face.

What meaning does the word "soon" have for a young person? Besides, then Kain will have no time for her. Now she's good enough, these are exceptional circumstances. Yes, she is coming straight out with it, because the wine is making it easier for her. Out there, she'll be pushed into a corner and will have to lead some timid existence. Does it annoy Eva, her saying all this?

"It does me good. I feel bitter, too."

It wasn't difficult for her, because she was going away with Kain. He'll write a big book about everything. . . .

"When . . . when you . . . go away with Kain . . . you mustn't be sad."

"Our friends are scattered all over the world—people who didn't necessarily find each other easily."

"You still have your brother-in-law here, Eva, that Werner whom I never get to see. He's like Papa. Papa is prickly too, and speaks his mind. But apart from that he's terribly nice, he's always giving the staff bonuses, he's helpful to everyone, and he's also registered as a benefactor to all sorts of organizations."

"Under the monarchy your Herr Papa also gave money away!"

". . . An angel walked through the room just then. I haven't been so lost for words in ages. You really know a great deal about our family."

"That'll have been an angel of death. Cheers, ladies and gentleman!"

"Please, don't talk like that, Herr Pilz."

"Be quiet, you toadstool, you! Can't you see that Eva is horrified?"

"Come now, come now, why so jumpy? We weren't talking about you."

"Calm yourself, Eva—do, after all, we were only talking about Papa, and I'm not superstitious."

"May I inquire as to the grounds—or the underground—for your fears, Eva and Hilde? I fail to understand the meaning of what you are saying, nor the point of it."

It was all Pilz's fault, said Hilde. With his angel of death. An angel of death passes through the room, he had said. That had scared Eva. She is so easily frightened these days.

"And are we all going to die now? I don't quite understand."

"Whoever is superstitious is afraid of such talk. And there's no shame in that. Napoleon, too, was superstitious. And certainly not a coward or uneducated. You only have to read his testament, there was greatness and intellect in that."

"He had style," asserted Hilde, giving Herr Pilz what she felt was a withering look. "One has to show consideration for people who are superstitious, especially women, and you don't let nuns into their bedroom. I'm certainly not superstitious, and I'm terribly fond of nuns, I feel so sorry for them. Anyway, we were talking about Papa, so there's no reason for Eva to tremble. Because, at the worst, death touches only the person last spoken of."

"In women's heads," said Kain, "logic takes some strange twists and turns. But as far as this sinister instance is concerned, the talk was, as far as I can see, about Werner, and I'm easy in my mind about Werner." And he laughed. "Werner will never die. Werner is flesh turned to stone, and I mean that in the best sense. Firm and never to be ground down. And nicely colored, too, like a rock with a high ore content. He lives for himself—he has no friends to drive him to an early grave. Not even enemies, nor, for that matter, a wife. He eats everything up by himself. He cannot understand people, but turns his clear eye on them and they understand him. Perhaps not his eccentricities, however. Forgive me, Herr Ingenieur, I'm drawing a portrait of my brother. He's a confirmed bachelor and though a little grumpy, in no way without feelings, quite the contrary; he could go away any time he liked, yet will not leave his homeland at any price."

"I like the man," said Herr Pilz, and drank to his health.

"I like him too. He is something out of the ordinary. He has character, even in these times. And who can you say that about without reservation?"

"And at a time when things are made hardest for people with just such character," said Eva softly.

You couldn't get the better of Werner. He had no weaknesses to make him vulnerable. The angel of death would certainly not touch him. Werner would defy the gloomy image.

So, Herr Pilz wanted to know, what did the angel of death look like?

"Like an undertaker," said Hilde drily. "With death's-heads and horrible bones. These gentlemen are also known as *Sturm-Staffel* or SS-men. Is that not so?"

Yes, that was true. Did she have any other questions?

Kain had something he wanted to ask. Leading so broad and varied a life, going on expeditions, flying high above the world as a pilot, how did he come to find himself in the narrow confines of this situation?

"What narrow confines?" Herr Pilz was baffled by the question.

Well, here he was, sitting with them, even though he was an SA-man, sitting here because he knew how to appreciate it. He appreciated intelligence and courage, and that's why he was sitting here. So why go along with this farce? Woe to the vanquished—you divide up the spoils, you plunder them. But to deny them any honor, the vanquished, that was unworthy of a civilized people, that was barbaric.

"But they don't have any honor."

"You wouldn't sit down at the same table with us if you could possibly believe us to be without honor."

"You mean . . . well, yes . . . you are exceptions."

"And the others?"

"The others live by the Talmud. It says in it that they have to kill us Christians."

"Only the Orthodox ones know the Talmud, Herr Pilz."

"Besides, Herr Ingenieur, there is nothing of the sort in it. A great deal lends itself to all kinds of interpretation, but the same thing is the case with the Bible."

"Surely no one lives by the Talmud, Kain."

"They're all living by it and are a threat to our lives. That's why we have to wipe them out, so that they don't kill us."

"What are you doing, Hilde?"

"I'm looking for a poisoned pastry for Pilzy, I put poison in it specially for him. You've got to eat it now, right away. Come on, open wide, eyes shut. Right, now you're going to die."

"In your arms, I hope. The dying warrior."

"Among the books I'm leaving behind I have the Talmud upstairs. I'll bring down a few volumes and you can show me a place which will back up your claims."

"That's a good idea, Herr Doktor."

"I'll come with you."

"No, you'll stay here, Hilde."

"Now isn't this nice, here we are just by ourselves, little raven-haired lady. Why so silent? Did you make yourself so pretty for my sake? You've invited me to this fine supper, so I'd like to invite you out tomorrow. First, we'll meet by the pond, then we'll walk through the woods, next will come supper and then . . . let's arrange quickly what time you'll come, whisper it quickly in my ear."

"Come now, Pilz, surely you aren't going to fix a rendezvous with my friend while I'm here. I'm jealous, you know—and after all she is much older. Do leave her alone."

"You'll get your turn, just be patient. One thing at a time, otherwise Eva will be annoyed. I promised her first, so she comes first. Oops! You've poured too much wine into my glass, you little minx."

"Down the hatch, at once."

"So, what time tomorrow, my little Evie? Come here, I've something to whisper in your ear—what time shall we play Adam and Eve?!"

"Don't you feel well, Eva? Why are you holding your head?"

"Yes . . . I mean, no . . . it's just . . . so heavy."

"Have a drop to drink, and soon your little head will be rustling like the leaves in the forest, in the moonlight."

"I don't consider it at all right that you should promise her such things in front of me—after all, she's a married woman—so what are we girls to do if you go throwing yourselves at grown women? Eva, I'll tell your husband if you . . . Come on, empty your glass, Pilz."

"She keeps filling my glass all the time, this jealous little minx. I can't take any responsibility for what might happen if I drink that."

"Eva, Pilz is afraid of us. Down the hatch!"

"I'm not scared of anything—whoops—after all, I'm not Lot, and you aren't Lot's sons. Darling, whisper quickly in my ear when we can play Lot. . . ."

"Here you are, the Talmud, Herr Ingenieur." Kain had come back into the room.

"Yes, yes, thanks, very kind of you. If only I could read it! Hilde, the little minx, has poured me so much wine everything is rushing in my ears . . . just like in the forest. Hic! Even I can't understand what I'm saying, you must excuse me, I do beg your pardon, but I'm feeling quite dizzy . . . I know a little song, about the forest. . . ."

"Then it would be best if we call it a night and escort this young lady home, Eva, she isn't quite steady on her feet."

"Now you're leaving, just when everything's so nice. Take me with you!"

"I think you ought to sleep it off, Herr Pilz."

"Who wants to sleep when the moon is shining so beautifully, let's go for a stroll outside, up and down. . . ."

"Herr Ingenieur, we'll bid you good night."

"Good night, Pilzy!"

"Good night, Hildy. Wait, I've just remembered the ditty about the forest:

> Through heath and wood and glen,
> My strength through joy I spend,
> A hunting man am I!"

V. ABOUT FURNITURE

At the door, a young woman is standing. She has ash-blonde hair and is pale. She holds the door open and it almost seems as if she is about to stick her foot in.

"I'd like to see the apartment."

"The apartment has already been rented."

"To me. The apartment belongs to me."

"You are . . ."

"I'm Frau Pilz. When will the apartment be free?"

"In two weeks. We're just waiting for the visa."

"That's too long for me. Is there a lot to be done?"

"Not really. The hallway has to be whitewashed. I don't find this green color healthy. The kitchen will have to be freshened up."

"Can I see it?"

"Of course, you can see all the rooms."

"I know the big room with the balcony already. It's only this side I'm not familiar with. Oh, what *does* the kitchen look like! Like a greenhouse."

"It wasn't intended as a kitchen. That's why it has this wonderful view. The stove is not very good . . ."

"The stove is bad?"

"Yes. And I would seriously advise you to contact the gas company, sometimes the gas-pipe smells suspiciously."

"My God, how high the ceiling is! It must be very cold here in the winter."

"The kitchen ought to be divided up. It does get really cold in winter. Your husband has had his packing cases set up here in this pink room, while this blue room is usually very nice, but it's in a state of disorder at the moment."

"When people are moving that's inevitable. I know about

that. I, too, had to leave in a hurry. When my husband had to go to Germany. He fled to the legion, you see. I moved everything in six weeks. I went to join him."

"With your furniture?"

"Yes, of course. I only sold the old things. The amount of your stuff that gets broken."

She looks like a maid who has got herself married. It cost her a lot of effort to bring that man round to it. Now she is no longer a maid, but she had a hard job in achieving that. That, and the ash-blonde hair, suit her very well.

"Why is all your furniture still here?"

"I can't very well take it all with me, because we don't know where we will be able to settle finally. I want to put it into storage, because there are some valuable old pieces."

"Put it in storage abroad, that's the way I did it in Munich."

"I can't afford to do that abroad . . . we're only allowed to take ten marks with us, you see."

"But you'd have to pay plenty for it here too."

"That won't be a problem for us, because we have to leave all our money behind anyway."

"Do you have that much?"

"If it were a lot, we wouldn't be allowed to leave so easily."

"Is that all the rooms?"

"There are attic rooms upstairs. Your husband has a provisional bedroom up there. Do you want to go up to see him? You can get there from here, you don't have to go out into the corridor first."

"No, I've already been upstairs, and he's not at home. He was on the night-shift yesterday."

"He's not at home?"

"This is the bathroom?"

"The furnishings are mine; I'll be leaving them here."

"I'm certainly glad to hear that. It will have to be repainted, but my husband will do all that himself."

"Well, that will keep the cost down."

"It takes too long for my liking."

How unjustly life has treated her. There she is, with such an upright personality, married to that buffoon. At a loss, and with austerely pursed lips, she looks around her.

"Do you maybe want to move in immediately? Take my room. In any case, I've been living on the other side since yesterday, in the little room next to the one with the balcony."

"You're living in the other side?"

"I'd be only too glad. We'll certainly be leaving soon, it's all a question of the visa."

"That won't suit my husband. He doesn't want me to come before he has redecorated everything. He wants to give me a surprise . . . you see, he's . . . not . . . the way people might think . . . he's a good man . . ."

"He speaks so nicely about you. I only cook breakfast here in the mornings and make tea in the evenings. You'd have the kitchen all to yourself. I'd be only too happy; I have so much to do with the packing and you could keep your part of the apartment clean and that would save me a lot of work, if you see what I mean."

"That's true, but . . ."

"You could move into my room, the paneled room, it's charming. I'll show it to you. It's been compared to all sorts of things—a railroad compartment, a candy box. See?"

"It looks like a washing trough. There's someone sleeping there!"

"Yes . . . I can see . . . in fact . . ."

"Jesus and Mary! That's my husband!"

In the little wood-paneled room, which had reminded him of a booth for private assignations, Herr Pilz was indeed lying asleep. He was sleeping on the bed, fully clothed, in his uniform or, rather, what was once his uniform and now resembled nothing more than a crumpled, dirty, brown tangled heap, twisted crookedly about his body. His trousers afforded an embarrassing view of woollen underwear, sticking out but drawn tight by a buttoned waistband. His legs hung down from the bed, but he was sound asleep, his face bathed in sweat and his open mouth revealing a row of blackened stumps which, in his waking state, his long upper lip kept hidden.

His wife shook him awake, meanwhile glancing angrily at Eva, as if she had forcibly laid Herr Pilz on the bed and tied him to it. Then she hit him on the shoulder and he struck back, but then awoke. He no doubt recognized his wife, yet still befuddled by his dream he imagined himself at home and inquired rather stupidly what kind of mood his mother-in-law was in today. She reprimanded him hastily and none too gently, so that he jerked into a sitting position. He looked at the room and its owner, who was standing, undecided, by the door, and then tugged at his clothing. The sight of his uniform brought him back to his senses and he apologized to the lady for the disarray.

This politeness enraged his wife inwardly, but at the same time she moderated her tone and, instead of giving him the full benefit of her candid opinion, she merely asked how he came to be in this room, whether his attic bedroom had collapsed; had he fallen downstairs into this bed or had he lost his way, since he must certainly have been drunk to come and lie down here.

He had been slightly merry, that was true, he said, and admitted that he could have manoeuvred himself up the stairs and into his own room only with great difficulty.

So had there been so much drink on hand during requisitioning last night?

He hadn't been requisitioning, but rather there had been a pause in operations, a day off, he said. So he had accepted an invitation, from the Herr Doktor, to a refined supper. It was first class, and the household very friendly and informal.

She was glad to hear that, came the reply. Because she too was moving in here, indeed had already completed the move, which had cost her no more than the decision, a yes or a no, and she had said yes, so here she was.

She couldn't do that, he protested. Not everyone could move in immediately. There was no room and that was no way to behave.

But she was able to call on the Frau Doktor for support. There she was, standing here, and she directly requested, indeed begged, her to stay. It would be a relief for her, who had enough to do on account of their move. She would be taking half the apartment off her hands.

He sat there open-mouthed. Looked at his wife, and then across to Eva, who maintained an embarrassed silence. Then, artfully, he lowered his gaze.

"That's marvelous," he declared. "The Frau Doktor begged you." That changed the whole picture. From beginning to end. If she had been begged outright, then she must stay. In fact, he insisted upon it. Even though he had wanted to introduce her into the house, as was only fitting, into a house that had been freshly painted and newly refurnished.

At this, both women blushed, although each from a different emotion.

He had a surprise for her, he said. Could she guess what? Impossible. Well, he was going to start at once. With the distempering, with the painting. Let the whole world hear it, that didn't matter to him. The walls will gleam, he would turn the apartment upside down, put the furniture out in the corridor. So that he would have elbow room for the battle.

That was something he most certainly should not do, the tenant of the apartment allowed herself to remark. For the landlady was fussy about her corridor, the neighbors were tyrannical, and that was her furniture that he wanted to put out there, so all the complaints would land on her head if it got in the way. Having said this, she left without waiting for an answer.

She needed no answer, she knew enough.

She had wanted to be clever and secure a happy conclusion for herself. And had brought about the conclusion. She could guess what was being decided in that room, which in fact was her room, after all.

In that room, Herr Pilz was holding his brown shirt in his hand, because it was crumpled, stained, torn, and his wife was also pulling his woollen undershirt over his head. But then he slipped it back on—there was no other one handy to change into and this one would be just fine for his painting work.

At this, he held his wife tightly, but she fended him off with a sullen pout that made her look like a child rejecting, out of defiance, the chocolate it would love to have.

He interpreted her movement correctly and expressed his regret that this trick had been played on him and he had to let his wife move into a house that had not been suitably prepared to receive her.

But here he met with resistance. She knew, she said, that it was not consideration for her that had delayed her moving in. She hadn't yet been completely taken in by him.

He protested and asked her to show some taste. All she had to do was look in the mirror (by the way, not bad, that mirror with the ornamental gold frame) and compare. Was she black-haired and no longer young? Most certainly quite the opposite. The whole room was not at all bad, and free of charge into the bargain. And why did she talk so obsequiously to that expellee, that subhuman creature? She should behave with more vigor and not let it be seen that her father was a tram-driver, but instead make it clear who her husband was. What a membership number! "Just look at it, that number, not bad, eh?'

"Leave me in peace," she said, and declared that she was not going simply to take everything away from these people, but would buy it cheaply.

He was infuriated by this. And he dragged up every reproach he could think of—things that lay far back in the past. Was she not ashamed, had she forgotten, how things had been for her in earlier times? And what he had made of her? And if she had forgotten all this, he would refresh her memory. Was he to tell them in the Party about the kind of company she used to keep?

She became like an obedient dog. She admitted that she had not known all this. She had been pleasant to these people, because they had been pleasant to her. That they were to blame for the war, that they were to blame for the unemployment, that they held all the newspapers in their possession, that they usurped the capital resources, that they violated women and murdered children, all these things had been unknown to her. Even now, she still believed in exceptions, for example this writer here in the apartment was respected in the village, even held in affection. Nor could his wife be the worst kind, she even had a portrait of the Madonna hanging here.

She's trying to disown her tribe, having that there. An old trick. Besides, she should take a good look at what people care about up here. The uglier the motif, the more it appealed to them. That was the subversive thing. These cripples here! Painting cripples! "You'll take that out, and the Führer will go into that frame."

She was not yet altogether convinced. The evening before, after all, he had been sitting here with these people and heaven knows what he had said because he talked a lot when he had been drinking.

He had had something to drink, he admitted that, but because he was worried. He had to drink away a problem which he wanted to confess to her now. Incidentally, he had her brother to thank for the whole regrettable business. From A to Z.

"Because you let him get away with so much. Because you slip his wife everything, even the leather armchairs."

The one thing had nothing to do with the other. It was true, he said, that her brother had involved him in a piece of business, a fine mess. Even now, the very thought of it gave him a toothache. He alone, of course, had been the one to suffer, since he, as a superior, was responsible to the Party. And had to get all the money together by himself.

He had been on a requisitioning mission. There had been foreign currency, bundles of it, heavy gold chains, thick as your finger, diamonds as big as cherries, silver tableware, they only ate off silver.

"Would you believe it?"

All this was gathered together and wrapped in tablecloths, several of them, one couldn't hold them all.

Admittedly, the owner kept on shouting that he was a Catholic, an Italian, and a member of the nobility into the bargain. His wife came running in, but she was fat, with dark skin —enough to give you the creeps—her nose crooked, with hairs growing out of it, she cursed and complained till she was foaming at the mouth, her husband ran to the telephone, it had been cut off, and he, as the superior officer, confiscated the gold, diamonds, currency, silver, and damask, while the brother packed everything up.

As they left, they were followed by a volley of swear words and a promise that this was not the end of the matter.

They met next at the Italian consulate. Because the alleged Jew-boy really was an Italian, who would have believed it! Dark, small, with flaring nostrils and a fat belly. And then came the worst of it. The zealous brother, her brother, had had the gold chains melted down immediately and the Italian insisted they were old pieces, antiques he called them, and what's more, family jewels, valuable mementos, and he would be acting very decently if he were to demand only ten thousand marks. Melted down, the gold brought in next to nothing, a few hundred marks, and that was all your brother's fault!

"And all that, when we're giving them South Tyrol as a gift," said Frau Pilz.

"That's the way the Italians are. They're not black-haired, crooked-nosed, small and ugly for nothing."

"And absolutely unpatriotic."

So what did he intend to do?

Confiscate. By the sweat of his brow, he would requisition until the money had been raised.

Half an hour later, Herr Pilz was standing in the kitchen eating a pudding. Chewing slowly, he watched his wife ironing his uniform blouse. He was also stirring the paste heating up on the stove. Then he fetched large pots from the kitchen cupboard and poured the mealy paint into them. This he now mixed together with water and paste. He carried the pots into the anteroom. Here hung a work-coat in a brightly colored floral pattern, the kind women wear. Herr Pilz slips into the coat; it is too short for him and dangles about his knees, but it's good enough for painting in.

He paints the dirty, stained wall in the hallway without cleaning it first, and in this too he resembles his model and Führer. Because he is painting over the dirty, stained wall in brown.

He paints, takes a step back and scrutinizes the effect. He paints, and the furniture gets in his way. He splashes it, sees this and thinks, Stop, not a step further!

The furniture is good, light-colored stuff, everything in this house is made of hardwood. It will go well with pink, so it is pushed into the pink room. The big wardrobe with the lidded trunk, the three-piece chest of drawers and the old farmhouse cupboard. A fine piece, that rustic cupboard, a piece of craftsmanship from the old country, something patriotic, a showpiece for visitors. Eighteen hundred and thirty-nine, it says on it, yes, those were different times, a hundred years ago. A modest age.

Herr Pilz pushes the furniture into the pink room to join his crates, and in doing so, puts some dents in them. But he has no wish to ask his wife to help; it's supposed to be a surprise. He goes back into the hallway, but then has second thoughts. To be on the safe side, the hallway should be painted last. Although there is now nothing standing in his way, not even the umbrella stand, which he also carries into the pink room, along with the silk gentleman's umbrella; it's as good as new.

Once again, Herr Pilz stirs some paint, white this time, as white as innocence, and he paints the bathroom with it. Satisfied, he smiles at himself. No one insults the SA-man Baldur Pilz, low Party number and sensational character, and gets away with it. The real sensation will come when he holds his first reception in this noble house. They'll be amazed, all his friends and colleagues.

Frau Pilz is having exactly the same thoughts at that moment. She is taking over her wood-paneled room and improving it. The pictures on the wall have to go, who would think of hanging cripples like these? Whoever painted that? That sort of thing is printed off and sold by the hundred! "Breughel," the man's called. And this tattered Madonna in the frame! My God, but this Christ-figure is hideous! The wood is all rotted away, and in the face, of all places. And dirty—they don't even think of washing it down.

Herr Pilz, too, is angered by dirt. By the dirt behind the bathtub. The plaster has all crumbled and fallen off back there. He goes into the kitchen to mix some plaster. In the kitchen stands Eva, looking at her vacant hallway, baffled.

"Where on earth has the furniture gone?"

"It's in my pink room, next to the crates full of ammunition. That kind of stuff explodes very easily. If you're not afraid, you can go and get it back."

Eva left the kitchen without answering and knocked at the door of her paneled room. No—no longer her room. Her eye falls on the table with the pictures and the small Gothic wooden figure. But she looks away again at once, as if the whole thing has nothing to do with her. She goes to look for Frau Pilz.

Thank heaven, thinks Eva, she's blushing. She can still blush. With a look on her face to suggest she has something else on her mind, she asks whether Frau Pilz needs any furniture. Furniture for the hallway and a rustic dresser.

"I could certainly do with them."

"They're already in the pink room."

"Surely not," she cries, and is all sweetness again, forgetting all her dignity and going to have a look at the pieces of furniture.

Eva goes off, well satisfied, to her rooms at the front of the house. Frau Pilz has been won over and Herr Pilz has been outsmarted.

The newly-won Frau Pilz was busy helping the outsmarted SA-man push the furniture from the kitchen into the pink room, over to the wall, next to the rustic dresser.

"The pink room will have to accommodate the whole lot for now," her husband explained. "After all, it's well protected by the ammunition, so nothing will go missing. You can safely leave the furniture from your paneled room in there, it belongs to you now, but just be careful with the ornamental mirror, it's worth a lot of money. We'll show that hussy. No one stands in the way of an SA-man. Inviting my wife into my own house! When it's not yet ready to receive her! She did that to you deliberately."

"But I can't simply keep the furniture, just like that. It's mahogany. We must pay something for it."

"It seems to me that you too are now intending to defy an SA-man. Do as I tell you and go to your boudoir."

When Eva went into the kitchen to put on the kettle for tea, there was no longer any kitchen there. The furniture had disappeared, and on the stove, paste was bubbling away. The smell left a sickly-sweet taste in the mouth.

Once more she knocked at the door of the paneled room. It was only ajar, and swung open. Frau Pilz was sitting at the dressing table dusting her face with dabs of pink powder. Startled, she hastily wiped the powder off her face with her apron and stood up.

"I wanted to ask where my kitchen furniture is."

Frau Pilz went red and hesitated with her answer.

"I'm only asking because I'd like to give it to you as a gift, too. Don't you want to have a look at it?"

"Oh, yes, thank you," she stammered.

It has to be said, to the credit of the human race, that Frau Pilz was now slightly ashamed.

"May I ask what price you would be asking for this furniture in here? It's pretty old, but I could buy it from you all the same."

"The fact that it is old increases its value. These are antique pieces. But I'm not asking you for anything for them."

Eva closed the door to the paneled room behind her for ever and went to the front side of the house. Here at the front, in the study, everything is chaste, imperious, and untouched. The atmosphere here is one of strict order. Kain will not so much as notice what is about to happen next door. And a whole lot is going to happen. They are being pushed out, before the appointed time. They are being dispossessed, and forcibly. They are going to have to move out before they can travel. That much is obvious. This cup, too, they are going to have to drain. To take Kain out of his peaceful study, down into the cramped surroundings, into the dangerous city, where no one knows him, where he is an outcast. He will have to live in one room with his brother, who will be no agreeable partner. Yet they must be grateful that this brother exists, with his small apartment and an obliging janitor. The janitor is lord over each and every tenant and one cannot be choosy. One can pick and choose nothing any more. One could move into a hotel and be taken away from there and locked up. One could move in with friendly Aryans, happy to be able to rent out their rooms, but after a few days the Aryans would be punished and one would be taken away to a concentration camp. To move in with Jews is not possible, for their apartments are being taken from them, they are being evicted and whole families are being crammed together in single rooms.

A cold sweat stood out on her forehead. All this she has to try, little by little, to make Kain understand. He's sitting down there in the garden with no notion of what is going on here. Placidly, he bends over his work. He has been able to maintain his dignity here in this house. Isn't that worth everything—the fact that he has retained that dignity? Now it is a question of acting prudently and making a peaceable withdrawal. It will be necessary to speak to Werner, today, and alone. And Werner will have to come and take his younger brother, complaining, down to the city. First, though, she has to calm herself. That is possible if she goes out on to this balcony and lets her gaze wander into the distance. Because the far distance has no conception of these cramped conditions. It is unmoved and surrounded by the blueness of the skies. It stretches as far as the Alps and the Alps stretch right into a foreign country. And the foreign land is the good land; the homeland means enmity, hostility right down to the flag on one's own balcony. The flag which already hangs in shreds and has been turned brown by rain and sun. But Herr Pilz no longer rearranges it, he now has too much to do with his thirst for revenge and with his new possessions.

What do possessions matter, what do even the little things in the space in which one lived matter? What do even the paintings matter, torn out, degraded, what do the colors matter that are being left behind, or the fragrance, all the smooth and rounded surfaces? There are greater things to be retained.

What do possessions matter when greed is sated on them, when greed is dazzled by them in order to dazzle with them?

Eva stood there for a long time, looking at the mountains, the blue skies, the trees, and she became altogether calm and, with a smile, went down into the garden, to Kain.

He was reading in the *Odyssey*: Odysseus so harassed, so harassed, tormented and disappointed and how noble is his suffering . . . as if transfigured, he raised his head and saw Eva standing before him.

"Only the dog recognized the homecomer," he said to Eva, into the midst of her turmoil and her cares, still intoxicated by the poetry.

"Do you believe that's possible?"

"Yes. Since the events of this year. Since familiar faces have changed beyond recognition. Since many a loyal face might now conceal secret falsehood. Since many a countenance itself has changed . . . yours too, Eva, although not in a base way . . . it has nevertheless become harder, more difficult to decipher. How a long life changes things! Are you coming up to our room with me? Odysseus has lifted my agitation—I'm eager for work once again."

Slowly they walked through the large garden.

When Kain opened the door to his study and went in, however, he no longer recognized the room. There was furniture standing there, one piece leaning on another, armchair piled on armchair, and a bed had been pushed in, his bed, from the next room, from the bedroom, the last living space left to them: on his desk lay, in total confusion, his reference books, and, short of clearing everything off the heavily laden desk, they would have to sit on the bed.

In fact, Herr Pilz was already painting in the next room. He was painting Kain's bedroom. He was painting it blue, like the sky, and later there would be stars in it, golden stars.

The two of them sat on the one bed, the one free space in the room. They sat in the same position, both leaning forward with heads bowed.

VI. AN AIRPLANE TAKES OFF

The next day, Herr Pilz has already painted a great deal. The kitchen is white, the bedroom blue, with the stars still to be added. Now he is standing in the hallway, putting on the brown. The doors to the corridor are standing open so that the paint can dry better.

Up the steps to the corridor comes a young lady. Beautifully dressed. And pretty, too. Her hot cheeks plump, fresh, ripe, her hair in disarray. That's a wild woman, that's the right one. Now, in summer, she is wearing a fur coat. But he knows this woman. At her neck hangs a string of pearls, as long as a watch-chain, which she waves around like glass beads. She approaches him.

"I've come to you," she says in intimate tones, "on account of the airplane. I want to buy it."

In his astonishment, Herr Pilz drops his paint brush and has to put down his paint pot before he drops that too.

"You want to buy it?"

"Of course, that's why I'm here. You will help me, won't you, and then take me out of the country. You did promise."

"That can be done all right . . . Have you spoken to your Papa?"

"Yes, and he is in agreement."

"He agrees? Tell you what, come into this room. There's such a mess here in the corridor, and besides we can't talk in peace here. And you'll get your lovely fur coat dirty. In here. No one will disturb us here."

"In there? Into that powder keg!"

"Yes. Still, it's better than my wife. Now there's a real powder keg for you! If she finds out I'm doing you such a favor, I'll be in a real fix. She'd have me up before the Party."

"So where is your wife?"

"She's here. Moved in, she has. That's something the fine gentleman let me in for, the Herr Doktor. I believe he's after my wife, what with the wife he's got."

"But Pilzy, the day before yesterday you liked her so much."

"When I was drunk. Then I see everything double. When I look at her today, it makes me feel sick. Such a black-haired little creature. Now, you should see my wife, she's tall and blonde and smart into the bargain! She's getting into everything! He'd just better look out, your friend, before all this really gets under my skin. For that sort of thing he could land in the concentration camp, and a bit more besides."

"But, Pilzy, am I small and dark?"

"No, not you, I'm not talking about you. You're pretty, a pretty little doll, God knows how your Mama managed it, your turning out like that."

"There now, you see, Pilzy? If Doktor Kain wants a tall blonde, he can always . . . have me. He doesn't need your wife."

"They can never get enough."

"But Pilzy, he doesn't want me at all."

"What cheek. Now listen, don't you put up with that. If I were you, I certainly wouldn't have any of that. The way he spoke to you!"

"I have a confession to make. You can believe it or not, but since that evening, I no longer like him."

"Oh, yes indeed, I can believe that. The way he behaved. No real man carries on like that. He must have something seriously wrong with him."

"You're quite different."

"Go on with you, you're just saying that. I know you people, I just don't believe you any more. And that business with the plane, you're just saying that, too."

"I'm quite serious about that. I've even brought the down payment."

"With you? Well, so where is it then? Out with it. How much have you brought?"

"I haven't any money on me, I've . . . I've brought a diamond. Papa paid three thousand schillings for it. It must be worth at least three thousand marks by now. Mama says it's worth much more than that even. Jewelry has gone up in value a lot."

"Let's see it. Now that's worth a tidy two thousand marks, quite handy as a down payment. We could drive out there right now, take a look around, and in three days you can have your kite. When will you bring the whole amount?"

"That's just it, Pilzy. Not this week. If Papa decides on something, it always takes a while. I'll bring one installment next week, and then another a few days after that."

"If your Papa wants to buy an airplane, does he think he can pay in installments? How does he make that out?"

"Is he the one that wants to buy it, Pilzy? He most certainly does not! I want to! And when I set my mind on something, then I see it through! After all, he did buy me that meadow. He has half agreed already, but not altogether. But I'll get him round to it, you can be sure of that. Surely, Pilzy you can trust me to manage that. If not Papa, then Mama."

"Oh yes, I certainly believe that once you get something into your head you'll achieve it, just as you've managed to talk me round into getting you the plane. You don't think I'd do that for just anyone, do you? But this is taking much too long; you won't have the money together for two weeks."

"So why are you in such a hurry? I don't need it right away."

"Me? I'm in no hurry. Not in the least. It's none of my business when you want it. I'm going off, on my expedition. It's you that wanted the plane, not me. As far as I'm concerned, you don't have to buy one at all. Don't I have enough trouble of my own? If my wife gets to hear about me wanting to do a favor for an Israelite woman!"

"But why are you so bad-tempered, Pilzy, she won't find out.

That's something between us. By the way, can I take somebody with me when you fly me out?"

"Aha, so what do you know! So you want to take somebody with you. And who might that be?"

"Well, for instance . . . my friends here."

"You want to take these two with you? That's a laugh. Then we'd have to stick another zero on the price of the plane. Why do you want to take them with you, when they're leaving anyway? In a week's time, they keep saying. Or can't they get away? Will nobody let them in anywhere? I can easily imagine that."

"Of course they're leaving. The notice of their visa has already been given, Pilzy. I was only asking. I wanted to put you to the test."

"Put me to the test! This gets better and better. And what kind of test would that be?"

"Well, I wanted to know whether I can count on you."

"Count on me, fine, but if anyone gets wind of this, it'll all come to a bad end. Maybe you think I'll take your money and run off?"

"How can you think such a thing! I just wanted to sound you out, to see if you would do me a favor as a friend. Of course I know I mustn't tell anyone. That's in my own interests."

"I'm only too happy to do you a friendly favor, but only once we're up in the air. Just think how great that'll be."

"Do you loop the loop? Don't people fall out when you do? Why ever not? Oh yes, because the cockpit is closed in. But then, don't you fall on to the roof? Or do you fall on your head?"

"Come on now, silly. If I were to fall on my head, then we'd both crash. Don't worry, I'll make sure nothing happens. No-body's ever dropped me on my head!"

"You're sweet, Pilzy. There's something else I'd like to ask you, but don't be angry. Will you be angry with me?"

"Of course I won't be angry. Who could be angry at you, you little silly?"

"Just why are you being so horrible to the two of them, I mean, to Eva?"

"Me, horrible? I never even see them. As far as I'm concerned, they . . . I'm not in the least bothered by them. I'm in my apartment, getting everything sorted out, and I don't give a damn for these people. I'm letting them go on living there. How do you think the others would go about that?"

"I know, of course, that you're something special, but at first you were so nice, and now . . ."

"Begging your pardon, but he was the one who brought my wife into this house, when I wanted to bring her here only once they were gone. What kind of reputation will she have, living under the same roof with that circumcised man? If it weren't for your sake, he'd be living somewhere else by now, I'm only being nice on your account, because of our plane trip."

"Oh come on, now, you're such a sensitive person, you couldn't bring yourself to harm a respected writer, one with such a good name, especially abroad. After all, you're an artist yourself—and politics have no place in the arts."

"Now there you're very much mistaken. These writers are stirring up the whole foreign press against us, it's a scandal what they cobble together, nothing but reports of atrocities. If I had my way, not one of them would get out!"

"Pilzy, I've got to go now, and next week I'll come back and see to it that I drum up the whole lot."

"Well, yes, certainly I can't do anything with the stone, the best I can do is put in an application, I mean, they're selling like hotcakes, are the people's airplanes. You won't find anything like that in any other country."

When Hilde visited the second set of tenants of that apartment, or rather, of the one single room left to them, they were sitting on the bed, caught up in a discussion which seemed strangely touching because it was so remote, bearing no relation to them and their situation, even though everything about the room filled with furniture and dust pointed directly at their situation. What had happened was that Eva had let slip a remark about what would become of those children—what a hostile brood, what a belligerent phalanx against everyone who did not belong to it, to their "race," as they called it. The way they were growing up, these children, with hatred, inculcated for all eternity, against their fellow men, hatred for either their religions or their convictions.

This "for all eternity" was challenged by Kain. It was true that the new pedagogues were feeding poison into the minds of the children, drip by drip. Toughening them with poison. First and foremost, however, that poison was being directed against the teachers themselves. But that was not the point. What Eva was overlooking was the unpredictable. The fate of each and every human being. One's fate does not follow the lines of precepts in school, nor of the teachings of the masters. Fate acts arbitrarily, driving people where they do not want to go. Fate has already broken many ground rules and caused many intentions to run aground. That fate is now leading the oppressed (and who is not?) into the arms of the others. Yes, merciless fate—however strange it may sound—reconciles.

Just as, he went on, fate reconciles nature's orphans, those who exist at the margins, life's wallflowers—now they have been allotted a status. It tugged at his heartstrings, he had to admit, whenever he saw a young woman like that—her age indeterminate, because she belonged among those who, even in childhood, had not been adorned with the soft down of youth. Whose sex was barely discernible, because feminine charm was lacking—whenever he saw a girl like that these days, with a gleam in her eyes, a glimmer of something upright, almost ready to laugh because she was no longer thin, yellowish, freckled, with straggly hair and grayish teeth, because she was now ennobled, she was uplifted, she was "Aryan." And the swastika, a brooch, a pin or a hat adornment on her otherwise mediocre appearance, was not a badge of aggression, it was a sign of help-lessness which, he repeated, touched his heart.

Hilde's appearance interrupted his flow, although in the pres-ent circumstances there was no chance of the conversation being about appearances. Instead, the girl pushed and squeezed her way between the pieces of furniture towards the couple, finally landing by the window next to the balcony—the windowsill offered possibilities for a young girl. There she sat, legs dangling, and talked light-heartedly of her latest victory over the National Socialist Party next door, of the airplane project, of the probabili-ties. These she had firmly in her sights, indeed they were certain-ties: going off abroad with her two friends, without a visa—that ridiculous rubber stamp which was so decisive and yet such a mere nothing in a plane, which was taking ages to arrive and which had placed them in this terrible situation here.

Her report had its effect. Any way you looked at it, her ludi-crous, childish plan was bound to bring disaster, Eva said with some vehemence. She was losing her composure as her own words heightened her annoyance. And so the girl, still confident of victory, turned to Kain for support.

But now, now it was becoming clear to her: she was being left completely in the lurch. Like Nora in the Doll's House, she thought, and searched within herself as to whether she was still fond of him or whether it was all over, as with Nora. But unfor-tunately it was not all over. She had been abandoned, by the originator of her foolishness, innocent though he was. She real-ized that Kain did not feel moved, even by her flushed cheeks and moist eyes, to voice his agreement.

Should she manage to get the money together, she would never set eyes on that airplane, that much was obvious. If she didn't get the money, which was to be feared, then she would drag them all into an abyss. But she would raise the money, she insisted, and, in her fury at him and at herself, she twisted her kid gloves into a knot. Most certainly she would raise it. And what could go wrong then? At worst, she would be swindled. What did losing the money matter if it had helped to stuff the dragon's jaws? She seemed infatuated by this dragon metaphor.

Even that possibility makes no sense, he said. Because people of that sort, who acquired possessions dishonestly, also applied dishonest means to defend their possessions.

If he were challenged, she replied. But she wasn't thinking of doing that. There should certainly be no cause for contention between them.

Here, Eva backed her up. What she had started was undoubtedly foolish, she said, even if well intended. However, if she were in a position to see it through to the end and to put all that money at stake, she could at least secure everyone's peace of mind.

At that, Kain became vehement. If the girl distorted the facts, that was pardonable. But Eva was old enough and equipped with sufficient psychological perspicacity to be aware that something dangerous was being set in motion here. Something dangerous, yes, he stood by that expression. Whichever way you cared to look at it, it was dangerous.

Now there was a lull in the conversation. Because here, in this topsy-turvy confusion of piled-up furniture, in this dirt, dust and disarray, in this discomfort, each found it difficult to regain some composure.

We'll move down into the city, Eva then declared. They couldn't wait up here for the visa. The foe's passive resistance was like an attack; she was even fetching drinking water from the garden in order to avoid the kitchen.

The visa must surely arrive any day now, Hilde said soothingly.

But for how long now had they been hearing that? Eva objected. Under the terms of the order and the signed ordinance, they had to leave the country in two weeks' time. And now on top of that, all this as well—this fear that it would not arrive in time, this fear.

Which was quite unfounded, she was brusquely reminded. In such cases, foreign countries made considerable allowances. A photograph of the police order existed abroad, in two capital cities, and she was multiplying their difficulties for no good reason.

It was clear from his tone of voice that he was not as confident in his mind as in his words.

Hilde, happy to shift the topic away from herself, asked about the new lodgings. They were pretty primitive. Nor was the landlord very pleasant. Still, they would be living in Werner's place and, hidden behind his rough and ready exterior, there lay more warm-heartedness than behind the unctuousness of a paid landlord, who would be hard to find anyway, since there was no room for outcasts in that city. They felt they were in good hands with the brother, who, by the way, already had a subtenant staying with him, one who had been compulsorily billeted in his apartment.

Eva went on to explain how it had not been at all an easy matter verbally drafting the lease agreement. The way Werner sat there calmly, giving no answers, as she herself had to apply to move into his house. The way he stared the whole time at a flower pot, and not one with a plant in it, but just damp soil, into which he kept digging his fingers. The way he turned his head this way and that, feeling in the soil and picking out stones. The way he—instead of giving any response to her pleas for accommodation until their departure, which was bound to come soon—looked up and said: "There is a story of a head, buried in a flower pot," and turned his clear blue eyes towards her. It was obvious he had not been listening. Then, however, when she repeated her request, the way he became almost warm in his agreement with everything, without, however, creating the impression that his mind was quite on the matter in hand.

"What a charming person he must be," said Hilde.

"You can't really describe him like that," Kain laughed. "But he is his own man, and there's something about him. I feel drawn to him, perhaps precisely because we are so different. I could never imagine the world without him. I don't have to see him often, but he has to be there, must be in this world. In short, I'm fond of him."

There was a knock at the door, which opened to the accompaniment of a sob. Outside stood Frau Wlk. She came straight in, although it was not her habit to pay a visit when the Herr Doktor was present or to give voice openly to her concerns. Far less to sit down, as she now did. Yet the totally unfamiliar chaos, the lady and gentleman sitting on the bed, the confusion in this sanctum, armchairs piled on armchairs, the young Miss on the windowsill, bare-legged, all this gave her the courage to sit down on the chest by the door and to launch straight into her story.

This was that her boy had run away, with two others of his age, so she had been told. He couldn't write to her, he hadn't a penny to his name, and that was that. The work on the farm was hard, the food watered down, and the promised payment was not forthcoming, not even a first installment. They had all grown weary of this, so they all up and left, the older ones first, and now her boy was roaming, she sobbed bitterly, all over the place, from farm to farm and, exhausted by his travels, had first to earn his food and a bed for the night through hard labor. But the worst thing was that she had no idea where he was at that moment, in what corner of the world, otherwise she could raise some money and send it to him. "The Jews would lend me the money," she added, without a trace of respect, so absorbed was she in her despair.

Eva consoled her as best she could. The boy was not all on his own, she said, he wasn't an isolated case, and all the others before him had made their way home safe and sound. His experiences would toughen him for life, and anyway, he wasn't lost in some far-flung country—and it could be worked out on the map which way he had gone. And she opened the concise atlas lying under a film of dust on a pile of books and gave Frau Wlk a rough idea of his route.

Perhaps it was the shortness of the distance as represented on the map. Perhaps the reassurance that a simple person derives from seeing it in black and white; Frau Wlk examined the lines in the atlas, dried her tears and declared it a scandal the way respectable people had to live, while those (and here she came out with a swear word) act as if they owned the very air itself. But they'll pay for it, just as they'll pay for tormenting the Czechs. And now she related once again the story about the ballot box and the Czechs, because she was forgetful. Then, however, came a new occurrence, about which they all had to laugh.

This was the story of an attorney, to whom she used to be in service. A famous attorney, a fine gentleman, she would testify to that. Two policemen, who had known him for a long time, came up to him as he was stepping from his carpeted entryway into his car. They had come to search his house. Naturally, Frau Wlk said, he had already burned or disposed of everything and had kept only one bundle of documents, which lay in his desk drawer; the destruction of this bundle would have meant the destruction of certain people's very existence.

So when the two policemen entered his house, he did not act nervously as people normally do, but remained self-assured and demanded sternly and with dignity what was the point of all this and how could it make sense to them, men of the law, that in a well-ordered state in Central Europe a respected attorney—his reputation impeccable, his incorruptibility a byword—should have his home ransacked like some criminal. They were cowed by this, hoped to ease the embarrassing nature of the situation by means of polite words, but nevertheless, with silent determination, proceeded to search the library, the shelves of files and the folders on the desk, but without finding anything incriminating. Finally, the attorney unlocked the desk drawers for them, three at once, and they looked through these drawers. By the fourth one, their search had become only cursory. In the fifth drawer, however, lay the bundle of papers upon which hung his freedom in this life, and perhaps his life itself. He pulled it open with the expression of a minister who has been accused of having purloined ten pfennigs. He lifted out the thick bundle and held it up: "I don't imagine this will be of interest to you," he said scornfully without letting the files out of his hands. Respectfully, the two bowed and left his chambers, full of apologies. He was saved.

That story, said Kain, reminded him of the experience of a poet in a village who had also rescued himself from a tricky situation through his cool-headedness. But he did not get to tell this story, because there was another knock at the door.

In came the landlady. She entered with a friendly smile, but then blushed, ashamed by the state of the room, which she remembered differently. She even faltered in the middle of her greeting and directed Frau Wlk, who had leapt to her feet to offer up her seat on the chest, back to her place with a pat on the shoulder, even though such intimacy towards her servant was alien to her nature.

She had come to say goodbye. The final farewells could not take place outside the house here—a great pity, she said. Still, radically new situations did bring profound changes for everyone, she herself was compelled to go along with many things, but for the sake of the cause. Because now at last her South Tyrol, her homeland, was coming back into the fold of the Fatherland. Herr Pilz, who was now lodging here, had given her his firm promise on that. Having waited, as she had, for twenty years, she could wait a few more weeks.

At these words, Frau Wlk cast such an eloquent glance at all present that the landlady could not miss it. What some people—women of exaggerated maternal instincts—were putting about should not be taken too literally, she said. The youth of today don't know the meaning of hard work, they only want to eat the best food and to be well paid for their idleness into the bargain. In her day, things were very different, she had had to go about her work, much worse fed, and without any hope whatsoever of being paid.

Whereupon she took her leave, with a firm handshake for each and every one, instructing Frau Wlk not to linger too long: all sorts of jobs were waiting for her. And then she left, and on her way out she ran her hand over the door panels, on which some paint was flaking away.

Behind her back, Frau Wlk retorted that that was how people spoke who had no children. She was a good soul, the landlady, but all the same she was an old maid—she should have gone into a convent and given up waiting for her Tyrol. It was like a sack with a hole in it, that Tyrol.

And then she gave the Frau Doktor a piece of advice; she shouldn't report a change of address for her husband, shouldn't change their registration up here and shouldn't report any new address down in the city in the meantime. Those fellows had their lists, and anyway up here the Herr Doktor was in everyone's good books. If he were to appear on a list down in the city, then God knows what kind of mischief they would cook up.

Eva found this advice excellent and not at all difficult to follow, if she knew the kindly landlord of the apartment down in the city. But instead of voicing this, she replied with a piece of advice of her own, urging Frau Wlk to secure the furniture in this room quickly, before the Pilzes next door came and helped themselves. Whereupon Frau Wlk assured her that two sturdy men would come up from her place, she could depend on that. They would take everything outside right away, load it up and not leave a stick of furniture behind. And with that, she threw her arms round Eva's neck and thanked her effusively.

In great detail Herr Pilz was explaining to the tenant farmer: they were going to do it like in the country. They'd send word to the neighbors to ask, how much did they need? For sure, they would not be able to satisfy all of them. Meat is scarce here, he laughed. They could offer it for sale with due ceremony, even generosity, but they could also sell it in one piece to the butcher down in the city, but he would pay only half as much because he earned only half. A gold mine, by the way, a butcher's shop, he'd exchange his cinema for one any time. Naturally, he himself would buy some of the cow, whatever he had space for, his sister-in-law would buy some, his mother-in-law, too, would there be much left for the neighbors then? Because the landlady would put in her bid and he, the farmer and owner of the cow, along with his family, would certainly carve off the finest parts of the rump for themselves.

But the cow wasn't sick, protested the farmer. The vet had examined it, and thoroughly at that. The milk yield was meager, but pure; the beast was not very productive, not very strong, but that was all. The cow was not sick.

Herr Pilz objected earnestly. Did the farmer think he had been awarded his high rank because of his height? Certainly not for his girth. Or that he hadn't earned it? It was his custom to reflect before he acted. The cow was sick, one had to have the courage to come straight out with it—and to lift its eyelid. Its eyes were sick.

This time the children are standing well back, and the red-haired girl is standing over by the wrought-iron gate, next to the little handcart on which her parents have placed their suitcase. Today, the little girl does not look so ugly. Today she is smiling and her mouth is no longer so big. Her thin skin has a pinkish glow—she is no longer tense—her limbs are like ivory, her once red eyes are brown, and they are shining, and her cheeks are full. The little girl looks back on the extensive garden and there is not a trace of regret in her features. Because she is going to go on a big ship, out on to the sea and to a distant country where her father will be a gardener and plant trees, and she will run around the whole garden and no one will scream at her, "Ruthie, now you've got to be called Sarah!"

She shouts all this to the children and they come running. "I'm going to the sea," she says, "to the New World."

"We've got a sea now too," says Horst, the eldest, "and a new Reich. We're by the seaside too."

"Yes, but your cow is going to be slaughtered."

"I won't allow it!" cries Horst.

"So what can you do?" says Ruth. "You're not a grown-up. By the time you're big enough, it'll be dead."

"She's not going to be slaughtered," says Horst and starts to cry.

"You mustn't cry," says his little brother, "otherwise you'll not get into the *Jungvolk*."

"I don't want to get into the *Jungvolk*."

"But then you'll never get into the Hitler Youth."

"I don't want to get into the Hitler Youth."

"If you don't want to be in the Hitler Youth," says Ruth, "then you could come to us. By the time all the trees are big. Then I'll write to you and you can come."

"He won't be allowed to come," says the little brother. "Mama wouldn't let him."

"When the trees are big, he'll be big too, and then he can do everything big people do."

Her father is already pulling the cart away and Ruth has to run after him.

"You'll have to learn English," she calls back to Horst. "Because when I get to the New World I'll be able to speak English and I'll write you an English letter."

"Can you speak English right away there?" Horst asks.

But she can no longer hear him. She runs off, her cheeks flushed, trembling with happiness.

Her hair was burning like fire.

Not everyone who was leaving that house on that day was of the same mind as the little girl. There are, among all the others, some people who have both feet planted firmly on the ground, and thank heaven most people are like that, they cling to essentials, stride forward, look reality square in the eye, reach out for what is tangible.

Then there are some who walk as if in a dream; they stumble, because everything is a dream, they take refuge from waking, cling on to what is lost, grasp out for the unreal, grope about inside their dream and fall on the merciless ground.

These people are thankfully a minority, they are variations, isolated cases; they are known by various names, and they are also called poets.

And just such a poet was, on this day, taking his leave of the big house, the garden, the mountains, the hidden corners, the pointlessly barred windows, the almond trees, the slopes, the little stream and the roof garden. The place you are about to leave forever becomes, for that reason, a thousand times more precious. You are woven into that spot, you hear secrets in its corners, you whisper secrets back, the place dies a little because you are leaving, and you die a little with the place.

For the second time, Kain did the rounds of the garden, the house, the sloping drive, he went up into the tower, which did not belong to him, he walked through the round, milk-white lobby and, practically climbing up the pillar, he looked at St. Florian, he gazed at the Venus who danced on one leg, and then he was stonily reminded to set off on his way at last.

For down at the wrought-iron gate, her features cold, dressed in dark clothes, in hat and gloves, stood Eva, and from her hat a veil hung over her face, arming her thoroughly against what she was leaving. She was leaving the place the way you avoid the spot where a loved one who will never come back again once walked with you, the way you avoid that place because it exhausts you and churns you up and brings your pain to glowing heat.

"Doesn't it hurt you, Eva?"

"I'm not going to sing 'The Last Rose of Summer,' and if I were to sing it, it would be in English," she said, her voice hard.

Slowly, they went down the hill. And just as a young animal on a leash keeps on turning its head in one direction, in the direction where freedom is, Kain kept turning his head round all the time, walking almost backwards.

She could see the movement in his fine throat, the secret sobbing.

And then she felt her knees giving way. She stopped. The weakness passed. And now her features softened. Running towards her came two little lads. In blue blouses, with impudent eyes and rosy cheeks. They clasped their arms round her knees, those trembling knees, they hit her and pulled at her hair and tugged at her skirt. Behind them appeared, bright and beautiful to behold, their mother. She approached Eva, grasped her hand and shook it vigorously.

Eva almost thrust the little boys away. She nodded without speaking.

"I don't like this place," the mother said yet again, and again she took a child on each arm and carried them away, so majestically beautiful, like some biblical maiden carrying her pitcher.

From an open window came the strains of the second movement of the *Pathétique*, out into this chaos, into so much insanity, into a life that was cold and in turmoil. She stopped again. And suddenly everything was transformed. Suddenly everything became warm and intense and dreamlike.

"But you're crying, Eva!"

The tortoise lives in a hard shell, but is robbed of it because it is so beautiful, it protects it no longer, and leaves it naked.

Its secret is its serenity. It lives off nothing, off air, off leaves. It can be cut up, dismembered, torn apart, and yet it lives on, silent and solemn. But it needs warmth.

Without warmth, it is bound to die.

If the vulture spots it, it is bound to die. In its cruel claws, the vulture carries it high into the air and smashes it on a rock. Now its flesh is the vulture's flesh, now the vulture devours its flesh.

If the tiger spots the tortoise, it is bound to die. It turns it over, and now it is doomed. The tiger tears it to pieces and devours its flesh. The tiger rushes about and with its ferocious strength brings down everything, everything it finds. It leaves the tortoise lying on its back, and a tortoise lying on its back is bound to starve to death.

Unless, that is, a man spots it. He admires its shell, shining so beautifully. The man heats the animal until it glows, so that the shell detaches itself and his dream is fulfilled. Is this then a noble wish? The man is careful, he soon notices that the fire reduces the shine. Instead, he prefers to throw the animal into boiling water so that the shell suffers no damage. The shell is saved, and the animal creeps away, mortally wounded.

If the man wants its flesh, then he cuts it off the living body, fine and fresh and tasty. And he sees the animal's wise eyes and thinks: its head darts to right and left and no doubt it tastes very good, too. So he cuts the head off and takes it home and watches the head moving and snapping, that cut-off head.

For the tortoise does not die so quickly. It also has an inner shell, and that is why it does not die.

If one cuts its heart out, the heart goes on twitching for a long while. If one detaches its brain, it goes on creeping.

But then, of course, without warmth, it cannot live.

Part Two

VIII. MOVING IN

Werner Kain had an apartment in the city, consisting of one room and a kitchen. His meticulous, sound work as a geologist brought him no more as a reward than this one room, but neither did he need any more. What he needed were the long walls lined with shelves all filled with rocks, with carefully cleaned rocks, polished ones and dull ones, gray ones and bright ones.

Whenever he came home, his blue eyes would roam over the shelves, the work of many years. It may comfort a tree when one new layer of bark after another encases it. It comforted Werner beyond words to delve ever deeper under the surface of rocks, into the secrets of the earth, of its millions of years.

One day, his eyes flitted around, now suspicious, as if a foe were lurking among the shelves, now with a shimmer of hope. Yet, in the end, a look of confusion remained, clinging to him.

Those carefully excavated treasures of the earth, those finds, every one with a label attached, like a patient with his case-history, had, that day, been devalued. Who would be able to appreciate their sparkle, their shape, their meaning, their long ancient history?

Werner had been dismissed. Thirty colleagues in the scientific institution had reached that decision, and not a single one had had the courage to tell him to his face. So they had left a letter on his desk and put a stone on top of it. For the first time, Werner had regarded a stone as a stone and hurled it out of the window. Then he rushed home and, with clenched fists, threw all the rocks off his shelves with such force that, had they not been so hard with age, they would have smashed to pieces on the floor, and fell to his knees. Then he began to sob, a dry, tearless sob, and then he slowly picked the rocks up again and gently laid them back on their shelves.

It has to be said that his colleagues discharged him all too unwillingly. In their meeting, called because of him, they all agreed that he had to go. He was small of stature and his nose was not Roman. Yet there was something about his eyes that would make even stones melt, and no one among them could or wished to claim that he had, for so many years, sat over his rocks or searched for and excavated rocks because he was looking for gold. Indeed, when he had to leave, they even promised to meet up with him again. In the grave, when they had all turned to stone. And that was the consolation with which they sent him on his way, that they would all decay into stone, less than that, to ashes, to dust, to an insignificant amount of dust, to a mere nothing, and in an insignificantly short period of time, measured against the years, the venerable age, of the rocks.

Of all the inhabitants of the unhappy city, this man was the unhappiest. Those people in their rooms, cramped and confined, gagged and bound, were *waiting*. They were waiting for the great moment when the train would pass through this corner of the world, the border between unhappiness and peace, death and life, disgrace and freedom. Werner shuddered at this prospect; the border was, for him, part of the earth, wonderful, living earth, which he loved, which was his work, and which he would never, never leave.

Now he was standing out in the street, outside his house, waiting, as a mother waits for the coffin which will be carried out and in which her child lies dead.

Meanwhile, upstairs in his one room, the attendant from the museum was bending calmly over a packing case which he was unhurriedly filling. Werner himself had called him here and had himself shown him how each rock was to be handled, how it should be wrapped in cotton wool and, according to its number and the shelf it came from, bedded down in the crate. But then he could no longer bear to look on, and went to wait downstairs. The other people who lived in the house passed by, he didn't see them. He looked away, but even as he did so, his eyes became more piercing, boring into something, and it seemed advisable to avoid them. Two little boys went past, dressed in the brown shirts and the red armbands of the *Jungvolk*, *Pimpfs*, as they were called. They were singing a song about his long nose, straight to his face, but he didn't hear it. They became more brazen and threw a stone at him. Strangely, as the stone landed at his feet, he awoke from his evil spell, looked down at the stone as a child gazes at a kitten, and smiled. Even *Pimpfs* had no idea of what make of this kind of person, so the two went off about their business. Werner's smile remained for a while longer, but suddenly he was startled half to death.

The coffin was being carried out. The coffin and the earth's heart.

The attendant was standing in front of him, bent almost double. With a grunt he pushed the crate on to a cart, pulled on a rope, tightened it and, wiping his brow, took a letter out of his breast-pocket. The letter shone, remarkably clean, as it was drawn from his stout body.

In the letter, the director of the museum was making an application, in extremely polite terms, for Werner's name to be entered in the commemorative book, which was opened only on very special occasions, only when great services to the museum were considered to merit the honor of such an entry. However, this ceremony did not come about, because Werner stuck the letter in his pocket, unopened, and forgot to read it.

The cart moved off, and, with it, the soul of the man who stood watching it go. The earthly husk of the man remained behind and moved, as slowly as a tortoise, back up into the apartment.

It was, after all, perhaps just as well that Herr Felberbaum shared the room with Werner. For Herr Felberbaum (to whom this accommodation had been allocated because his own apartment had been confiscated, or rather, requisitioned) had so little understanding of his companion's sufferings that he was unable to share them with him, but rather, in a sense, chopped them into rough pieces. He talked such inconsequential stuff about stones that Werner would fly into a rage and threaten to throw him out, while Herr Felberbaum listened with gentle eyes, without feeling in the slightest offended.

That was very nearly enough to calm the geologist down, had not Felberbaum said, with the doggedness of a Moorish servant, "You think I have a heart of stone."

"Sir! If I must look at these empty shelves here and have before my eyes not their rich contents, but instead the contents of your thick head, it would be advisable for you not to touch on things which you are too addle-brained to comprehend."

Herr Felberbaum smiled in bewilderment, his enormous mouth spreading still wider, and then he patted Werner silently on the shoulder. Helplessly, he stood beside him, flushed and embarrassed, searching for words and finding none and then slowly went, shame-faced, into the kitchen.

Before Herr Felberbaum's billeting there, this kitchen had been a vacant room, with traces of the fresh lime-distemper not altogether cleaned off its floor tiles. The sink with running water for rinsing crockery served in this household as a niche for washing in. When he had moved in, Herr Felberbaum had brought a gas stove with him and set up a cooking corner opposite the washing niche. Now he stood in front of this primus stove, because some soup was simmering on it. He tasted the soup and was satisfied. He turned off the gas and poured the soup into a tureen, which he carried into the other room with a washcloth because it was hot. On the uncovered brown wooden table stood two wooden spoons and two earthenware plates.

Herr Felberbaum poured the soup straight from the tureen into the plates. There were pieces of sausage, potatoes and parsley floating in it and he started licking his lips, so good was the smell the soup gave off. When the plates had been filled to the brim, he took the arm of his companion, who was standing completely vacantly in front of the empty shelves studying a label with a blue border, which had been forgotten and was still stuck there. He drew the strange man towards the table and, sure enough, he complied, allowing himself to be led, sat down, distractedly reached out for his spoon and ate his soup without knowing what he was doing, why he was doing it, or for whom. It is obvious that this Felberbaum was the very embodiment of the commonplace, one of that annoying species of contented people, but it is also obvious that here, he was saving a man's life.

While the other absentmindedly cleaned his plate, equally absentmindedly allowed it to be refilled without raising his head, remaining bowed over his plate like some small animal, Felberbaum reflected on what he could say in order to distract this unhappy man from his thoughts. However, he could think of nothing and so he placed the plates one on top of the other, laid them in the tureen, with the wooden spoons on top, and carried the whole lot out into the kitchen.

In the kitchen, incidentally, stood a bed, as of today. It was a golden-brown wooden bed with a light blue counterpane. He was unable to go past this bed without skirting round it reverently. Now, after he had rinsed both plates in cold water and wiped the greasy ring clean with the washcloth, he remained in the kitchen for a long while. He brought out a mirror which had been standing in the corner by the sink, and hung it above the basin. He unfolded a screen which he stood in front of it. He unwrapped a picture from its brown paper, a painting of a hunter in the forest, bending over a stag, shot and bleeding, and he reflected for a long time on the best place to hang the picture. In the end, he decided in favor of the wall above the bed, over its bright blue cover. He drew a nail from his vest pocket, reverently pushed the bed aside and knocked the nail in. The picture was hanging slightly askew, but that was easily adjusted with a piece of cord. The bed was pushed back and now, for a good two minutes, he stood contemplating his work with satisfaction. Then, from the hallway, he fetched a little table that had been standing there bearing the telephone book and all sorts of brushes. The telephone directory was laid on the floor, the brushes went into the drawer of the table, he dusted the tabletop and spread a white serviette on it. The table was pushed over beside the head of the bed and now he laughed happily as he brought out a vase, a vase painted with delicate, greenish-blue flowers of indeterminate type, into which he would later put some forget-me-nots. A strange effect was created when he now unrolled a carpet and laid it on the tiles, as if to protect the bed from the bare floor. He walked on the carpet a few times to enjoy its softness, but with broad strides so as not to damage it with his heavy tread. Delighted, he looked around, and everything pleased him enormously. With special pleasure he looked through the window, the panes of which he had cleaned, with infinite care, that morning. Except for one rather greasy spot which grew bigger and bigger the more it was rubbed, so that it was better left alone, the panes were sparkling clean. His expression became even more satisfied, and anyone seeing it would not have imagined that he found himself in a city where he and his kind ranked far below the dogs.

But there was a reason why he allowed events to come at him with equanimity; he had no need to fear events: they had already befallen him, at the start, six months ago, as a purple patch under his left eye testified. With a black eye, however, he could be said to have gotten off lightly; he had already been locked up, beaten and released again and could now be glad to be alive. While those who shared his misery had to accept, with ninety percent probability, that their turn was still to come, he could go through life with ninety percent security, and the ten percent probability that he would be picked up again dented his sanguine temperament only slightly. Mostly, he was so preoccupied with other people's fears that he had no time to think of himself at all.

And on this day he was in a celebratory mood. This was due to the new lodger who had been registered, for whom he had snatched the carpet from his sister-in-law and the screen and the mirror from his mother-in-law, for whom the picture hung resplendent above the blue bedspread (in actual fact, it was not resplendent, it was dirty, dirty green and dirty brown; nothing, absolutely nothing about that painting was resplendent), for whom he had bought the painted vase, a blue-green vase with blue-green flowers on it, because this was no run-of-the-mill kind of lodger. Not a tenant like himself, who had just brought in a bunch of forget-me-nots from the windowsill where it had been kept cool. And, putting the flowers in the vase, he beamed as he thought of what kind of tenant this was.

The erstwhile kitchen was intended for a lady. A real lady, one you could spot from ten miles away. One who put you in a state of great wonder even without fully understanding her. One who spoke a different language from yourself, even though she was using the same language. One who thought, walked and lived differently from other people. One with a gaze that could look through walls, looked somewhere far off where he had never reached. A lady, the like of which you might perhaps come across in the theater, yes in fact, when Herr Felberbaum had once been to the theater, twenty years ago, there stood, up on the stage, just such a lady, with black hair and an extremely white face and a very weary, cultivated voice. Right up in the gallery you could smell her fragrant body and he wondered at the time whether that was possible or whether it was maybe a trick, whether that perfume was being secretly wafted about by the management, from the stage, so as to overpower the fascinated spectators completely.

Such a creature was, as of this evening, going to be walking about here and for that reason he stayed on in the kitchen and laid out on a platter the finest cold cuts; he sliced little gherkins and added radishes; it was now the fashion to eat such raw vegetables at mealtimes.

Yes, into Herr Felberbaum's flat and toneless life change had come. First in a nasty sense, for one day he had been dragged off, jeered at, beaten and locked up, and then in a good sense, just as day always follows night, sunshine comes after rain, fat years after lean. What he was now experiencing had sound, color, smell about it; it was like music in the forest, like rose-hedges here in the room, like all the silken colors in the silk shop down below on the corner.

A discussion had preceded the lady's decision. She had come by one day, and sat in the room with them, next to the disgruntled owner of the apartment who, despite obvious efforts, nevertheless just could not cast off his stony crust; and she had talked, in that, for him, totally alien language, with words as carefully chosen as in the theater; she wore white lace around her neck, snow-white, as if bought in the shop only moments before, and she turned those eyes, which could see through walls, on him and showed him the oval of her face.

Someone then came to collect her. A very tall man, in full possession of his powers, with a strong face and speaking the same language as her, so that you were reminded of the scene in the play when, just like this, the hero was sitting with the pale woman on the divan, carrying on a conversation. Only the man in the theater was a slim gentleman with, for his taste, a rather too flashy splendor about him, whereas this strongly built man had a bright radiance with something lively about it, something sunny, so that Herr Felberbaum told himself beatifically that if he belonged to the same strain as this man, then he was determined that he should be ostracized along with him.

Not that he had no role to play whatsoever and was taking no part in the conversation. On the contrary, he was the real host, for the silent man, to whom this role rightly belonged, did not feel up to it; he was incapable of grasping who was sitting next to him and would soon sit next to him day in and day out, who was about to move into his house, to light it up, and what preparations had to be made. Just in time, Herr Felberbaum removed a chair which was creaking under his guest's firm grip, because it was in danger of falling apart. He brought in fruit on a broad platter. He brought in a little methane burner and prepared some mocha for everyone, he handed out serviettes made of Chinese silk paper and laid out cigarettes. He fetched photographs from the drawer in the table, snapshots of Cairo in which he himself could be seen, minutely tiny at the feet of the Sphinx. Finally, when he noticed how well everything was going so far, he turned on the radio, but that was a bad move on his part, as a voice, as if from deep inside some ventriloquist, boomed out. Felberbaum smiled in embarrassment and apologized for the poor joke. It was "our" Führer.

It goes without saying that, in the course of the conversation, he expressed his willingness to move into the kitchen and put the room at the lady's disposal. But here, he came up against resistance. His roommate's eyes turned glassy, and it looked as if he would be unlikely to leave the room alive, and then *feet first*, as he said himself. Embarrassed, Felberbaum took refuge in the lady's glance, from which all reserve had disappeared, it was close to him, all too close, it almost gripped his heart, and then she said, with that look which he felt expressed such kinship still fixed on him:

"It's charming of you to wish to give up your bed to Kain."

Him. Felberbaum. She was calling him charming, and the other one she called "Kain." Strange that she should call this man Kain. "Abel" would have suited him better. But that wasn't the right one either; a man like that doesn't get struck down. But what say does any man have about his name . . . ?

As Herr Felberbaum now reflected on all this in the kitchen, he remembered that the second pillow on his bed had not yet been covered, because the brother, that unhappy man, had refused to give it up. So he immediately went back into the room on tiptoe, because the poor fellow had fallen asleep from exhaustion, he was lying on the same divan on which Felberbaum would be sleeping from now on. His feet were dangling over the edge, sweat was beading his brow. He straightened his feet and spread his jacket over the sleeping man, with the result that he himself now stood there in shirtsleeves. Next, he opened a drawer and took out a pillowcase. He pulled it over the second pillow from his bed, which he had brought with him from his own apartment. By the time he had finished with it, the pillow had taken on a rather round shape, because the corners wouldn't fit, but it looked clean and, more than anything, he would have loved to lay his head on it there and then for forty winks. But there was still a lot to be done, and so he tiptoed over to his cupboard and picked up a large box from its floor which he quietly carried into the kitchen.

Once in the kitchen, he was startled. Only a moment ago, he had left a little paradise here, a cozy warm home, and now it seemed to him cold, empty, gloomy, all thrown-together, and only the forget-me-nots in the vase looked at him in a friendly way. From the flowers, his gaze moved to the carpet; it was soft, with cheerful colors and a thick pile. From the carpet, he glanced over to the blue silk bedspread, and now his dark expression fled, the bright silken covers gained the upper hand, and, beaming, he examined his work, placed the box on top of the gas stove and started rummaging. It contained, for the most part, photographs of scenes from films. Not that he was a great cinema enthusiast. If anything, the contrary was the case; figures flitting past which could not be grasped made him uneasy, figures which, at the end of the film, no longer existed, and had, as it were, melted away like those dreams which annoy you on wakening because none of it was real. Naturally, he knew that these figures did in fact live, that they even came over from far-off America and showed themselves in person. He himself had even seen such a film star with his own eyes, yet that had served only to heighten his misgivings, because that famous lady, who had come sailing across the sea, had had nothing about her of all that she displayed on the screen, so little that he was downright appalled.

His relationship with films was a business one, or rather, had been, before everything was turned on its head, distorted and lost. He himself had had to do with films for a time, when he had taken a lease on a cinema, because that was a profitable thing in those days. Those times were over. The souvenirs here in this box acted as a last testimony, a kind of diary, each with notes written on the back, and these referred not to the quality of the film—he was no judge of that—but instead they indicated how well it had done at the box office, and in that his judgment was unerring.

He drew out one scene, showing Greta Garbo as a courtesan, in a loose gown, kneeling on a rumpled divan; she was talking to someone in a far corner, who could not be seen but who, judging by her expression of triumph, must have been totally crushed. With satisfaction, he laid the picture next to the gas burner. Then he thought that perhaps the lady who was now going to have to live in a kitchen would be happier with a fellow-believer from the fairy realm of the cinema, and looked for a picture of Elisabeth Bergner, but couldn't find one. He came upon a love scene under a bower of blossoms, nothing special, two completely unknown actors, but the bower brought spring into the room, and so he laid it ready. He pondered whether a love scene in the lady's bedroom might be embarrassing and then remembered that she might prefer a film actor rather than an actress; after all, she was a woman, and so he picked out from among the stars a photograph of Hans Albers in jodhpurs, with his riding crop across his knees. Now it was a question of deciding on one of the three selected pictures. But he was unable to manage that, and so he installed all three pictures in the kitchen, placing the love scene over the sink, pinning the star in riding-boots on the wall at the head of the bed, and Garbo above the gas stove.

His fleeting melancholic mood had dissipated. Once more, the kitchen struck him as merry and festive, clean, colorful and bright.

But there was still a long time until evening, even though lunch had been delayed by the arrival of a museum attendant, and so he tiptoed back into the room, placed the box back in the cupboard, lifted his jacket from the sleeping man and laid a towel over him, very carefully, but the unhappy man was fast asleep. Best thing for him, and for everyone. Then he put on his hat, adjusted the rosette which identified him as as old front-line soldier, affording him just a little sense of security, and went out.

The street where he now lived had, like anywhere else, been affected by that destructive urge so approved of by the new Reich. The very finest shops had been plundered, among them one specializing in soap, of which he had been particularly fond, and he wondered in amazement just why these new potentates had to throw it into disorder, all the little boxes, laid out one on top of the other in a fan shape, empty boxes, to be sure, dummies they called them, but you forgot that when you saw the fine soaps all around, the filled little bottles, the colorful combs, the tubes of cosmetics, in first-class designs, the lipsticks and pomades. He was especially astonished to see so many brown uniforms today, which he avoided by ducking into the doorway of a house. Strange, he thought, in the war, we threw ourselves to the ground, now we run into doorways. When one squad had passed, he ventured out, but after only a few steps he spotted three more world conquerors coming round the corner. This time, he took refuge in a sweetshop, the owner of which he knew, and, despite her black hair, she was still in her usual place, probably a Hungarian or a Czech. Today, she didn't seem as chatty and approachable as usual, even though a fellow believer with a crooked nose was standing next to her and, to judge by his familiar behavior, was a member of the family.

Herr Felberbaum looked for some chocolate, driven as he was by the emergency of his situation to make a purchase. He decided on some chocolate candies, which he could serve up this evening on a plate. It was in fact the eve of one of the principal feasts, which was very apt for the new guest, the next holiday of the year, and one which even he commemorated with reverence. It was such an exalted feast that the harassed people in that unhappy city could take a deep breath, because that holiday gave them some relief, even if nothing else in the world gave them protection any longer.

"It's terrible," he said while he helped his acquaintance to pour the sweets into a bag. "There they go again, running about and making people nervous." Since his words evoked no response, he looked up and saw the confectioner woman winking at him with one eye. So he looked at the man beside her; he wasn't wearing a swastika and looked like the shamas from the synagogue.

"This is our leader, the commissar," said the woman, only to be barked at by the man: "Don't give any warnings, or else . . ."

He didn't hear what followed, because he threw down a mark, picked up the little bag, didn't wait for his change and hurried away. So that's the famous commissar, who looks like any three other Jews, an avid Nazi at that, whom everyone fears because he disguises himself so well.

The woman will end up telling him my address! "No, not at all," he thought confidently, "our people don't do that."

Nevertheless, he no longer felt quite so comfortable out there in the narrow streets, so he set off back home. As he went, he reflected on how he should prepare for tomorrow's feast-day in a manner that was halfway fitting and fairly dignified. His wife had gone away, she had accepted a job as a maid in Manchester, but the purpose of that journey was to get him to England too. His mother-in-law no longer cooked, instead she prepared herself for the feast by living off the handouts for the needy. He wasn't allowed to go into a restaurant—without a swastika and with a nose like his, he would be turned out of there. So, suddenly, he stood there in the street, at a loss, too frightened to move a step.

Then he remembered a coffeehouse which belonged to a fellow believer. This café owner had fought next to him in the World War at Lvov and had lost half his head there. Not from fear of the battle, but in reality. The back of his head was made of leather and iron, and he didn't exactly hold it high. Now, though, he has his recompense for that, thought Felberbaum with satisfaction. Because everything in this world brings its own reward. The man had not been expelled from the country and wasn't out of work like all the rest, but was allowed to continue working, and in his own coffeehouse. As a waiter, admittedly, and that was not easy for him, what with that heavy head of his. But it was better than if the children were left starving at home. In fact, you were doing the man a good turn by going to his coffeehouse. Even though no coffeehouse, let alone his, was safe from attacks by the brown heroes.

Delighted at this happy way out, which enabled him to get ready for the high feast, Felberbaum turned into a side street leading to the main thoroughfare. In the main street, where the café was situated, he saw a large throng of people. Accustomed to fearing such crowds like shrapnel in the war, he slipped into a doorway opposite.

The crowd had built up right in front of the coffeehouse where he had intended to have his evening meal. Outside, on a ladder, stood his comrade-in-arms at Lvov, the owner, now waiter. But at that moment he wasn't being a waiter either. At that moment he had by his side a bucket full of paint and was painting something on the shop window. The crowd let out yells and threats and he had to wipe it off. He started again, the crowd remained quiet, watching, but then it shouted and cheered for joy. Felberbaum craned his neck and discovered a triangle, which the old man had drawn in paint on the window of his coffeehouse. He couldn't understand why this triangle should arouse such rejoicing, but then he realized it would turn into a Star of David. The man painted on, the people around him let out whoops of delight. The back of his head with its metal plate stood out grotesquely. Felberbaum looked at this military decoration and strained fearfully to see a part of the face of his comrade-in-arms, who was very susceptible to attacks of vertigo. He was now painting the declaration of his faith on the coffeehouse window and insisted on adding a proud "e". However, this was forbidden by the man with the death's-heads. He was obliged to turn "*Jude*" into "*Jud*," and did so reluctantly, while the people around him went into ecstasies. After he had finished, he took out his purse and paid five marks for the use of the paint and the brush. Then a placard was hung round his neck and he had to walk up and down with it on.

Felberbaum had had enough. He slipped back into the quiet lane. "It is a wonder," he thought, "they didn't smash in his head while they were at it, that half a head, after all the things their leaders are having printed in the newspapers."

It was beginning to get dark. He went into a little grocer's shop. There you were as welcome as a silver coin, you weren't asked about your religion and your race. Butter and cheese stilled your hunger and it was served up to you, since people don't like serving themselves on a high feast-day.

In the little establishment, there was neither butter nor cheese today. But the friendly woman had hidden away a fresh ham, for her regular customers. The blonde creature with the rather pale face cut off a juicy slice of ham and spread it on three bread-rolls for him. Herr Felberbaum asked permission before sitting down on a crate. The rolls were fresh and tasted delicious. He also ordered a glass of beer; you were supposed to fast this evening, until tomorrow evening, an eternity. It was a custom, a commandment, reputedly even good for your physical health, but that could be just a ruse. His system usually was slightly upset by it, he would suffer from the effects for three days, but God wanted his sacrifice.

He would have very much liked to strike up a conversation with the woman, one was only human, a fellow human, they were all human beings, but he remembered his experience of half an hour previously and ate in silence. By the time he was on his third roll and she was refilling his beer glass, he could stand it no longer, but asked politely about how business was doing.

"The big apartments have all been emptied," said the woman, "and those in the small apartments don't buy anything."

"So, not altogether satisfactory." He swallowed his beer hastily. He hadn't been expecting that response. You had to be wary of such a reply, because if it were overheard, the punishment would fall on him. He paid in a hurry and only once he was out in the street did it occur to him that it was a gratifying sign, that complaint, that growing dissatisfaction, gratifying for their decendants. His like would not live to experience it, they were old, worn out and beyond measure marked out by fate.

Shadows came over his features at that thought, and also because what he had done was not right. He had made himself ready for the high feast-day in a stranger's establishment, without consecration, and on pork into the bargain, no, that wasn't right. That had been gluttony on his part, he should have made do with bread and cheese. Even though one well knew, these days, that such prescriptions in the Bible stemmed from an out-of-date-expediency, and in other respects no one obeyed the regulations or paid them any heed. . . .

Even the death's-head people were rushing about today! The murderer had free rein, and he was granted a memorial. They were pillaging for all they were worth. It was only envy that stopped them from stealing everything, absolutely everything. The envy of one towards the other which turns them into spies against their own people. Envy is what keeps them in order. Had anyone ever heard of such a thing! Black uniforms, looking blacker than the undertaker's robes, silver death's-heads on them, horrible to look at, skulls and crossbones!

Thank heaven, there was still this evening to come, these guests, genuine guests of honor, they will magic this whole deathly specter out of fearful hearts. With a sense of relief, he turned in at his own doorway.

VIIIa.

Beautiful and placid lie the vineyards on the outskirts of the city. They flourish symmetrically and opulently, and when ripe their grapes are taken off. Their juice is pressed out on the spot and immediately drunk, just as it is, by the people in the taverns. The connoisseur, of course, waits for its transformation and has his glass filled once it has fermented. Then he pays for it and that makes the winegrower happy, and most of all he is delighted by the strangers who come and have large tankards set up, they sit out in the garden in the shade of the trees and, at a sign from them, the pitcher is brought out. They drink heartily and order more, the strangers are in good spirits, laugh and look around. The fruit trees fan the air with their twigs, plums gleam, blue and velvety, inspired by this new life, the lady lays her soft arms on a battered wooden table which doesn't even have a cloth on it, and the atmosphere is complete: blossoming bowers, fireflies that flit into your hair, and rough-hewn tables with pitchers on them. The wine flows, and the silver coins stream into the big winegrower's fat purse, the heavy lumps of metal pulling his belt down below his paunch.

But at this moment, the belt is tight. The big leather pouch is yawning, it just will not fill up, its contents are meager and the winegrower stares glassy-eyed around the tavern. It's full, his inn, with heavy cigar smoke obscuring the view, there's not a table to be had, the room is booming with laughing voices, the garden is full to overflowing, the money is rolling in, yet the pouch does not fill up. Because this nickel coinage that these new customers leave behind drops into the drawer of the cash register, but it does not turn into silver, it remains nickel, the vintner gazes grimly at his patrons, swallowing down a response to their "Heil!" which would land him in prison.

From time to time, he goes over to the glass door leading to the special side-room. It is the one place where business goes on as before, where wine splashes on the tables, where glasses break, where customers no longer keep count of the number of pitchers and throw the money on the floor. But how small that room is! Four tables, he counts, four tables have to make up for the losses from the customers in the garden.

Today, not even those four tables are occupied, because the weather is dull and the free-spending gentlemen have remained in the town.

In this little private room today sits a gentleman who is not afraid of the rain, because he is afraid of nothing at all, and anyway he lives close by. He adjusts his swastika and pins on his pilot's insignia. He has just been speaking to the Gauleiter, who is not at all one for putting on airs. And here, Frau Pilz with her straw-blonde hair is blushing all over her face. For the Gauleiter has just shaken her by the hand and is now striding rapidly through the main room of the tavern, into the garden and out through the gate.

"But he doesn't kiss anyone's hand," the young woman in the side-room says to her husband. She says this because she is so happy but is trying to hide it. She takes out a mirror and dusts her flushed cheeks with pink powder from her new compact. A compact with a gold rim, housed in a wooden box like a washing trough, but the picture of the Kahlenberg is nice. It does gather dust in the wooden surround, however, and you have to be careful that bugs don't nest in it.

"Our Gauleiter is no Austrian, and anyway that's now being done away with in our circles; we are *Volksgenossen*, national comrades, and there's no hand-kissing, no discrimination there."

"That'll be why you took a seat in this expensive side-room, then, National Comrade!"

"You just have no idea who it is I'm expecting! It's a Party secret, and if you knew, you'd faint dead away. I'm sorry, my dear, you'll have to go now, these are important diplomatic talks and I can't be doing with you here. There you are, I'll kiss your hand, but now you have to leave; these people will be here any minute and I have to make a few notes and gather myself together. Off you go home, you have your apartment now, you have a boudoir with a beveled mirror, everything your heart could desire."

She stole a glance at the notebook her husband pulled out and from which he took a photograph, no doubt some military installation, and she begged him to let her stay, just for as long as he was making notes at least. It was all so exciting, she said, she simply couldn't get over all the experiences.

At that, he laughs, extremely pleasantly touched, and explains to her what he is thinking. The way blood-ties bind German brothers and the whole earth, and how they are going to defend that earth with their blood. It appears that the whole world is set on destroying the German Reich, because he sees it as a threat and assures her that they will rise as one man and show the world a thing or two.

"But surely in the end it won't come to war, the Führer promised that he isn't waging a war."

She's quite right there, he says. War is no rabbit hunt. Doesn't she remember the memorable words about the War Ministry: "Whoever wants peace, prepares for war."

"But what happens afterwards with all those soldiers if it doesn't come to a war?"

At such an argumentative attitude, his anger abruptly wells up. "Surely it's the Party which creates order in the country," she goes on stubbornly. "I mean, now they're carrying out arrests and requisitions in the Party's name too."

"The major battle has yet to come. Until the people realize that they are surrounded by enemies, until not one single Party comrade falls victim to a Jewish bullet, they will refuse to believe it."

By now she could understand so little that she pursed her lips grumpily.

"Do they still have weapons, then?"

"They have everything. You'll find that out when it comes to the supreme action. Because it is coming. This winegrower, he's another of these obstinate ones, he lets anyone and everyone into his inn. Yesterday, a girl walked through here, she lives in the villa up there, next to us. Her father's a fine example, a monarchist and not racially pure besides. It's enough to try anyone's patience. But now you'll have to go. After all, I can't very well look like a henpecked husband when there are major issues at stake."

The young woman dutifully got to her feet, slipped into her jacket, straightened the ruffle of her blouse, pulled on her gloves, closed her handbag and went away, leaving all this behind—everything that elevated and adorned her life, the proximity of fame and the importance of her own self—because in her kitchen she was nothing, nothing much, even though she could now walk about through several rooms, but then she didn't use them, since carpets wear out if you walk up and down on them and the finely polished pieces of furniture get so easily scratched if you sit on them.

Frau Pilz waited outside a little longer. To enjoy the sight of the important gentlemen, the big limousine drawing up, just like in the cinema. But she tired of waiting. She saw a young girl stepping into the tavern and was surprised, because that was not respectable behavior for a young lady. And then Frau Pilz set off for home.

The winegrower, too, is surprised at the young girl coming into his tavern. She's the one from the big villa, rich people they were, and good customers. He groans. Now the girl is going into the private room, yes, that's her, Hilde, she'll get a fright when she sees the SA-man. The vintner's eyes widen fit to pop out of his head. She's joining him at his table! Even as a schoolgirl she was a brazen young thing! The mind boggles! They're talking to each other!

The winegrower has to drag his fat belly out into the garden, where an argument has broken out. That's what you get with these Germans, nothing but loudmouths, know-it-alls, but they drink no more than an eighth of a liter of wine and annoy his customers. Now he is faced with the sight of one of his regulars leaving the inn, but fortunately he can catch up with his customer and lead him back in; that's all he needs, for someone to take his little bit of cash away. The insulted Austrian is greeted with cheers, a woman from the suburbs, with broad features and an ample bosom, lets out a shriek, her hair tumbles loose on to her breast, her hat falls under the table and is trampled on by her companion, an excursionist throws a bunch of meadow flowers into her lap, someone buys her a balloon and ties it to her chair. Next to her, a newly-fledged national comrade lifts a tortoise on to the table. The tortoise, he says in a Prussian accent, reminds him of the streetcars here in this city. And he bursts out laughing.

"It was the writer who brought them here, a whole basket full of them," says the Austrian, joining the Prussian at the table. He holds up the tortoise and now it sticks its delicate little head out and shows him its intelligent eyes.

"So that they wouldn't have to bear the mark of the cross!" the woman from the suburbs shouts boisterously and throws her meadow flowers invitingly to the Prussian, who thanks her with a bow and takes his cigar out of his mouth. He leaves the flowers lying where they are, but the Austrian picks them up and sticks them in his buttonhole.

"So where is he now?"

"He'll have gone by now," says the blonde woman, raising her glass to the German. He is much taller and broader than her companion and her compatriot next to her who has appropriated her flowers, she fancies him more and he knows it.

"Be doing hard labor, breaking rocks, he will," says the Austrian.

"He'll be crawling. Just like your streetcars here."

"The gentleman would do better to walk," the companion now speaks up and the Austrian straightens his posy and nods firmly.

"He doesn't have time for that," the woman laughs. "They're always in a hurry, these Germans!"

"We don't crawl around on our bellies, like this reptile here."

"They're dear little creatures, like snails," declares the fan of meadow flowers.

The woman assures him that he too is a dear little creature, and, at the sight of her, the winegrower can't help thinking of his own wife. She's no longer the woman she was, lying in bed with a weak heart, unable to work. Ever since the business with the flag over his premises. The one he had repeatedly torn down. He was born in this place, his father before him, and his grandfather was mayor of this place long before it became a suburb of the city. He's pretty well-built, this winegrower, he can knock three men over with one blow of his fist if the need arises, as people have found out here in his tavern. For his jacket, the tailor needs twice the usual amount of material for it to fit him comfortably. He's not afraid, but his wife was frightened. She thought they would demolish his house. And now they're all sitting here, those swastika boys, but that's not bringing in any money.

You wouldn't credit it: Hilde's still sitting there facing the brown SA-man. But she is drinking a lot of wine, the good lass, the jug is empty. Yes, she's dazzling that clown who doesn't practice what he preaches. Now he's even buying her something to nibble with her wine. What's she doing? She's pouring her wine under the table! He's never come across that in all his born days. And it's a French wine at that, just that it's sold as a new wine, a

Heuriger. The brown joker is ordering another jug. What kind of map is he showing her? No doubt one showing all Europe under the rule of the Third . . . It can't be a map, it looks more like some piece of military equipment. Well, well, look at that, isn't she delighted with it! Just what's Hilde up to? Now she's passing him an envelope. He puts it in his pocket and takes the picture away from her. By Jove, if that doesn't beat all! She snatches it from his hand and he must be afraid of something because he grabs it back—and it's torn in two!

How annoying! He has to move away from the glass door because they're arguing outside again.

Out in the garden, the new national comrade has been explaining his allegory by letting the tortoise creep across the table. The streetcar system in this city is bone lazy. Just like the inhabitants, he says, pointing to the slow-moving reptile, which has drawn its head back into its shell. The streetcars don't move from the spot either, but the Field Marshal will soon cure them of that, he assures the Austrian sitting opposite him, with total confidence. The Field Marshal will do it. There will be no more dawdlers like that moving through the city, dawdling will be abolished.

His neighbor at the table has lost patience. The posy flies out of his buttonhole, so quickly has he jumped to his feet. The pitcher falls to the ground, already in pieces, so violently has he thumped it on the table. And now he snatches the tortoise away from the Prussian and flings it back at him.

The blonde woman lets out a shriek, her ample bosom heaving.

"Don't worry, lady, they're pretty tough things," says the Prussian.

"That's for sure," retorts his adversary. And he punches him in the face.

But now they have to continue their fight out in the street, for the winegrower hustles them out with his massive body.

The fact that the fancy lady joins in with her umbrella makes no real difference, her umbrella gets broken, her balloon floats away, her shawl is torn from her shoulder, her escort receives a thump, all at once the whole assembly in the garden is now out in the street, two factions form up, one in favor of the streetcars, one against, a free-for-all ensues and the innkeeper is powerless. Anyway, they're no longer in his tavern, so it has nothing to do with him any more and he returns to his special little entertainment, to the SA-man with the forbidden fruit. But, oh dear, Hilde is on the point of leaving and the SA is already standing at the cash desk paying his bill. On the table in the side-room, the pitcher is standing, still full, and he has forgotten the picture, the military installation. The innkeeper leans over to have a closer look. It's a photograph, that's an airplane. The innkeeper snaps his fingers. Well, I'll be damned, it's not a real one! That's the papier-mâché plane belonging to the photographer down the hill, the one couples have themselves pictured in when they've had enough to drink.

Felberbaum was sitting at the table he had set. The distinguished couple occupied the places of honor at the top, while he perched on the edge of his chair, since he was busy passing round the platters, with cold cuts, slices of bread (which he spread for the lady), topping up the tea cups, and feeling awkward because he was an outsider, not participating, embarrassed on account of his custom of observing the day of fasting, an utterly ridiculous custom, incomprehensible to such educated people, and, on top of that, an unhealthy thing at his age. He was altogether ridiculous, he well knew, but in the end he laughed up his sleeve at himself, grinned to himself, a feeble but happy grin.

For it turned out that these new friends were not looking down on him, the two, that is, who mattered. If anything, they were delighted by his zeal, it did them good, that was very clear, and even his comical remarks cheered them up, he knew.

And the lady was smiling.

The unhappy man, sitting at the farthest corner of the table, couldn't control himself. He poured scorn on the feast day, the well laid table, the tablecloth and, naturally, on Felberbaum, who was fasting. Wood, he said. To cover wood with a tablecloth, wood that would one day turn to stone, was crass. Just as crass as a man, who looked like a fat sack of flour, fasting. Fasting was right and proper for the monk with stony features and not for fat flesh.

At this, his brother countered with the name of Luther, but Werner paid no heed to the objection and went on grumbling. You had to have a fair amount of sawdust between your ears to call a day a holiday with the streets swarming with brownshirts, arrests coming thick and fast, and cattle trucks rolling through the streets loaded with people beaten to a pulp.

Here, the lady heaved a deep sigh which cut Felberbaum to the quick, and he pulled himself together. Arrest wasn't the worst thing, and he wasn't just talking off the top of his head, but from experience, he had that behind him; and besides, did anyone believe that people were being arrested only here in this country? He himself had been arrested in Cairo, and why? Because of an old rag wrapped round a filthy piece of wood, because of a mere nothing, because of a bit of rubbish. How interesting, the guests said and begged him to be more specific, and so Felberbaum told the tale of how he came to be arrested in Cairo.

One day, a stall-keeper came running after him, carrying a mummy, the mummy of a small child. That is to say, at first he saw before him a few filthy rags of faded dressing material wrapped round some wood, and he waved it away. When the man demanded twelve pounds for the filthy object, it began to interest him—what it might contain—and, back home, he looked up in his lexicon what it could possibly be that cost so much.

The next day, the trader scurried after him again. Herr Felberbaum now knew roughly what this bundle represented, and ran a curious eye over it. The world is quite mad, he thought, and has no interest in anything other than digging up corpses and stuffing them. Then these would be sold at a high price and sold on again. The dealer had noticed his searching look and refused to leave his side. By the time they arrived at the great Sphinx, the price of the mummy stood at no more than two pounds. Then the man, who was in a state of great desperation, asked for only one pound. Felberbaum bought the mummy for a pound.

So now he looked forward to enjoying his purchase and to discovering the true value of his find, because he knew from his lexicon that a mummy was worth much more than a pound. Therefore, with the mummy in his arms, he set off for the museum and searched through the rooms for mummies. At last he found the mummy of a child, which suffered by comparison with his own; it was closely similar, which pleased him greatly, but his seemed far better preserved. He carried it in both arms, very carefully, as one carries a newborn infant, into a second room, the one with the large mummies. He was standing in front of them, scrutinizing and comparing, when suddenly he found himself being roughly grabbed and, in short, being arrested by two museum guards. Ignoring his wild protests, they took him to the director's office, where a severe-looking gentleman stared coldly at him. Terrified and bathed in sweat, he started to tell his story, convinced that he was being arrested because of some theft from the museum someone else had committed, or at best because of his questionable purchase. Then, all of a sudden, the director smiled, laughed even, dismissing the two guards with a haughty gesture and a reproachful glance, and revealed to Herr Felberbaum that the scraps of cloth wrapped round the mummy dating back thousands of years probably came from the very factory which Herr Felberbaum represented in the area.

This tale produced the effect of a sack of gold thrown into a beggar's house. There was indeed a city called Cairo, there were mummies, dead bodies preserved by people of culture—just how would they protect the living, the prisoners? We are protected elsewhere, abroad, that is obvious, here they keep an eye on us, who are deprived of all rights, the newspapers pose a threat to peace and tranquillity—you could never set eyes on these newspapers, without hearing the grinding, the gnashing of teeth of the helpless, yes, the helpless out there. Let them carry on their wanton vandalism here as much as they liked. This was the only solace, the only protection for anyone in a land where the leaders encouraged murder, in which the custodians carried out robbery as a profession: here they were, in Cairo, in Egypt, far from this town in which no god struck down the sinners with the ten plagues. They were here, in this peaceful room, safeguarded by the hearty laughter of Herr Felberbaum from the Handelskai.

Still, Werner raged on. It was significant, he said, and absolutely typical of certain people that they should go after mummies instead of going to feel the Sphinx, to touch it with their finger-tips, millions of years that one could breathe in, overwhelming forms and materials, called diorites, porphyries, basalts, granites, the Sphinx divulges its secret, and this fool bought a mummy.

His brother steered the conversation away, believing that Herr Felberbaum had found the happy solution: it was more stimulating and more appropriate to the holiday if each of them would tell a story. He himself was prepared to take it from there and, since imprisonment and arrest seemed the order of the day, he would tell a tale of imprisonment. The man arrested was—a writer, who lived alone and isolated in a small village. He was very well liked in that village, as he had been for a long time. He was pretty well established, settled there, he left the place only seldom and briefly, liked living there, worked away, brought honor to the village, was something of a showpiece, a rare part of the place. He would greet the natives as friends, join them in the inn and pay for the whole company's wine.

When, therefore, the new regime issued the decree that arrests were to be made, there was embarrassment in the village. The only people who lived there were the villagers themselves, and it seemed impossible to arrest any of them, since they were like one big family, intermarried, related by marriage or by blood, each one sticking by the other. In their awkward situation, the police hit upon the idea of locking up the one and only outsider in the place. It was no pleasant task, there were no real grounds, but orders from above were reason enough. The warden of the jail himself was delegated the task, for he was the hardest man in the village, as was only fitting for his difficult office.

Early in the morning, he knocked at the door of the learned gentleman, who immediately showed him in. When the hardest man in the village found himself face to face with the distinguished gentleman, who was always giving his little daughter cherries, or whatever fruit happened to be in season, he stood twisting his hat in his hands, embarrassed. After all, talking was not his strong point, he talked with his fists. Fortunately, a policeman had come along with him, who was good at reeling off stock phrases, especially where transients causing a public nuisance with their cars were concerned, and so this policeman said, "No offence, Herr Doktor, but we have to place you under arrest."

"Arrest me? And why?"

At this, the warden gave a shrug, while the policeman, quick-witted as his profession demanded, searched for a response and found one.

"There's a warrant for your arrest."

The poet was deeply shocked; he could think of so many things that could give this new regime reasons for committing him to prison that he had no idea what was to become of him. He cast a despairing glance at the writings piled on his desk, which might provide evidence for practically anything frowned upon these days. It could be his pacifism, his friendship with a cardinal; his latest essay on modern art; his membership card from the party which had still been the government in power only a few months before; the sketches by a world-famous caricaturist: all these amounted to so much that the rest of his life (which was already half behind him), would not suffice to atone for all these sins, from that other, and as he hoped, better, more noble half. With bowed head, he walked off between the warden and the policeman in the direction of the jail.

Now this jail was nothing more than a room in the warden's house, because it was not worth the trouble of setting up a separate prison for the extremely rare occasions when crimes were committed in the little village; any robbers and murderers were hauled off to the capital in the green van, and that happened but once every ten years. Petty thieves were simply locked up, in short order, in the warden's house where he had them at his finger-tips and this saved space.

Since, in this case, there was no charge of theft, fraud, fencing, tax-evasion, smuggling, drunken excess, vagrancy or anything whatsoever—to tell the truth, there was nothing at all against him—the warden left the door to his living room open, so that the warmth from his cheery fire could spread through to the cell. In addition, since they were dealing with a refined gentleman who was to be lodging here, the warden's wife had freshly made up the bed with her best linen, had lent her own eiderdowns and placed pots of pelargoniums in the window. Then she also immediately set about preparing a hearty meal of the sort reserved only for festivals and holidays.

So now the writer was sitting in this small room, which was hardly different from his own at home, gazing out of the sweet little window at the wonderful mountains, which, after a shower of rain, looked close enough to touch. Altogether, this wasn't so bad at all. What was bad, though, was the desk he had left behind, with all that material or, to put it in technical terms, with all those incriminating documents, those pieces of writing, his own and others', those letters and signed papers from authorities who were now all of a sudden being termed murderers, subhumans, traitors to their country, turncoats, and Jews.

Undoubtedly, his wisest course of action was to try to do something about it, and when the warden's wife came in, the gentleman got to his feet and approached her as she was stuffing a thick duvet into a crisp white linen cover. He fixed his blue, infinitely clear, infinitely gentle, eyes on her and said:

"I'm afraid I have been interrupted in the middle of an important piece of work. Would it be too much to ask, for me to be given my papers? They are lying on the right-hand side of my desk, among many other ones. I might as well be working here as sitting about idly."

The wife went into the living room, where the warden was sitting by the stove with a very long pipe, staring into the fire. Because that was *his job*, to sit there wearing a rather important expression, ready to clench his fists should the delinquent behave improperly. He listened to his wife's message, drew on his pipe, gave the matter some consideration and hit on the bright idea that it would be better if a prisoner kept himself occupied rather than snooping on his jailer's movements and thinking evil thoughts. So he deputed his wife to go and fetch the papers at once. The woman was delighted to bring this news to the gentleman in his room. After all, because of him, a festive mood reigned in the house. And no one wanted it to look for a moment as if this gentleman, who wore a silk shirt, was here to serve a sentence. Far from it: he added something festive to the place and such a fine fragrance radiated from him, such a warmth, his eyes rested so seriously on her, so steady, so strange. Only on one unforgettable occasion had she seen their like, when, two years before, the Herr Chancellor had passed through the village and fixed his gaze upon her. What they had here was another of those inconceivably refined, boundless human beings whose radiance lit the way to somewhere where one could only be afraid, where one sank down, deep down, out of awe and fear and reverence.

It was probably the case that the prisoner had some idea of the effect he had on the wife, because suddenly he raised his head, and looking her steadily in the eye, said, succinctly, that it would be best if she were to empty the suitcase in his room and pack into it all the writings and booklets and papers lying on his desk, otherwise she might pick up the wrong bundle, or mix some things up, all very delicate documents, and anyway there was such a mess there that he himself was unable to remember whether his work was lying on the right or on the left side of his desk. It would also be good if she could bring him some fresh laundry, at least six shirts, as well as his shaving things and toiletries which were lying on the washstand.

The woman obeyed him to the letter and returned very soon. She opened the suitcase, and in it she had packed everything, every single printed and handwritten item that had been in the house. Yes, even an old newspaper that had been lying around. The laundry had been meticulously wrapped separately in brown paper.

The writer had thus, as it were, localized the possible conflagration, yet the fire was still glowing, and all that was needed was the appearance of some malevolent official for the carefully guarded fire to blaze up more fearfully than ever. So he now began sorting through the papers, laying the harmless ones in a conspicuous place and tearing up the "evidence against him" into tiny scraps, all of which he stuffed into the coal-scuttle; he piled it full to overflowing and then sat back, greatly relieved. But now there arose a new problem. Where was he to put this enormous mountain of "evidence" now staring everyone in the face?

He peered through to the next room. The fire was crackling invitingly, the warden had nodded off in front of it; his long pipe, which had fallen from his hand, was standing erect like a walking stick. The writer took up a mountain of paper in both arms and carried it towards the fire.

But suddenly he stopped in his tracks. The warden's child, the little cherry-lover, who had been asleep in the laundry basket, woke up, caught sight of him and broke out into a happy yell, hungrily opening her little mouth wide. The writer retreated, because his guard was opening his eyes.

This was risky. If he were brazenly to set about burning the papers, arousing the suspicions of these guileless people, all would be lost.

In the prison cell, intended for miscreants and hidden behind a gray, stained curtain, there was a privy. So, with both arms full, the prisoner carried the shreds of paper over and stuffed them down it. He pulled the chain, the water came only in a trickle and flowed over the scraps, turning them gray and making the ink run, and the writer himself turned gray with the effort of trying to make them all disappear. He looked across to the huge pile that still had to be disposed of and then despairingly back to the old-fashioned toilet—then he jumped in alarm. Before him stood the warden. The forebearing man's features were going red with rage. "City folk just don't have an ounce of sense in their heads," he said, wagging his pipe menacingly. "Over there, there's a roaring fire burning, and here you're choking everything. Now, sir, if you don't mind, you just take all your trash over there where it belongs. That sort of stuff belongs in the fire."

The writer immediately picked up the whole box-full, and carried it over as fast as he could manage. With relief, he watched one pile after another of the evidence against him crumbling into ashes.

A few weeks later, he was released.

Herr Felberbaum thought the story was marvelous, and wonderfully told. A great talent. It all came out in the person of the teller, in the tale and in the language. Beside himself with happiness, he looked across to the lady, whose turn it was now.

"I'm not so good at storytelling," said Eva. "And certainly not a story from my own experience. But this one was told to me, in fact several times."

A Jewish woman took refuge in a park belonging to Prince Sch—. She had been chased in there, pursued in the process of a manhunt; she had that pallid, death-stricken complexion typical of prisoners facing execution. Here, too, a brownshirt spots her and barks at her to leave the gardens. This catches the attention of the old groundskeeper, a man with a reputation for being a wrathful watchdog: young people in particular preferred to give him a wide berth.

"My master, the prince," says he with the loftiest possible air of dignity (as is well known, servants love to play the part of their lords and masters, for their masters cannot be bothered), "my master, the prince, regards all visitors to this park as his guests and does not wish them to be harassed." His expression becomes so impenetrable that the SA-man goes on his way.

"A prince of a servant."

"And what happened to the woman, if I may be permitted to ask?"

"She remained in the gardens, Herr Felberbaum, while the groundskeeper looked out on all sides to see if anyone was lying in wait for her. Only then did he let her leave."

"Nice, very nice. It could well have turned out differently. By heaven yes, my dear lady. Altogether differently. I always say, we are all human beings together, and that being, created by God in His own image, is not facing extinction. A corrupt species may be trying to push its way to the forefront, but, God willing, it will not succeed. Another example of humanity in its purest form. It remains the victor in an unequal struggle."

"That's what I want to tell my story about," began Werner. "For many years now I have been working at our institute with a number of colleagues. They are Aryans, every last one of them. Quite a few of them are in sympathy with the new regime, some are dissatisfied, but all of them agree that the work being done there is valuable work, that it must be preserved at all costs, even if there is no prospect of carrying on any further. The rooms have been confiscated, the Hitler Youth is going to hold its meetings there, and a date has been set for vacating the premises. And another thing my colleagues agree about is that the valuable collection of rock samples must be saved. We decided unanimously to hand them over to the Natural History Museum, to which I have also donated my own private collection. An appointment was made for a museum attendant to come at twelve o'clock. At eleven in the morning, on that same day," said

Werner, a deep flush spreading over his face, "at eleven in the morning"—he was gasping for breath and Kain was looking at him anxiously—"the brownshirts arrived, those pillagers and desecrators of culture dressed up as clowns, and took away all the material—the valuable collection of stones, along with the institute's inventory—off to the garbage dump. . . ." He was panting, unable to go on, but then, all at once, he slammed his fist down on the table and shouted, "There on the trash heap out in the yard at the back lay our stones, our priceless stones!" Kain had leapt to his feet and dipped his napkin in a glass of water to cool his brow. The unhappy man thrust him away.

Then the bell rang, jarringly.

They all caught their breath. Even Werner had gone quite still, and it was as if this ringing had ripped the curtain of a fateful rage. It seemed as if it had brought him to his senses. Without further resistance he allowed his brother to place the compress on his fevered brow.

Eva hurried to open the door.

Felberbaum rubbed his hands with pleasure. Doubtless, this would be a most welcome visitor. Perhaps his friend, the precentor in the synagogue. He had already prayed, had eaten well in anticipation of the day of fasting, had prayed again; and he didn't usually make any visits on the eve of Yom Kippur, but then this was a state of emergency. Now he'd be coming to see how Felberbaum was doing, whether everything was in order, no arrests carried out and no new restrictions imposed. And no doubt he would have something interesting to relate.

Or it could be his mother-in-law, that was even quite likely, the solemn festival day gave good reason for hope. His mother-in-law would be bringing a letter from his wife in England, along with the visa. Very probably he was about to get his visa. Most of all, he would love to give it up in favor of this wonderful couple here, if such a thing were possible. For they had been waiting even longer than he, and they needed it more urgently.

They had had to sign a paper that they would leave, and couldn't get away. The deadline had arrived and the danger for the two of them was great, greater than Felberbaum would admit to them. The danger that they would be arrested, locked up—all that simply because they cannot get away. Terrible times indeed.— No, it couldn't be his visa, nor a visitor for him either, it was too quiet outside for that and the lady was away too long. It would be that beautiful girl, that Hilde, a friend of this dignified couple.

The door swung open. As it opened, it seemed to Werner as if there were no one standing within its frame. As if a black, menacing emptiness were yawning there.

The door closed again. Eva was standing in the room. How had she come in? Was that Eva? What had happened? She was trembling.

"Hadn't you better sit down?" asked Werner.

"What's the matter, Eva?" Kain, startled, rushed towards her.

"Is there someone outside?" Felberbaum inquired.

"You ought not to talk of the devil, Werner, or he's sure to appear. He was here a moment ago. One of those robbers dressed up as clowns, as you call them."

"An SA-man? Here?" Felberbaum's eyes widened with fear.

"Did he harm you, Eva?" Kain stroked her head.

She turned away from him and moved over to the window.

"So what happened, Eva?"

"We have to leave the country. All of us. All four."

"Leave the country?"

"And vacate the apartment within twelve hours."

"Who says so?"

"A man from the local administration was here."

"Did they also tell you how we are supposed to go about it?" She shrugged.

"Didn't you give him the answer they deserve?"

She said nothing.

"And what will happen if we don't leave the country?" cried Felberbaum. "What can they do to us? We're willing, all too willing. But no one will let us in anywhere. All the paths are barred!"

She propped her cold hands against the window frame.

Her tongue was cleaving to her mouth. She was unable to bring the words out. She could never have allowed past her lips, never have brought herself to repeat, the answer she had had to listen to. Never would she utter what that person had spoken through cold lips. And no god made a move, no avenger appeared, the ceiling did not fall in upon them all.

She had replied to him that, yes, they intended to leave. They themselves were desperate because it was not working out. And so what would happen if they were not after all able to leave?

"Then," he had said, "you will be shot."

X. THE INNOCENTS

To fall ill in a strange town, lying, a stranger among strangers, in an inn, is a serious matter. Because no one's sympathy comes winging towards you, you are someone with no name, a wanderer without provenance and destination, you have to count your pennies and you have no friend to vouch for you. And yet: the taciturn serving maid sees you lying helplessly there, she hears you pleading weakly for some hot tea, and she knows what to do. She hurries down the many stairs and comes back with the cheering tray with tea on it, she has toasted the rolls for you, you drink some tea, swallow a medicated lozenge and lie there, rather sad, rather forlorn, until the landlady comes upstairs. The landlady is very stout and brings plenty of spirited life into your little room. She asks you this and that question and, if you want, will get someone to call the doctor, who is at that moment sitting downstairs in the bar, drinking his vermouth, to come up and see you. But you are already halfway restored. The hot tea, the medicine, the bustling landlady, you can't resist all these, you have a cold, the way you often do, and here in the strange town and in the strange inn you have to get well again quickly.

The situation can be very different. It might be the case that you fall ill in your own hometown, that your financial circumstances are not straitened, you are not a stranger, indeed you are on friendly terms with quite a few, acquainted with many, you might be highly respected in your town, maybe you were born here, grew up here, you may well love your country, the people, you may have fought for this country, have gone to war, and yet here you are with a fever, but no doctor enters the room, for the doctor who wanted to come has been nailed to the cross. You are abandoned, like Robinson Crusoe, but not free. Your rights are called into question by everyone.

You are not even able to lie in your own bed, since your bed is perhaps no longer your own. You are sitting, feverish, in your coat, waiting. You do not know exactly what you are waiting for, you know only that you will be taken away and locked up, because you are supposed to leave and you cannot leave. It is also possible that you will not be locked up, but put out on the street and robbed of your possessions. Evicted and thrown out on the street.

A citizen of this city was sitting, with a high temperature, in his room. He had sent for the doctor, and the doctor did not come. His throat was burning hot, yet he could not sit still, but twisted in pain and groaned. It is a strange thing. Someone, who to such an extent had had enough of life, who was so shattered and defeated, was now rambling in fear about the door, the door which would open, open wide and black, with a death threat. To make him leave the country. The country he had no intention of leaving, as he says out loud. Says it aloud to himself.

In a lucid moment, he scolds Felberbaum, who brings him some soup. He wants an orange. But there isn't an orange to be had in the whole city. Then he demands to see his brother. But his brother is roaming up and down outside the local religious community buildings, waiting for information. About whether they were to be locked up, evicted or beaten. His rage at this brother who has left him on his own spills over on to the soup. In the kitchen, they are enjoying a chicken, he is sure, and they begrudge him an orange.

This was totally untrue. In the kitchen, they were eating nothing, certainly not a chicken, and certainly not Felberbaum, who was observing his day of fasting. And the only supplies in the kitchen were what the second precentor from the temple had hurriedly brought. The second precentor from the temple, a strapping man with bright blue eyes and a Bohemian nose, sometimes went shopping for Felberbaum.

Nor was there a serving maid there, no, not even a maid. No

such undemanding creature, who quietly and honestly went about her duties, the one and only female person entitled to walk about the streets. Admittedly, there was a woman there, a pale and self-absorbed person, but she walked up and down to no purpose, lifted and laid aside everything to no purpose, started in on this and that, all to no end, poured the boiling water into the pot, spilling it over the side, before at last bringing the steaming cup of tea, and dropping it. She was useless, that wife of his brother's.

Eva was no good for anything. She sat on her bed, staring fixedly ahead. She was thinking of a rubber stamp on a document, called a visa, which decided here whether you went on living. This visa had been promised for six months now. First by means of telegrams, then in express letters, then in long letters. These long letters kept on coming, but the visa did not arrive.

And suddenly she knew for sure that it would never come. It won't come. Kain will be arrested. They will beat him. He will fight back. He will be beaten to death, Kain. Suddenly she was certain of it.

A man cannot live his life the way he wishes. He lives it in an inferior way, a makeshift way, in the depths, under the ground instead of above it, he lives as a prisoner rather than at liberty, imprisoned in himself, in one of his own principal characters, he lives in fear, hunger and cold. At times, he does not live at all, sometimes he has no desire whatsoever to live, and here—this is what raises him above the animals—here is where his preparations begin. He puts his possessions in order, all his receipts, he crosses himself off the list, is in charge of his own soul, it is his final decision, and he takes the poison that sets him free.

That is what puts him above the animals.

And what if he is incapable of doing that? What if that moment comes when he does not wish to live and yet has to go on living? Because that, too, the Fates have woven into their bleak web. It is possible that a man does not wish to live, yet may not die!

Because he would take someone else with him to the grave if he dies.

Felberbaum had had an animated phone call. Had told Werner about it with great enthusiasm. Had watched with amazement as the color rose in his cheeks, but not the flush of a fever: it was joy, reassurance, that was clear. Werner threw off his coat, fetched a pamphlet which he had written himself, a geological treatise, and, earnestly and calmly, immersed himself in his publication.

Felberbaum called Eva into the room. But she did not hear him. She was sitting motionless on the edge of her bed in the kitchen, which served at the same time as her bedroom, telling herself that this is the bitterest thing: when a man is *not* at liberty to cast off his life, when he cannot avail himself of that privilege he has over the animals.

She sat there, as if turned to stone.

"Brilliant news, dear lady," called Felberbaum, rubbing his hands together. "Your husband called. No advance of the superior armed forces into our tabernacle! No exodus of the children of Israel out of Egypt! We do not have to leave and will not be shot. We can wait calmly for our visas. Everything has blown over, a minute ago. Those whom it has struck, may God have mercy on them, they have been evicted, robbed of everything down to the shirts on their backs, and are without a roof over their heads. We have been spared; one fasts, makes one's sacrifice, and the Lord accepts it."

But although Felberbaum relates all this with a broad, beaming smile, the lady is sobbing dryly. Even though it was all over. A period of calm could be expected, the storm had subsided, the hyena, too, was wearied, the mob had had its victims and before it could digest these, they would be gone.

He watched her step out on to the little balcony, this puzzling woman who was weeping now, now that all was well. He went back in to the cranky geologist who was, by this time, bright and completely restored, demanding something to eat. He, Felberbaum, was rather weary, because now at last his own stomach was grumbling. It was a day of fasting, and he had cleaned and cooked for the whole household. God may forgive, but the body did not. And the healthier a man is, the heartier the meals set before him each day, the harder the interruption is for him to bear, even though this holiday, called a day of fasting, was a precept from health treatises, a day of rest for the inner machine.

Incidentally, in his heart of hearts, he was convinced that, by dint of his act of piety, he had rescued himself and his fellow lodgers from the very worst.

Eva stood on the tiny balcony off the front room, overlooking the street. She wanted to view an extraordinary spectacle that, for days, had presented itself to her and had both drawn her and terrified her. But the tears veiled her eyes, tears that fell like rain in a thunderstorm.

On the second floor of the house opposite, the windows remained wide open, day and night, despite the mist and the cold. In one large room stood an old woman in a nightdress which hung loose on her aged body. She stood in the big, dark room wiping circles in the air with a duster, even though the huge room was completely empty, without a table, a bed, a cupboard; there was not even a chair in it to be dusted. In the total void of that room, the old woman was dusting off her furniture which had stood there just a few days before and which down through many years she had dusted daily, albeit not in her nightdress and not in the empty air.

Next to the room was a smaller bedroom. It, too, was completely empty, but for a chair by the window, on which an extremely delicate creature sat, the daughter of the old woman waving a duster around in the air. The young woman had her arms propped on the windowsill as she watched her mother, without comprehending what she was doing and without doing anything to stop her or even showing any great surprise.

First, her father had been arrested, and at that time her mother dusted the furniture in order to keep from thinking all the time. In those days, too, her mother would go into the kitchen and peel potatoes and fry them. The young woman's husband would already be sitting at the big brown table, and together they would partake of the simple meal.

Then the young woman's husband was led away. From that day on, her mother would go into the kitchen alone, while she herself could only sit in the bedroom and watch. A bag of bones, she sat slumped there, no longer moving.

Until one day the enemies arrived. Then she was forced to stand up, because they were taking the furniture away, and the armchair she was sitting in was made of leather. They also took the large pictures; the frames were valuable. They might have left the beds, but they belonged to a matching hardwood set. The men also explained to them why they had come and why they were punishing them. According to them, her mother was to blame for the World War and now she was agitating for a new war. She was a murderess.

The mother collapsed in terror on to the chair when she heard this. They forgot that chair (on which the emaciated creature was now sitting) and left it behind, with the mother still sitting there. Shocked at herself, she went about wiping the ignominy off her furniture. Her responsibility for the World War.

Eva dried her eyes. They had become red and swollen and were burning hot. For a while, she could not see anything, even though she strained to look across. So what was going on now? The windows were closed today, the frail daughter had disappeared, the empty room covered in sheets and locked shut. No doubt they had taken them away to a madhouse.

Then, all of a sudden, a black vehicle drew up.

The old woman had died.

Was that the old woman they were bringing out? No, it was the young one. Very delicate, very solitary, the thin limbs outlined under the canvas. But she did not remain alone for long. Behind her, followed her mother. Her mother was not going leave her on her own. Her body was still broad, still strong, not yet completely worn out; for one last time, her body protected her daughter. Now she has purged her guilt for the World War, wiped it out with gas, and she has taken her child with her. Now they lay there dead, and that was for the best, because they no longer had a bite to eat, not even the wood of the hard furniture.

"Are they not even going to grant them a coffin?" The two women were lying on a stretcher, shrouded in a canvas sheet. Eva herself was going out of her mind, talking loudly to herself. "Stop talking to yourself," she thought, "or you will go mad and they'll take you away." She rubbed her eyes. Perhaps the whole crazy scene would dissipate, perhaps it was all in her own fevered brain. Because you put dead people into coffins.

No. It was not her fevered brain which made this scene flicker like agonizing flames. They don't have coffins because there are no coffins any more. Because they cannot manufacture as many coffins, day in and day out, as there are deaths, day in and day out, in this city. That's why there are no coffins there for them.

Eva's eye was now caught by something moving quickly at the edge of her balcony. It was a fist. The fist was white, as if it had been blanched. The fingers dug, trembling, into the thumb. The fist hammered down on the wooden rail, making a hard sound.

Then she raised her head and became altogether still.

Kain was standing next to her.

"This time, we understand each other, Kain."

XI. ◼ THE GREAT FIRE

"**W**hat a disaster!" Felberbaum was wringing his hands. "The temples are burning!" He cried out the words into the air like an accusation, as if he were standing before Moses and complaining.

"The temples on fire? But that's . . ." Kain leapt to his feet. "Can you believe that's possible, Werner?"

"I consider anything to be possible."

"The temples are burning! All the temples!"

"Have you seen it with your own eyes, Herr Felberbaum?"

"Our neighbor saw it, and he's an Aryan, pure Aryan, so he must know! He was standing there! Standing at the main temple! He expressed his condolences to me!"

"I can't believe it."

"Because you always believe only what suits you."

"You're wrong, Werner, it makes no difference to me. But that they should commit such a gross tactical blunder . . ."

"You're still living under the delusion that they're proceeding according to some program. They're proceeding with pogroms."

"You're right again, unfortunately," Felberbaum looked fearfully up at Kain. "They're making arrests in every . . ."

"Don't say a word about arrests in front of Eva."

"What's that you're saying about me?" She stood, stricken with fear, in the doorway, looking from one to the other.

"That you're slaving away in the kitchen, Eva."

"Is it true that the synagogues are on fire, Herr Felberbaum? The janitor is talking about it downstairs."

"The temples are burning!" cried Felberbaum as if accusing all men and even God.

"The fire will spread to the neighboring houses—after all, everything is built so close together here."

168

"The fire will spread, but not the way you think, Eva."

"There goes my brother, being the prophet again." Werner was pacing up and down the room, regularly crossing the path of the brother he was mocking, who was doing the same thing. "It will spread, but to us. Got that? To us!"

"You could be right, if it were true, Werner. Only I don't believe it. One temple might have caught on fire, and people are immediately making a historic temple-burning out of that. None of you has actually seen it."

"But the janitor has come straight back from the blaze, Kain!"

"And our Aryan neighbor assured me! He even gave me a brandy because I was so shocked. How lucky we are that there's no temple nearby. Otherwise they might come for us to make us clear the debris away. Such a sin no one could bring himself to commit!"

"How lucky we are indeed. No one has ever had the experience of being allowed into a German consulate—but they let the little Jew in. As far as the secretary."

"The doorman at the German consulate once let me in, when I was in Paris," Felberbaum assured them, and they all believed him.

"The boy should be hanged. He'll land us all in the concentration camp. The real reason he fired those shots in Paris was because all the fanatics there were being acquitted. There's romanticism that's just perfect for you! Next thing, you'll be making him out to be a liberator, the Lad of Orleans!"

"You're mistaken, Werner, but the boy can't be altogether condemned as guilty. They took his parents to the frontier, the foreign border guards sent them back. There was nowhere they could stand, neither in their homeland nor on foreign soil. And they weren't allowed to sit on the ground, but were left hanging in midair. If it weren't enough to drive you crazy, it would make you laugh!"

"They weren't even allowed to hang in midair, Kain, that's what you should really be saying."

A bird flutters agitatedly about in a room and batters itself against the walls. Then it catches sight of the light and flies towards the window. But—how cruel. The air suddenly becomes hard, hard as stone. It won't let it out, out into freedom.

Eva went towards the window and ran her hands over the ice-cold, hard panes. The sky was bright and high. But they were prisoners.

A Jewish boy in Paris had fired shots at a man in the German consulate. On the life of the seriously injured man hung the lives of hundreds of thousands. Because the boy had carried out an act of revenge. Revenge for his parents, who had been driven out of their homeland. An innocent man was shot, and innocent people would pay for it. The injured man, the German at the consulate, had died. He was given a funeral with full pomp and ceremony. His fellow countrymen were now being given a lavish funeral feast. They were free to take whatever they wanted. Even the accoutrements of the synagogue.

They had lain in wait for a week, and for a week they had issued threats. What a week that was! They, his national comrades, were waiting for the death of the German in Paris. The Jews prayed for his life.

Eva groaned so loudly that Kain called her away from the window.

"He did the Führer no small favor, that boy," he said, turning towards her.

She was unable to say a word.

"Yes, the national comrades are now getting their pound of flesh, and they are throwing the meat to the dogs, as our good SA-man said."

"But the meat is poisoned, that was your answer, Kain."

"That reply is typical of him. Whatever happens to them later won't do us any good. We're sitting here in a trap. The temples are burning, and soon we'll be burning. What's happening here is called a pogrom."

"For heaven's sake, Werner, do you believe they'll come after us?"

"Nonsense, Eva. Don't let Werner harangue you. They have set fire to *one* temple at the most, and that will do them enough damage abroad. What interests me is, who gave the boy in Paris the weapon?"

"I might have known that would interest you. That detective story is of no importance. What is important is what's going on outside. For days now, those people in their clown costumes have been hanging about every street corner. The fact that people take these outfits seriously speaks volumes about the mentality of the populace."

"Have there been arrests? The janitor gave me such a funny look."

"Not a single arrest," Felberbaum declared, resuming his role of the kind-hearted protector. "No question of that. Nothing but arson."

"You wonder that the city allows it. This city has not become that inhuman."

"The people are enjoying the blaze. They stand by watching, but apart from that there's nothing happening, not *one* arrest."

"There you have it." Werner looked at her grimly. "There you have the city which has not been dehumanized. It will all backfire on us. We have no rights and no protection. Left to the mercy of the rabble."

"You're certainly taking them very seriously, your clowns."

"As seriously as you take a pack of hungry hyenas if you don't have a revolver. My janitor took mine away from me last week, so that they won't be able to find any weapons here when they search the building. They're looking all over the place for weapons now."

"What a nice chap."

"He used to be the National Socialists' most ardent supporter, but since his disappointment with them, he is sticking by Werner. He told me all about it himself."

"A janitor like that is worth his weight in gold. He protects you like a policeman. Up where I lived in the second district, they've all turned. They get into such a rage when the SA people come. Because they take everything away from the Jews and don't leave them enough money for tips."

"And because the SA-men deprive them of their power over the building. I mean, in our city, up until the putsch, the janitor was the absolute ruler—over the tenants and the building itself. That's been taken away from them now. What they have to do now is 'permit forced entry into the building,' and they don't like that."

"We should have bought a Dutchman for ourselves," said Felberbaum now, and he meant it in all seriousness. Nor was he misunderstood for a moment, indeed even Eva nodded.

"We haven't enough room," she said quietly.

In fact, a Dutchman had been offered for sale, but the price was too high. People become quite outrageous with their demands, especially in times of unrest. Only in the last few days, the price for foreigners had risen ten- to twenty-fold.

That made Felberbaum think of a story, which he now told to distract the disturbed lady.

A wealthy cloth merchant had bought himself a Swede, because a Frenchman, even on the marketplace, would have been too expensive for him. This Swede squeezed a hundred marks a month out of him, and, on top of that, a nice room, full board, a bath every day and a regular box at the theater. All this was granted him without demur, and, in addition, the merchant's gorgeous niece would sit in the garden with him on warm evenings looking at the moon.

The Swede, who had not been exactly spoiled in his own home, where, in fact, he lived off nothing but a kind of salted fish for six months of the year—not exactly everyone's taste—began after a time to step up his demands. Special menus had to be cooked for him, the domestic staff of the household was sent running hither and yon, and every evening, when he took his footbath—he suffered from corns—two basins of water had to be brought to him, one for each foot. He demanded a camera, and within a few hours it was in hand. He demanded a home movie projector, and that was acquired for him. But then he wanted a roof garden. For the cloth merchant, this was not only a considerable expense, but a pointless one into the bargain. They were fully expecting to lose their villa, to sell it, so to speak (such was the common euphemism for theft from a powerless minority), and on top of all that was the fact that such a luxury was bound to antagonize the already hostile neighbors to the right and left. So the Swede did not get a roof garden. This made him angry, he saw red, and not even the sweet whisperings of the merchant's beautiful niece could dissuade him from leaving that very day and moving in with a competitor, a silk merchant, who offered to pay him double.

"I don't quite understand," said Kain, as if waking from a dream. "Does it really make such a difference, having a foreigner in the house?"

"People imagine it does," replied Felberbaum. "It's like with Coué: nothing will happen to me, nothing will happen to me. If he keeps telling himself that, nothing really does happen to him. The fact is that no houses have been looted with foreigners living in them. From a good country, naturally. A Yugoslav or a Romanian is worth nothing, a Czech even has an adverse effect, but an American is worth his weight in gold."

"I don't understand that either," said Werner, turning to his sister-in-law. "People let foreigners live with them and even pay them for it?"

"Yes, and I would too, if we had room and I could afford it. Any foreigner is a form of protection."

"It just goes to show that they do fear opinion abroad," said Kain.

"Cold comfort," retorted Werner caustically.

"It's a considerable comfort," declared Felberbaum. "They immediately chased an Englishman away from the main temple because he took pictures."

"Were you there?" asked Eva animatedly.

"Our Aryan neighbor told me about it. He left at once, he couldn't bear to watch."

He was aware that he was skirting round the subject of greatest interest here and now. Since his words were being listened to, he went on. He described the eviction of the two women from the house opposite.

On that occasion, it was not actually an eviction, because they were let back into the house, albeit empty, both the mother and the daughter, so that the old woman then had the compulsion to go round dusting the air. They had carried her furniture out into the street, where it was sold to any and every passerby. Because for weeks there had not been a furniture van to be had, not in the whole city, since they had all been booked in advance for evictions. For the "punitive" eviction of people who were to blame for the World War, like the old woman and her daughter. Most of her furniture was bought by the girl who worked in the dry cleaner's on the ground floor. She went and stood outside the front door, and behaved like a raving lunatic. For a few marks, she acquired almost the entire contents of the household and had everything put in the shop. All the while she let out fierce yelps, because there was no one there to prevent her depriving two helpless women of their last possessions. Spitefully, she twisted her face this way and that, becoming alternately pale and red with rage, but with only a meager audience. She was too young for such venom; perhaps she was so nasty because she had a squint. People like that are often embittered.

But however kind an explanation Felberbaum might offer for

people's bitterness, his hosts were listening to him with only half an ear. He noticed this, tried to change the subject, started stammering and, in his embarrassment, began talking of precisely the topic he had wanted to keep quiet; namely that he himself turned up as a buyer, stood by the raving shop-girl and bought back a bed from the brownshirt, who was obviously in a hurry to get rid of his wares. He left this bed standing out in the street for a while and only later carried it back into the building and up to the old woman's front room himself. To be precise, he had bought two beds, but as he was laboriously dismantling the second one, so as to take it back up piece by piece, the shop-girl rushed like a wildcat out of the dry cleaner's to protest, making menacing references to his nose.

At this, Werner spoke up. At the outbreak of the World War, he had been very young; he enlisted, because you had to lay down your life for your fatherland. Mountains of dead bodies lay around him, literally mountains, you couldn't count them any more. His unit was in a particularly exposed hillside position in the Dolomites, they had been pinned down for days by heavy Italian fire, all communications were cut, and they could not remove their dead. It was horrendous. All around him the dead, with the worms crawling about on them at night, crawling towards the living; there was no possibility of digging a grave for them. One friend after another fell, fatally wounded, and could not be buried. They had given themselves up for lost. Yet all this had not seemed pointless to them, had not seemed to be without dignity, it was all happening for the sake of their homeland, the country had to be defended, and you died on the field of honor. It was dreadful to see young men dropping, to be unable to dig a grave for your friends, the stink of decomposition was awful and the mark of death and its horrors at such close quarters was torture to experience at such a young age. But it was not as awful as what was going on here and now in this city.

"You are right, brother."

A transformation had taken place in Werner. Perhaps because his younger brother was around him every day now, assuring him on a daily basis that without him he had no wish to save his own skin, that for him it was no deliverance if he were to leave the country while Werner remained behind. They were, once again, the inseparable companions of childhood. Werner no longer shut himself off, he raised his clear eyes and recognized with amazement that he was fond of the three people around him.

When he had finished speaking, he turned to Felberbaum and said, "What you did, with the bed, was an act of decency. It wouldn't have occurred to me."

The recipient of this remark felt deeply moved by praise coming from this harsh man and strove feverishly to think of some other soothing tale to tell, but nothing would come to mind.

"You can't imagine the things my mother-in-law talks about," he said guardedly, because in this company, people were very precise. "A rabbi from Palestine has arrived, with a British passport, and he is negotiating with the Gestapo; he'll pay in gold, and in no time at all everything will settle down." He believed this himself, so convincingly had he said it.

"Did she watch the main temple burning herself?" asked Eva.

"People haven't the heart. They feel like criminals. They believe the temple will strike them down if they watch and don't do anything about it."

Eva looked past him, as if he were a stranger, and said, "We shall remember this November, when we are all being punished because a child went wrong and was led astray, and in France at that."

"It's interesting," affirmed Kain, "that people never cease to play school. I consider school to be the source of all subsequent evil in a person's life, even though it does have something to be said for it. But it does more harm than good. School impresses the receptive minds of children to such a degree that every child becomes narrow-minded for the rest of its life, striving after rank. Among adults you find nothing but inspectors, headmasters, star pupils and sycophants. Anyone who does not toe the line is impoverished and wretched and is well and truly and sadistically tormented and stomped down. This desire, to play school forever, finds its most striking expression in militarism. Especially here in this country. The way they make such demands—some of them fair, some of them sadistic—in the schools is just the way they act in the army. Certainly, in countries where the schools are institutions of distinction and where posturing and misdirected ambition are frowned on, playing school does not by any means have such a bad effect as here in this country."

"Where people are divided up into generals and other ranks," said Werner.

"Correct. And even that is not enough for them. Here they play their parts even more precisely, Führer, Gauleiter, Kreisleiter, blackshirt, brownshirt. Everyone is divided up into classes—and they call themselves socialists."

"If only Hilde would come," said Eva out of the blue. "She is such a breath of fresh air among schoolchildren, such a fine specimen, not to be cowed, and not in the least exemplary."

The doorbell rang.

But that's not Hilde, she thought. That will be the sadistic headmasters in their black uniforms. That will be them now!

Shivering with fear, she went to open the door.

It was Hilde.

Kain heard her young voice and cheered up, as he always did when she arrived and took their minds off everything with her blossoming appearance. But when she came in, he was stunned by her expression.

"What's going on out there?" said Felberbaum, looking at her anxiously. He was the only one who stood up politely to welcome Hilde.

"The temples are on fire!" Hilde sank on to the chair which he pushed towards her. It seemed as if this had absolutely nothing to do with her, so strangely did she say it.

"So it really is true!" exclaimed Kain, searching her face to see if that was what was disturbing her so much.

"They've arrested Papa!" She burst into touchingly childish tears and buried her face in her hands. "This morning, they took Papa away!"

XII. THE AIRPLANE CRASHES

The adventure had turned out badly, the adventure with the airplane. Terribly badly. It was no longer an adventure, it was a tragedy, after a long series of humiliations. It was an infamy, it was an agony without end, but the end came, and the agony remained.

Hilde did not relate the story in sequence. She did not tell a story at all. She stammered out wild descriptions and details. She accused herself, put herself in the wrong, her features displaying a new and so profoundly felt experience, that Kain furrowed his brow.

"The man had bad breath," she said in disgust. Only two of those in the room could understand her, the two others had no idea who or what was being talked about. Werner fixed his clear gaze on her and was mystified. It was said that such girls existed. Who could be bought. That's what people said. Girls who lived for adventures and admitted it, outright, without shame. Inexplicable and indecent.

Felberbaum, too, looked on in bafflement, yet he sympathized with her in her misfortune, even though he could not understand a word. He found the girl superb, she was a real beauty, much more beautiful than the threadbare stars he knew from the movies, her voice was warm and full, warm and full were this young creature's eyes and image and every movement.

"He kept jumping to his feet, rushing to and fro, and wanting the money," she went on, rather more clearly now. Her words renewed Werner's astonishment; those girls actually received money, as far as he was informed, although he could be wrong there.

"From the subject of money, he moved on to his feelings,"

she added, with irony. Not that he had used that term, he talked only of fatuous things, in totally meaningless clichés. They had been sitting in a country inn, he poured some wine, a dreadful concoction, by the way, insisting that she drink up, turning nasty, until she got to her feet. Then he leapt up and came abruptly back to the initial topic of their conversation. Sickened, she promised to get him the money the next day, firmly determined to throw it in his face, even though she had not the slightest notion of how she could come by it.

The next day, she did manage to get together a large sum. An old friend of her father's helped her out, a childhood playmate of his who sold her last remaining jewelry. She no longer dared ask her parents for help, since they had always been against the plan, "thinking just as you did," she said, and she would have softened the heart of any savage, sitting there so innocent and exhausted, weighed down by a great burden of cares that had nothing to do with her, yet that she herself—with the most altruistic of intentions, one might almost say out of magnanimity—had created.

She brought this large sum to the inn, he took the money, counted it and seemed dissatisfied. Because in fact it was short by almost half and she had the impression he needed this money urgently. Not for her airplane, of that she was already well aware (she spoke these words like a child making a confession, and it moved her three friends), and if she hadn't been dealing with that scoundrel, she would have been inclined to believe that some debt of honor which must be kept secret was involved, so importunate was he becoming. She faced up to him and, with a light quip, promised to bring the rest on the following day, even though she did not know where in all the world she could possibly lay hands on the remaining sum, which amounted to some thousands.

Her light-hearted tone calmed him down, and he started into his dreary courtship, but this time she excused herself hastily and rushed away.

She ran home and became sick with agitation. She lay in bed with a fever, meekly allowing her parents to lay cold compresses on her brow and give her iced water to drink. No matter how she looked at it, getting the rest of the money together seemed impossible. She had run out of sources of cash, out of any ideas, and out of all hope.

With a dry throat, she did nevertheless go to the inn the next day, driven by the fear that he might send her a dangerous reminder. If only she had not gone. Things couldn't possibly have turned out as badly as they did. Distraught, she begged for more time. She lost her composure to such a degree that he became suspicious and, with furtive glances and in a menacing tone, ordered her to come to her senses. This time, because of his greed, he had no desire to soften his rage. Now she was really afraid. Because it was clear that he was capable of anything, indeed, to judge by the horrible sight of his face, capable of many things she could not begin to comprehend or even imagine.

At this point, Werner interrupted her. He understood now that there was more at stake here than some haggling game, some mere tawdriness, and he wanted to know the story of what had gone before. His brother took over this task, briefly and impatiently (he wanted to get to the end of it), but with a great amount of noble consideration for the girl; he put her actions in such a pure light that Werner was left wondering why such an upright creature hadn't gone into a convent or become a maid rather than disfiguring herself with cosmetics and silken lace.

Her friend's words now made Hilde's heart grow even heavier and led her to confess the rest. And so she continued, now telling her tale with intensity and in the order of events, as if driven on, telling of how obsessed she had been with the thought that her life was at stake, her parents' lives, and worse still, those of her friends here. These were her very words, and they were accompanied by a glance at the man she was specifically referring to, so that they went straight to his heart and Eva bowed her head, abashed. Because she herself had escaped all this and had, to a certain extent, put the burden on this inexperienced girl.

Back home, Hilde had been overcome with the desire to confess everything to her mother and to shift all the worries on to her, so despondent did she feel. Yet she was so afraid of worrying her mother, who got into a state about the slightest thing, and anyway there was no way out of it all. Her mother did not have access to large sums of money without her father's consent, and they would never obtain that, certainly not, indeed especially not if he were to hear the whole dire story. The time for the rendezvous was drawing closer and with it, it seemed, the end of the world. She could see such disaster looming, all the result of her failure to pay off a sum of money on time, the kind of thing you so often read about in novels, she foresaw arrest and death, so that she resorted to the most terrible way out, she went to her father's desk—and here she sobbed so much she was unable to go on, because this was the point at which she was forced to lay herself bare, to besmirch herself before the very person in whose eyes she always wanted to seem pure, the one who had led her to achieve purity of spirit, who had led her to something higher, to much more than she really was—and yet it all had to come out, she could bear it no longer. She wanted to be rid of it, wanted, herself, to be away from here, away, out of this city, out of this country, forever.

"And you opened the drawer containing his money." It was Eva who now spoke, calmly, spoke with an expression that suggested it was quite understandable, as if it were no sin, as if it were not something despicable. In fact she spoke thoughtfully and seriously, as if that seemed to her the only solution, as if she herself would have taken refuge in that solution.

The girl nodded gratefully, and now her weeping sounded more like a release; she had been forgiven, here she had found forgiveness, she was no longer humbled and ridiculous, and only her pain remained. She drew a deep sigh and seemed to rest now for a moment as if after an arduous walk.

Felberbaum took advantage of this pause to relate how he, too, had had an experience with such a monster. This man had had him secretly locked up, then, adopting a saintly mien, had called on his family, had secured for himself all the family's possessions and finally posed as his saviour. He had literally opened up the prison walls, had appeared before him, the prisoner, persuaded him to sign a paper, a mere formality, this signature, since he had already taken over the premises: no castle, no parliament, nothing more than a cinema, which now belonged to him. In no way did he bear this man a grudge, he insisted, after all he had been freed in return—this man had, in the end, got him out, a thief capable of a noble gesture, whereas usually they go straight ahead and stab you.

During his tale, Kain looked up and was about to ask a question. But the girl had recovered her breath and went on with her story.

Yes, she had indeed taken the key from the desk and opened the safe. In it lay the bankbooks, four in number, each in one of their names and protected by a secret password. She knew the password for her own bankbook, her savings were invested in that account, as her father had proudly shown her often enough, and she herself was occasionally allowed to deposit sizable sums in it. She took out this bankbook, locked up the safe and set off on her fateful way.

The man was visibly reassured by the bankbook. He even suggested they take a walk to the pond, telling some romantic story as they walked round it, with a chivalrous end to it. But she had had enough. She waved down a taxi and left him standing there, speechless.

The next morning, everything went smoothly. She was able to withdraw the money from the bank.

"That's amazing," Werner broke in.

She hurried to the little coffeehouse which had been selected for the winding-up of this strange piece of business. She threw the money on the table, not feeling it at all necessary to continue any further with the airplane farce, and left him hastily, incapable of concealing her contempt.

"And today,"—she groaned and laid her arm on the table and her head on top of it, which disturbed the company beyond all measure—"today, they arrested Papa! Papa had absolutely no idea . . . he kept protesting the whole time . . . that he had not withdrawn any money without the permission of the authorities . . . they showed him my signature . . . and I'm standing there . . . I'll never forget the long look he gave me . . . as they took him away . . . he didn't make a move . . . just looked at me. . . ."

"And you see that as the motive for his arrest, that he had withdrawn the money?"

She looked at Kain, unable to understand.

"A pity," said Felberbaum, "that it wasn't my SA-man, my acquaintance, my thief of the noble gesture: I might have had a chance to intervene. You can reason with that man; he would get your Papa out, returning a favor, as it were."

On that score, Kain with some sarcasm assured him, he could put his mind at rest. Judging by the way things happened in real life these days, which was indeed more interesting and more involved than anything that the imagination spawns (perhaps precisely because *everything* starts off in the imagination), it seemed highly probable to him that all this did come from *his* brownshirt. From a remark which Felberbaum had, quite by the way, let slip earlier, Kain concluded that in fact the same scoundrel was behind all this. Could he, Kain asked, remember the man, his appearance and his name, the man who had exchanged the cinema—that's what it was, wasn't it?—for his freedom?

Of course he knew him, knew him very well. In the past, in

what were still the good times, he had often bought a painting from him, that picture for example which the dear lady had taken down in the kitchen because the sight of the dead stag depressed her. The man had in fact been a painter, before his present career; he was tall, very thin and ugly, and he was called, what was it?—Schwamm."

"If his name is Pilz, then we are talking about the same man," replied Kain, and Felberbaum, highly delighted and amazed at the perspicacity—the very genius—and talent of the most learned Herr Doktor, agreed that, yes, quite right, Pilz *was* his name.

In the wink of an eye, he had transformed, as if by magic, a grieving girl into a bright and happy one. Because youth is like gold, wipe away the dust, and it shines beautifully again, happy and full of hope, and it is right in this, for youth itself is still there, is itself the fulfillment. Felberbaum bet her any amount she liked, he would liberate her Papa.

Not that Kain had any wish to disturb the calm just breathed into the turmoil of the young girl's emotions, but the situation was so serious as to compel him to raise an objection: he did not see Pilz in such a rosy light. In his view, there was no doubt that Pilz himself had ordered the arrest. The best way a thief can protect himself is to play the detective. This one here was playing the informer in case the whole business were to come to the attention of the Party.

Felberbaum made so bold as to disagree. That was the reasoning of a man of imagination, whereas Pilz was far too simple. "Much too simple," parroted Hilde, as if forgetting what misery he had plunged her into.

Eva gave her a suspicious look. "What do you say to him when he asks about Kain?"

"That you've all left. That's what everyone back home thinks."

"That explains why they haven't been coming with reminders, even though the deadline has passed."

"Of course that's the explanation," cried Felberbaum brightly, genuinely relieved. "But now I must be on my way and pay our Pilz a visit."

This decision, to go out on such a day, did not come easily to Felberbaum. There he was, sixty years old, and having come through all sorts of things. But on the other hand, it seemed to him to be to his own advantage, too, to talk this Pilz round. You never knew what sort of things might happen, what with the temples already on fire. And so it could be useful to freshen up his weird friendship with that rascal.

Now it was Kain who spoke up and said, to the astonishment of all, quite brightly, "Burning temples and the fanatics standing by, that's not something a writer gets to see every day, but now he can see it and he is not going to let it slip through his fingers."

It happened only infrequently that Werner pushed himself to the fore. Even then, he did so shyly and only to share an experience with his brother. It might well be that he was in a more relaxed frame of mind, or perhaps the girl's revelations had impressed him by their candor; he now came out of his shell and spoke up excitedly.

"If reason deserts people who have so little of it to fall back on anyway," (here he was becoming personal, but Felberbaum was already deep in animated conversation with Hilde over by the window and was neither looking at nor listening to him) "then there is no further point in arguing. A blind man will fall into the ditch because he will not be led. But that my brother should take leave of his senses, that is alarming."

"Now here I must protest, Werner, in the words of the greatest German poet: He who does not lose his reason over certain things has none to lose."

"And what would these certain things be? Burning buildings? Or is it the *canaille* standing around them? Aren't you ashamed of yourself, providing an audience for such a spectacle? I am

amazed at your wife. Normally, she goes out of her mind whenever you go out. But women always have their hearts in the
wrong place."

"Do you mean, on the right side, Werner? That's where
mine is."

"I'm not at all ashamed," said Kain. "I didn't set fire to the
temple. I will admit however that this atrocity does fill me with
satisfaction. It is a symbol of the intentions and the actions of
these new people in power, crucifying and burning feelings and
beliefs. It is so very symbolic that even I, a complete non-
believer, can see the end of these sinners approaching. And so do
the people! Because the population is terrified. When places of
worship burn, cities fall silent. The small crowd outside the temple is not the people.

"But I have another confession to make. First, though, I must
mention an experience from my childhood. As a child, I saw a
monastery on fire. I can still see it before my eyes. It is flaring
with a peculiar kind of fire, because it is broad daylight and the
fire is competing with the sunlight. Only gradually does the
monastery die, it dies quite slowly and once it is no longer ablaze
and glowing, but black, I feel utterly miserable. But from the day
I watched that huge inferno as a child, I have been a fire-
worshipper, and at times I fanatically wish for a blaze."

"If your shameless heart is not touched by stones being torn
from their seams and reduced to glowing embers, how is it that
your mind turns to the story of the monastery? What we have
here is a novel being destroyed, an atmosphere being disturbed;
that part does not bother me, but the fact that it leaves you so
cold worries me. Especially as we keep hearing from you, daily,
hourly, that atmosphere means everything to you."

"But fire stirs me to such a state of intoxication that I for-
get the story. Perhaps this intoxication makes me cruel. Perhaps
I even feel the story burning as well, and I smother the thought.
Anyone presumptious enough to investigate all mankind's

emotions—and their justifications—contains all these emotions within himself. I have them all in me, I admit it. How to come to terms with them, for example, with the criminal within me, that is my affair. And I have to say, I find it difficult. I just cannot cope with the lazybones in me. I can understand him and call him a dreamer. I find the drunkard as difficult to escape from as fire. Intoxication is all an artist can wish for, and it is not for nothing that our relaxed state after consuming wine is called intoxication, it conjures up freedom."

At the word "freedom," Kain saw himself cast back between the gray walls of life, and his tone became almost sharp:

"I am not ashamed of my defects, indeed I need them. The stones, when they are glowing hot, are too remote from me, even if they are your stones, Werner. I am pained by what happens to everything that I can still recognize as living. If someone burns a swastika into the tortoise's shell, that sets *me* afire. Not to mention the torture it is exposed to when someone removes its shell."

"There's a lot to be said for tortoises. They cling to cliffs, the ancient eternal cliffs. They blend in with the cliff. If I had the choice of living in this world in another form, then certainly it would be as a tortoise."

At that, Eva and Kain laughed.

"The rigor of the tortoise, its toughness and calmness provoked me," Kain said charmingly, "into comparing you with it."

Which comparison Werner accepted, rather like a ballerina accepting the compliment that she dances as graciously as a fountain plays. But he did not allow himself to be diverted:

"So what do you think of the people living in the building that is on fire? Of the loss they suffer?"

"For me, back then, after the fire in the monastery, punishment followed swiftly. Two monks burned to death. I can still see, even now, my horror, which tormented me for a long time. They had been overlooked, and so they must have been fully aware of their predicament. That was my first grievous blow in life. Of course, a healthy adult shares even more vividly, in his own thriving body, the sufferings of the dying. But life does not teach this to a small boy."

"Yes, I too, find it distressing, Kain, that they had been forgotten about and knew what was happening to them."

"If someone has to die," said Werner, "then it is better they are aware of it. I already have my coffin prepared. Made of granite."

"Oh, come now, Werner!" Kain burst out laughing.

"The coffin has been carved out to fit my height and my girth, it is broad and rounded on all four sides, it has a stone lid, like a sarcophagus, and I shall lie comfortably in it. Those are no empty words, for I have already lain in it to try it out. By means of that coffin, I shall submit myself to the earth and its transformations. With that coffin, I shall put a stop to slapdash procedures, to the crematorium, which arouses in me the same despair that the prospect of being ripped apart by a wild animal arouses in you."

"I must say, that truly is the most terrible prospect for me, decaying only once inside the carcass of an animal. But that you should be against the most rapid means of approaching the nature of stone is illogical, Werner."

"You seem to be unaware that ashes disintegrate into nothing. I shall decay in stone. In granite."

"It also seems logically consistent to me that we should not disturb the earth's well-being, and our own—not work counter to its natural process. But we don't merely subside, Werner, we hand ourselves over to Man. Who does not shy away from setting up our hollow skull on his desk. Given that, it's preferable to decay into ashes and dissipate into nothingness."

"You ought not to talk of 'hollow skulls.' That could lead to misunderstandings. Especially when you are thinking of your own head. By the way, and, with some *schadenfreude*, I note that you are becoming less trusting."

"This year, in this city, I have lost the ability to trust. I admit that with bitterness. I can feel, ripening within me, what I call the weapon of the little man—disparagement."

"And I have made a good bed for myself. In granite. I shall pass over into granite. But if you would like to do one last thing for me and set up a monument to me, then I would want it to be in the shape of a tortoise, walking up and down on my grave. One made of stone, it goes without saying, for that, for *me*, is the genuine kind, to the endless amusement of my sister-in-law. I hope you will not permit women to walk on my grave."

"Even in all friendship and brotherly love, I cannot promise anything, Werner. There is nothing in the world I know more certainly than that you, even though you are the older of us, will walk on *my* grave. You will, brother, and no doubt with some stone amulet, which you will place in my grave with me. You see, you have built upon something with consistency, and you should not lose that. I, however, have built upon mankind; how fallible is its soul, how fallible its form, how endangered and dangerous it is."

"Instead of bowing before your self-knowledge, would it not be better to revolt and to rise to higher realms? Why do you give mankind up for lost? Change it. You have the scepter in your hand, your pencil!"

"But that is the great misfortune! The thinker has only the scepter and not the power. The powerful, on the other hand, cannot rise to a single thought. The synagogues are burning, Werner. Everything happening in this land will spread like the plague. What is going on here is past hope. It may well lead to war, but how hard is that way out! The painter with his brush, the poet with his pen, the orator on the podium, they have all pointed out the horrors of war, and Man has understood. He shudders at the thought of war. But then the violent criminal steps up. He stirs up the earth, he will always appear and destroy, because there will always be violent people. He who clings to the surface of the earth is doomed."

"You are right, I'm sure, but why you, for that reason, are bound to die first escapes me."

"Because this knowledge is gnawing me away."

"You are not doomed, Kain. Once we are on that island you will once more see people untouched by all contemptible urges, generous even towards their foes, courteous towards their friends, brave and quiet, even in the face of danger."

Was that cloud-cuckoo-land she meant? inquired Werner grimly.

She choked back her response and stood up from the table. In the window alcove, Hilde was deep in conversation. Her new protector was noting her details on his cuff, while she was already holding his gold watch in her hand, snapping it open and shut. Then Felberbaum assured her he would transform Pilz from a poisonous toadstool into a button mushroom. And when his eye caught Eva, he went even further, declaring he felt as if he were at court: he had just been standing with the princess, and now the queen was approaching.

Werner, however, was not in the least upset to find himself alone with his brother; he still had something else which he would prefer not to say to him before witnesses.

This was, to ask how he could go so far as to doubt others, since he had so much reason to begin with himself. Werner blushed to the roots of his hair as he said this. What he missed in his brother, he said, was character. And that was why everything in him was melting away, and the world with him. He himself possessed character, even if it was immodest to say so. What kind of state was he really in, his younger brother, who in every respect was the more favored, by nature, by their mother, the one preferred by the gods, the one whose very breath was incense. In what state was his character? If someone took something dry and harsh as his model to look up to, there was no need to worry. There was, however, cause for concern if someone felt himself possessed of *all* qualities, and even boasted about them! A moment or two ago, he had failed a test. After that honest girl (who, by the way, was leading an unsuitable life) told her story, then he, on whose behalf she had lost her father, ought to speak up in place of that father and demand his release. Because, strictly speaking, he was to blame for that man's arrest, even if not directly guilty of it.

Kain bubbled over with pleasure. To see his brother's renewed self-assurance, to see him personifying blind justice, did not simply mean for him that this brother had been saved, had been restored to his old self, it meant that he, Kain, had saved him. Because Werner was taking him down a peg. Because Kain was setting him alight, preventing him from growing cold, prodding him, kneading him and breathing new life into him.

To be sure, he replied lightly, he was the cause of this misfortune. Yes, perhaps he was not altogether innocent. But there was something odd going on here. And he could never bring about the release of the old gentleman, but instead would only create even more confusion and unhappiness.

That was not what it was all about, blind justice insisted. What really mattered was how one feels about oneself.

And at that, something happened to Kain. He himself could not have explained what compelled him to do it, but he suddenly leant over his much smaller brother and embraced him. As he did so, he became increasingly brighter. He was most certainly not going to put himself in the hands of the murderers, he said, nothing was further from his mind. But the fact that he, Werner, was there, now that was something. And if there was anything that was capable of breaking down Kain's contrariness, making him more relaxed, perhaps even restoring him to life, then it was just such an original character, whom he would not wish to be without. In the end, the tortoise is proved right, as they knew from the fable. The hare cavorts about and takes his time, but the tortoise reaches the goal.

"Dear Andreas," said Werner, very moved—much to his annoyance—and making an effort to conceal this. "If you cannot be dissuaded from rushing out into this hostile town, instead of sitting, safe and in peace, at home, as I do, then you can rest assured that *I* shall be the one putting the tortoise on *your* grave."

"But in that case, it will have to be made to a different design. One that you can open up, so that the hollow inside will form a censer, in which you can burn incense every time you come to visit me," cried Kain with a laugh. "Because that's my favorite aroma, isn't it?"

XIII. MISTAKEN IDENTITY

After Hilde had waited a long and anxious time and Herr Felberbaum had still not returned, she had to go home. Because, back home, her mother was becoming frantic, and her brother was going the rounds of his Aryan schoolmates to see if one might be willing to help him. And the domestic staff was upset and reluctant. This, however, was not directed against the master and mistress, far from it, everyone in the house was fond of the old man. The servants knew something their employers did not know, something the manservant had told them. He had been coming up the hill just as his master was being led away. He saw that the old man was bleeding from the mouth, went up to him (in itself a courageous thing to do), and wiped the blood off his face. He could see that his teeth were hanging like loose stalks in his mouth, he could see his distraught expression, but then he was pushed away and had to leave his master to his unhappy fate.

Eva, too, was getting ready to go out. She wanted to go looking for Kain, she was uneasy. He would be standing by the nearest synagogue, staring in wonder at the blaze, his head held high in the air.

She asked Werner what he wanted to do and, before going out into the street, she looked out from the front room to see what the weather was like, when she caught sight of two men in uniform standing outside the house. She had the urge to flee quickly out of the apartment, but, too late, they were already entering the building. She went and stood in the living room; opening the door was her responsibility, but she was overcome by weakness. She did not feel up to cross-examination now; she deemed it wiser not to let herself be seen, to ignore the ringing of the bell, to leave everything to Werner. He would deal with these people in short order, known as he was in the district as something of a crank, as someone who minded his own business and wouldn't hurt a fly—he was well liked.

Indeed, the bell did ring, and she rushed to the tiny balcony next to the kitchen. It was very narrow, really no more than a projection with a balustrade, but she was able to squeeze herself into a corner where she couldn't be seen through the door, which was made of glass.

The bell was already ringing for a third time, and only now did Werner, thinking she was no longer at home, finally stir himself to answer it. In the doorway to the outside passage stood the two brownshirts. She saw them come in.

She could hear them talking, but could make out no more than snatches of conversation. Much more clearly, she could hear Werner's offended tone of voice. It was all a mistake, he was saying, he was indeed Dr. Kain, but not the one they had in mind. The one they were thinking of was his brother.

Had he written books, he was asked.

Indeed he had, but not the kind they meant. He was a geologist and his books dealt exclusively with geological matters. His brother had written novels.

Whether he drew maps or wrote things hostile to the state did not matter a bit. The fact was, he had to leave the country—and right now. He had given his signature to that effect. And it was high time, past time.

No, declared Werner, raising his voice. He was not going to leave the country.

So he was admitting it, then! That was all they needed! He himself had put his finger on his mark of Cain! He was indeed the one they were looking for! The one who did not want to leave the country. He had signed, the deadline was up. What did he have to say to that?

This was infamous, it was monstrous, that's what he had to say to that. The nerve! A barefaced calumny! He had never signed any such thing! His brother, yes, he wanted to get away, but not he himself. This land belonged to him, who knew it, every stone of it.

"We'll soon give you a different area for your geography studies."

"I have nothing to do with geography! You ignoramus! But with rocks! Can't you understand that? With rocks!"

Oh, he'd have plenty to do with rocks, as much as he wanted. And now, if he would be so good as to get ready, and be quick about it. He was going with them.

Now she heard Werner shouting angrily and the two of them just as enraged interrupting him. They seemed to be rummaging around in his desk drawers and in his cupboard. Only when he protested that it was his brother it was all about could she once more clearly hear what he was saying.

"And where is this brother?"

Oh, if there is a God! Eva's lips moved in prayer. She herself did not know whom she was praying to. Perhaps she was praying to the tormented man out there.

Did they take him for a scoundrel, Werner was shouting, who would betray his own brother? He didn't know where he was, and even if he did know, he wouldn't tell them.

If only she had run out to him! Had thrown herself before him and thanked him, thanked him on her knees! How she regretted later not having thanked him on her knees!

Because Werner was taken away. He was taken away in place of his brother, to prison and then to the concentration camp.

Kain turned for home, exhausted by the day's horrors. He cursed his fiendish curiosity and inwardly praised his brother, who had this time proved to be the wiser one, by staying home. Because pillaging and robbery did not bring any sound knowledge. What was happening here screamed of revenge, and where else would this be granted to the great masses but on the battlefield of honor, sanctioned by the international courts?

For the first time, he was looking forward to that little room where his arrival was anticipated, looking forward to the cramped restrictions of that room, the very closeness of the conversations; all this distracted him from his febrile thoughts. He looked forward to Eva, too, whose strong personality outshone that fraught atmosphere, he was looking forward to the brightly-laid table and his wife's hospitable movements, he was looking forward to Werner, whom he was increasingly winning over to himself and to life. Even Felberbaum brought a smile from him, that kindhearted, ordinary man.

As he opened the door to the apartment, a letter fell to the floor. Hurriedly, he switched on the light and, filled with bright presentiment, tore the letter open. A hot flush rose over his face. He suppressed a shout, read the letter once more and, with a cheer, burst into the room.

The room was in darkness. The table was black, the cupboard yawned blackly in the gloom, the desk had been thrown open, the shutters tightly closed, letting no light in, only one candle was burning. With the result that, at first, he could not see Eva. When he did catch sight of her, he knew that Werner was missing. He did not imagine for a moment that he could have walked away by himself, that he would come back. He knew that Werner was gone, and for good. Nevertheless, he stammered out the question.

"They've taken him away, Kain."

"What reasons did they give?"

"All part of the general course of arrests. Because of murder."

"Were you here?"

"Yes, Kain."

"Where have they taken him?"

She shrugged.

"I've got to go to the police at once. He'll be in the town prison, they don't have any more room in the camps."

"You mustn't go, Kain."

"Am I supposed to leave my brother to die? What are you saying!"

"You mustn't go, Kain, you won't find him."

He grabbed her by the shoulder and shook her. "I hate you when you talk like that!"

She stared at him, mutely. Her face was no longer her own, so much grief was showing in it.

"You mustn't go away. They'll arrest you."

"I have to, Eva," and he stroked her hair compassionately.

"Werner has been arrested . . . he's sure to be taken to Dachau. Don't torture me this way!"

"And you're telling me that only now!"

"He's been arrested instead of you, Kain."

He let out a groan and turned white as a sheet. Then his eyes closed and he slumped over the table. The candle fell over and went out. She groped her way to the switch and, in doing so, bumped into his body. The light flared up harshly. It's like a magnet, that light, she thought, a magnet to those thieves, who will come straight back to see what is still here that can be taken away. And there's nothing left to take.

She tried to lift him and drag him towards the bed, but she didn't have the strength. She bedded him down where he lay, and listened to his breathing. She called his name.

From his cold hand fell a letter with the imprint of the British consulate. She did not have to read it to know that it was the visa at last.

XIV. NOVEMBER

As Herr Felberbaum, immersed in his conciliatory thoughts, was heading out of the city towards the suburbs, he could see shop shutters being hastily rolled down, in broad daylight. People were running into the entrances of buildings, exactly like during the war, and, without pausing to think very long, he hurried to the streetcar and waited in the tumult, waiting his turn among the knot of people.

He stood there, pushing forwards with the others, when he felt himself grabbed from behind, just like back in Cairo, he thought. His arms were bent back, then twisted out from his sides until he moved forward and was standing by a cart, a cattle truck, really, and he was hoisted up on to it before he could think what was going on. Once he was standing up there, he was amazed at himself at first, at how he had clambered up there, on to this truck, no mean feat at his age, and then he found himself being pressed in on all sides by people who had landed up there just like himself.

However, he did not remain silent like the others, but yelled down from the truck at a company of uniformed men. They were standing by the truck, looking imperious, and he shouted, not directly at any particular one—because he did not know which one was responsible and which one he should tackle—that he had already been arrested, already been locked up, thoroughly interrogated and set free again, with a good testimonial and a clean reputation. He expected this to be taken into account, his departure was imminent, and his visa, which his wife was obtaining for him in England.

But all this had not the slightest effect on the faces in front of him down on the street; instead, he heard shouts of "Murderers!" and, although this did not apply directly to him, but to the whole cattle truck full of men of every age and rank, the sweat of fear beaded his forehead and he developed shadows under his eyes, black shadows, his childish, at times stupid smile seemed now, as always, about to melt into tears, so that it was tempting to imagine that he would immediately burst out crying like a schoolboy. Helpless, with his arms pinned to his sides, crammed in tightly, he was standing next to a man, tall and blond and in all other respects outstanding, who was winking at him. This seemed to calm Felberbaum down, so much so that he raised trusting eyes and, to his great joy, recognized the second precentor from the temple, who had been herded in and loaded on to the cattle truck with all the others. Felberbaum was so relieved that he now recovered his full composure at the sight of the second precentor, who, after all, was now a prisoner, just like him, as helpless as himself, who could do nothing more than wink at him. Prudence dictated that he say not a word, because further back in the truck a man was being savagely beaten for looking up towards a window. At the window stood the prisoner's wife, leaning far out, as if she wanted to go with him; he shouted, "Be careful," for which he was beaten almost to death. How stupid of the man to use such words, which could be misunderstood in such coarse times. Naturally, a criminal must take care, but someone who has been grabbed in the street and wants only to prevent his wife from falling out of the window—what should he be careful about and what had he to hide?

There was no time to bother about the poor man who had been beaten, because towards the front of the truck someone collapsed. But this was not because of the heat and the excitement. As Felberbaum could now see, blood was flowing down the man's chest, trickling down in big fat drops, his shirt had been torn open, his hair matted with sweat; he did not seem to notice this, but was trying to stand upright. However, he slumped down, not to the floor, because there wasn't enough space for that, but reeled backwards and fell on the men behind him. They propped him up as best they could, he begged for water; strangely, no one wiped the blood away. The men lifted him down from the truck and laid him on the street, where he was left lying. His lips were closed, only his eyes were open, flickering back and forth, he pleaded for water, unable to understand why he was not being ministered to.

Those in the cattle truck pursed their lips too. But behind those lips, they seemed to be murmuring. Whether prayers or vows of hatred was impossible to tell.

Felberbaum cast a sidelong glance at the man dying of thirst and then at the people gathered on the street corner. They were wearing swastikas and looking timidly and anxiously towards the dying man; none of them dared to approach him, not one.

All at once, there was a jolt and the cattle truck moved off. It picked up speed, and those at the edges of the vehicle clung to the ones in the middle. It headed in the direction of a district familiar to Felberbaum. Inquiringly, he pursed his lips, looked his friend in the eye and put his ear close.

It was all because of the murder in Paris, the man whispered to him.

"God Almighty!" said Felberbaum, once again moved to a state of fear and agitation. But he had neither space nor time for his feelings, because they had arrived at their destination. They had to get down, no easy matter for a man over sixty, but he jumped down without hurting himself and went in along with the others. From the huge building they were met by a pleasant, moist coolness and, at the same time, a smell that, in the countryside, emanating from cows, is described as healthy. This smell came from horses; at that moment there were no horses in the ring, only their odor lingered. Men were lying all over the floor, similarly brought here by cattle truck and deposited like cattle on sand which was not too cold and not too damp.

Felberbaum also had his coat with him, which he spread out and shared with his friend, whom he had not let out of his sight.

He lay down, for he was tired, on the floor next to the others and his friend, and when he looked round the enormous horde of people, more than he had ever seen at any single moment, he calmed down, telling himself, quite logically, that it would be far too complicated a business to execute thousands of people at one time.

Just as he was calming down, the big well-built man beside him started to groan. Anxiously, Felberbaum inquired whether he had been injured. That wasn't it, and God's servant was at first unwilling to speak out, but then he did admit, by only a hint, that he was suffering from a natural need which, under normal circumstances, would not cause him to groan. At that, Felberbaum asked him why he didn't simply go where even the emperor goes on foot. Without a word, the precentor from the temple nodded towards a long line, to hundreds of men standing waiting impatiently and with pained expressions for the one little room in the whole arena to become vacant and offer them relief.

Felberbaum became very serious. He was not just sorry for his neighbor, but reminded himself that he, too, would soon be in the same predicament, and he started looking for a solution to the problem. And he found one. He hit upon the idea of standing in line, just in case the need arose. Even before he took up his place, he, too, was feeling the urge, and sensed that, in a few hours' time, he would be glad he had done so. And that was how it turned out. In fact, he stuck so strictly to his plan that no one saw him anywhere except standing in line for the small room in question.

Late in the evening, he lay down on the sand next to his friend, with half a coat for protection. Usually, before going to sleep, he was in the habit of placing a small Star of David, which his mother had given him, under his pillow, and set about doing just that, because that star had afforded him protection for so many years. He was about to take it out of his purse, when he remembered that he didn't have a pillow at the moment. So, he pushed it, along with his purse, under his head, where it dug itself into the soft sand.

He was extremely tired. Despite such a hard bed for an old man, he fell asleep at once, breathing deep and peacefully. Suddenly, he was dreaming that he was being massaged. It was the attendant from the Diana Baths, who was usually very good at finding the right spot, but this time he was massaging him so fiercely, buffeting and jabbing him so hard, that his eyes snapped open, even though it had been so blissful to keep them shut. The thumps still did not subside, even as he rubbed his eyes in the darkness, telling himself that it was all a dream. No, it wasn't a dream. Somebody really was tugging at his watch-chain, then snatched the watch from him, snatched his wallet, too, hissing at him to keep his mouth shut, and made off.

Felberbaum fumbled for his purse and the star; they were still lying buried in the sand. He ran his hands over his body, rubbed his eyes again and, still half asleep, hoped that it had indeed all been a nightmare. He searched for his watch, the one that told the date as well, a memento of his father, but, finding neither watch nor wallet, lay back sadly.

"Even my own brothers are stealing from me," he thought, and that thought depressed him even more than the loss of his watch.

But, that night, a few thousand men lying there were thinking that same thought, only to find out differently and to keep their mouths shut in the morning about their missing ready cash, the loss of which hit Felberbaum especially hard, because he carried all his money about his person; it was supposed to cover both the cost of his trip to London and the waiting time here in this country until the visa arrived.

The next day, he was brought before the tribunal. It consisted of women, because the men in the new Reich had more lucrative work to do.

The young woman who finally interrogated him looked rather youthful for the kind of questions she was asking him. In fact, they were so embarrassingly detailed that he was unable to understand quite a few of them properly and he became flustered and stammered, and then preferred not to say anything, for fear of incriminating himself out of ignorance.

With a quite definite and clear "No," he answered the question as to whether he had ever had any close relationships with Aryan women. He could also assert in all honesty that his wife was no Aryan, even bore the given name of Sarah, that she had never had an affair with an Aryan man, he could swear to that because she had been a virgin when he married her, of good family, respectable and faithful right to the end. What this Portia then asked him about his wife was so far beyond his comprehension that he confused the word she used with a different one, one which he had been hearing used very freely in the arena, in fact one to do with the little room he had stood in line outside, and he very nearly answered with a yes. He remembered just in the nick of time, however, and remained silent. Portia came to his aid, asking why he had no children. That he could understand, and he was saddened, because they had always wanted children.

He then told his story of how he had already been locked up once, securely locked away, quite definitely imprisoned, and subsequently set free again. When he gave his age, and repeated it, he was given the prospect of release. He now had to sign an assurance that he would not say a word about the proceedings and the conversations in the circus, and that under penalty of death. He signed in large, clear letters and hurried back to his spot with his old smile on his face, but with deep shadows under his eyes.

His companion in the faith, the precentor from the temple, was no longer lying next to him, but had settled near the smallest room, where the others had readily made way for him, an honor that was his just due, since the man was suffering from severe colic attacks because of all the upsets and was not able even to stand in line.

But, the next day, Felberbaum was set free.

When he stepped out into the open, the fresh air took hold of him, the light hurt his eyes, the firm ground was too hard after the damp sand carpet in the arena, he staggered and would have liked to sit down on one of the benches which stood vacant in long rows along the avenue. But he did not dare do this— there was a notice strictly forbidding it—and so he searched in his rescued purse to see whether there was a little money still in it. And, sure enough, he collected a few marks together, much to his delight. He stumbled into the nearest automat, where vending machines served you, where no human face scrutinized you inhumanly as to where you were from and which tribe you belonged to; there he sat down at a little table, took a deep breath, drank a large glass of coffee, then a second one. It tasted delicious after the period of starvation in the circus, in point of fact a real circus. After the second coffee, he considered his situation; it was rosy, despite the fact that he was now destitute. He still had his wife abroad, a good woman, she was working, she was already earning money, pounds at that, and his friends here wouldn't leave him in the lurch since he could pay them back over there in pounds sterling. But how his fellow lodgers would gape in amazement at his tales. And the lady! Yes, it had to be admitted, Herr Felberbaum had forgotten his oath. The oath he had sworn to keep quiet about everything, the events in the arena, Portia's questions, the conversations with his fellow believers; he had forgotten that oath, forgot the risk he would be running if he were to tell them, trustingly forgot about his fellow men's thoughtlessness, merely thinking, with a grin and a great deal of contentment, of how he himself had now become something of a personality in that circle, overnight, an interesting figure in possession of priceless secrets.

When he came out again, the air gave him strength, the light brightened him up, the ground gave him stability, and he decided to stroll home on foot—after the cramped confinement in the arena, it was just too beautiful out here in the world, and the farther he went, the more contented he felt. He was increasingly moved by his situation, ever more grateful to his Creator, who had chosen him like Lot and repeatedly set him free. He suddenly felt the urge to enter a House of God and say his prayers, to sit for a while among his own kind and talk things over with them a little.

But then, of course, the temples had been destroyed. He knew that. But not all of them, he thought with a smile. The little synagogue he had attended since his childhood lay hidden away in an exclusive residential area, among gardens, nestled up to a villa; that temple had been forgotten, as the precentor had confided to him.

Although it lay well out of his way, Felberbaum nevertheless stepped, happily humming to himself, on to a streetcar. The journey was marvelous. The weather mild, the avenue thronged and colorful, the time passed too quickly and there he was, close to the house of worship. Whistling a little tune, he got off and stepped into the side street. Then he felt himself gripped by the arm in a way familiar to him, and not just from Cairo. The tune died on his puckered lips.

"You're coming with me!"

Herr Felberbaum started struggling with all his might. He began to denounce himself, to unmask himself, saying he had a previous conviction, several previous convictions, calling himself a newly released prisoner, but the man in brown remained unmoved.

This had nothing to do with arresting him, he said, there were clean-up operations to be carried out; the rubble of a temple had to be cleared away, just close by.

Felberbaum forgot to feel offended that even his little synagogue, too, had had to meet its fate, he was so worried by this latest blow. He was a victim of persecution, a curse was weighing upon him, where was it all leading?

For a start, it led to his House of God. So why did this little temple have to be destroyed, such a little temple, he asked his guard without rhyme or reason, having no right to his irritation.

He learned that he and his fellow believers had been holding gatherings there, political meetings of a nature inimical to the state, and he shut his mouth.

All that was left of the temple was one wall facing the street, rising soot-blackened towards the heavens like a huge corpse. A man in a black uniform, watched in silent awe by a crowd of people, was painting enormous white letters on this cadaver.

Felberbaum was pushed into the garden, which now, of course, no longer bore any resemblance to a front garden, to the entrance to a place of worship, because all around lay rubble and bricks blackened by smoke, tattered Torah scrolls, mangled candelabra, smashed balustrades, their gilt shining through the soot, prayer books in ashes, red velvet cloths, singed and perforated, and yet all this might have reminded the casual observer not of a devastated temple but rather of a glimpse backstage in a theater.

Among the shovelers who had to load the debris of their temple on to a truck was a small man who loved conversation. He had been working there since morning, but was not complaining, because it was better that *his* hands were grasping the consecrated stones than those of strangers.

With a large number of others as well, he had been ordered to destroy the temple with pickaxes and hammers. They tried their best, convinced that the stones would detach themselves and strike them dead as a punishment. But the stones held firm. (This reminded Felberbaum, although even he could not trace the connection, of the Sphinx in Cairo.) At this, they were suspected of being obstructive, and their tormentors themselves took hold of the pickaxes. The stones refused to budge.

And then it happened. To the accompaniment of shouts of encouragement from the spectators, an explosive material was taken into the house of worship and there, in front of the altar, the temple was set on fire.

In happy excitement, the onlookers ran into doorways. The Jews stood babbling to one side. One of them, wringing his bony hands, murmured a psalm.

As the little man related this, he went on busily shoveling rubble together, and, with the aid of the others, the truck was soon full. The involuntary desecrators went home exhausted, while fresh bodies were sent for.

Felberbaum was not dismissed yet. He went and stood at the edge of the road to wait for the next truck. Dusk was approaching. The huge letters on the blackened stone took on a ghostly gleam. He looked at them with a feeling of foreboding, but strove to calm his anxious heart. It was still all right, he belonged to the oppressed. And he was innocent, completely innocent!

This thought filled him with a warm glow. Once again, he was reconciled, reconciled to his fate, reconciled with mankind, reconciled even to the black vision before him. He looked up at the gloomy stump pointing heavenwards.

Then, all of a sudden, the temple fell apart. The dark wall broke loose like a landslide, dust rolled down, enveloped him, the temple knocked him to the ground, where he lay on his back, covered in dust, under the ruins of the House of God and on top of soot and ashes, his face moist and still cheerful.

A streak of blood trickled from his forehead into his sparse gray hair.

Next to the dark pile of rubble which had once been a temple stood a small Swiss vehicle. It was standing there, dainty yet self-assured, something that didn't quite belong there and had no desire to belong there. Just as a tiny firefly swoops in wonderment over a marshy area and settles briefly. It lands, yet refuses to beautify the place. It doesn't belong there.

At the wheel sat a lady, while her partner occupied the seat next to her. Both of them, half turned round, were looking over at the ruined temple and at the goings-on as if at something totally alien, something they found incomprehensible. They looked away again, seemed to be making ready to move off, and the whole calmness in the fine vehicle had something frosty about it.

The old man, struck by the stones, lay prone on the black patch of ground, the blood trickling down over his brow, and when no one made a move towards him to help him up, the lady quickly threw open the door of her little vehicle and got out. The gentleman followed her.

The lady scrambled over charred timber, damp earth, blackened fragments and lumps of wall. She was careful, in her fine shoes, not to sink in or to trip and fall. The gentleman followed in her footsteps.

The lady approached the man on the ground, who was lying in the ruins and looking up at her, with astonishment in his kind eyes. His mouth was undecided; should it smile at the lady, the proper thing, or should it give free rein to his terror? She bent over him and laid her delicate handkerchief across his forehead.

Then she turned round. The people were standing ten paces away, reading with admiration the white writing on the wall. The man in the black uniform had finished. He climbed down the ladder, stepped back and viewed his handiwork. Then he glanced sidelong over at the man on the ground and the couple by him, and his features darkened. The lady heard him giving the order to one of his men to fetch an ambulance.

The onlookers were still following his every move with fascination. The old man on the ground did not move their hearts at all. To them, it was embarrassing that these strangers should make such a fuss of him, spoiling their fun. They were watching in wonder the young, energetic features of the SS-man who was in command here.

The lady, too, looked at the young man in astonishment. His

bearing was aristocratic and his face refined. Only when he spoke did an unbridled force cut savage overbearing lines in it. His dark eyes flashed sinisterly. She looked at the crowd, looked at their leader, and read the inscription on the wall of the temple.

THE TERRIBLE CONSEQUENCES EARTHQUAKE 1938

Blushing, she looked at the old man at the roadside, then, followed by her companion, climbed into the little Swiss car and hastily drove away.

XV. THE HOSPITAL OF THE SORROWS

Whenever someone seriously ill is put into an ambulance and taken to the hospital; whenever, lying on the stretcher, he lands in a large ward, in which one bed is free; whenever he sinks, relieved and somewhat comforted, into the pillows, something strange comes over him: all at once, he loses all the fears a hospital can arouse. He does not shrink back in the face of the long row of invalids, they are as helpless as he is. He is not suffocated by the air of sickness; what he can smell is the medicines which are going to heal him. He has no fear of the doctor's white coat, or of the nurse's harsh severity, for both of them, doctor and nurse, are going to help him to overcome his illness.

It is a very different matter for the visitor who sits down by the patient's bedside. He is startled by the white ward with its pale invalids. The neighbors, right and left, cough germs at him and spread them around the ward. The doctor is monosyllabic and keeps his gloomy diagnosis to himself. The nurse is dilatory and slipshod. It is terrible in this room, and the visitor waits for the hour to pass, keeps one eye fixed on the big clock and inwardly applauds the strict application of the rule limiting the time. At last, the bell shrills, and, with a sense of relief, he steps out into the fresh air.

In the hospital founded by Baron Rothschild, the regime was just the opposite. Those lying in bed looked bright and cheerful, well cared for and in a very good state. The visitors, however, sitting on the chairs, they were the ones who were dying. There they sit, thin, and as white as the walls. They sit as if they have become one with their chairs, as if they never want to part with them. When the rules bring the end of visiting hour, they look up at the hands of the big clock with a shudder of apprehension, seeing them moving on, much too fast and relentlessly. Because this period of time spent sitting here is the only time in their lives when they are safe from abuse, arrest and violent death.

Halfway down the ward lay Herr Felberbaum, his head bandaged, staring into space. Once again, everything had turned out wonderfully for him, fate again had treated him with favor. He had been injured, that was true, had a gash on his head, but the gash was healing, he could feel the itching of the scar already, something he was familiar with from wartime. He was feeling marvelous. Every morning, the senior consultant came round, accompanied by his staff, examined him, sounded his heart, his lungs, and shared his pleasure, because his heart, albeit a little too large, nevertheless was beating so strongly and his lungs were breathing easily and evenly. The most charming people, these doctors, even if at times not in the mood for conversation, and rather gruff, but that was as it should be, a doctor has responsibilities, wants only the best and does his best.

The nurse, too, commanded respect, and it did him good to watch her unhurried movements. It seemed advisable not to talk too much in her presence, since she was an Aryan and no doubt supported the enemy. So much more admirable, then, that she was devoting her services to the alien race. She was punctual and clean, only now and then did she lose patience, but was that any wonder, with eighteen patients to deal with? For all that, things were going along excellently, most patients were recovering and only a few died. You got your meals, breakfast, lunch and an evening meal, and for Felberbaum she poured the soup into a dish with a spout, so that he would not have to raise his head to drink. He was really getting along marvelously here. And considering how peacefully, without worrying about his daily bread, he could wait for his visa, which the religious community was going to pay for on his behalf, no one could close their eyes to the fact that he was one of the chosen, just like Lot.

Yes indeed, when he thought back over events, there was only one thing which still embarrassed and confused him: his promise to that dear girl, Hilde, to free her father. Here in the calm peace of the hospital, it weighed on his mind that he had, during his period of custody in the arena, been too much concerned with his own predicament. It bothered him a great deal. He went so far as to send his mother-in-law to the Pilzes as a mediator, since she had known them in better times. Well, she brought relieving news. Herr Pilz was away on a rabbit hunt at the moment and could not be reached. Which at least meant that Felberbaum no longer had to keep reproaching himself.

All the same, not everyone had escaped the battlefield so luckily. His mother-in-law could tell a few tales about that (she brought him letters from his wife, who had been spared the news of his mishap with his head). Once he was feeling better, the old woman confessed to him the news of the catastrophe: the arrest of his cranky landlord, who so loved stones, such a nice man otherwise, if a little neurotic, but then, everyone was these days. When he heard of the turmoil in the household, of the gap which the man's disappearance had left behind, he was so agitated that he almost lifted his head, but his mother-in-law prevented that in the nick of time, since it had been strictly forbidden—the nurse keeping a sharp eye on that, reminding him umpteen times a day not to forget himself.

One morning, however, to his amazement, the same nurse unceremoniously ordered him out of bed. He was made to lie down on the stone floor, on top of an extremely unhygienic gray blanket which had been hastily thrown down for him—and all the patients were ordered to do the same. All this without any consideration for those running a temperature and the pneumonia they could easily catch if suddenly snatched from their warm beds and deposited on the cold floor. Nor was any consideration given to amputated legs, legs in plaster casts, legs in traction, nor to the terminally weak or those in the throes of dying; all of them had to leave their beds and lie down on the floor. Those who were dying did not have to get up by themselves but were given some assistance.

In stormed some men with a cross on their sleeves, but not the Red Cross. Suddenly the room thronged with brown uniforms, moving amongst the sickbeds and the invalids on the floor; there were so many you couldn't count them. They pounced on the beds to ransack them, and as they did so they tripped over the patients lying beside them, but they didn't take this out on the invalids. They tore open mattresses, slashed pillows, the feathers swirled up; they couldn't reach as far as the heads of the beds, so they climbed over the sick people on the floor as if over corpses. They missed not one single bed, or pillow or blanket; they were looking for gold and money, and sent for the intern. Unfortunately he was black-haired and small of stature, and so he had to empty out the instrument cabinet. When they failed to discover diamonds in the syringe, they sounded out the paneling around the windows and knocked the top off the water pipe. And since they could find nothing worth taking away, nothing whatsoever, they arrested the intern and took him off.

The sister was extremely annoyed. Because they left her with the considerable nuisance of having to tidy up the beds again, since the patients couldn't do that by themselves, not the seriously ill ones. Those with no more than a slight temperature had already gotten to their feet and re-made their beds, and were now lying on top of wrinkled and twisted sheets, groaning and shivering with cold, their feeble hands tugging the blankets up over their infirm bodies, their faces now wan and minus that peaceful expression which had been their hallmark only half an hour previously.

Herr Felberbaum, too, had sorted out his bed and had laid

himself down again. But suddenly he no longer liked it here. Suddenly the room seemed strange and inimical, the walls were dreary and his head hurt just as it had on the first day after his accident; he felt leaden and everything seemed sad and hopeless. On top of all that, he could hear a patient talking in a monotonous voice, one who, because he was hard of hearing, always talked very loudly so as to be heard properly. He was dictating his will to the man in the next bed, something of no concern to Felberbaum, who was now most irritated and no longer interested in anything. But snatches reached his ears, whether he wanted to hear or not, and he gathered from the dictation that this will had all to do with the old man's suit, his nickel watch, his winter coat, his fountain pen; finally, he was giving instructions regarding his body, saying that his corpse was to be taken to the College of Anatomy. Then he instructed his neighbor to make a point of demanding that his son's emigration to China should be paid for. And although the neighbor knew perfectly well that no one was going to pay for a ticket to China in exchange for a subject for an autopsy, far less for the corpse of an old Jew, he promised him everything he wanted.

That day, it seemed as if they were all conspiring to throw the feelings in Felberbaum's great heart into turmoil and to keep on stirring them up. In fact, as he was sipping through the spout of his dish the yellowish soup—which, today, was not at all to his taste—he was barked at by the nurse not to raise his head: the same nurse who, that morning, had made him lie down on the floor. Just as he was putting the dish down and pushing away the dessert, a woman dressed in black entered the ward and made straight for him. He had no idea why he became so apprehensive, but he felt such a surge of trepidation at the sight of her, as if she would deliver a message to him, a secret to terrify him. Only when her eyes met his did he recognize her, and he stammered out an apology. But she nodded, as if to tell him she knew all about him, pulled the chair towards his bed, sat down and said not a word.

She remained silent, looking around the ward. And as she looked about, there was something of her former grace, when they had all lived together (had it really been so long ago?) and she had filled the house with her warmth and her perfume. He did not know how to begin, but a man had to be firm and not let things get him down, and so he started to speak. He thanked her for coming, in such difficult times and to such an awful hospital—and this despite the fact that she had been afflicted by such grievous misfortune.

She was not listening to him. She was gazing out into the room, looking at no one in particular, in fact she did not even seem to be taking in the patients but simply staring into space. After some considerable time, she remembered him, bent over and asked how the injury to his head was coming on.

Perhaps it was because she had rejected any direct personal address, or perhaps a sick man's insecurity, perhaps the relapse he had suffered that morning on having to leap out of bed—in any case, he started to complain, something quite contrary to his nature. He complained about the nursing treatment, about the food, about the events of the morning, about the man in the next bed, and about the doctor.

And then they both fell silent, because she could think of nothing to say in response.

He stole a furtive glance at her. What wonderful times those were, in the same house with this woman and her distinguished husband and the weird brother—the perfect example of a highly respectable man. Waiting for his visa had been easy for him there, but that was now all in the past, and his landlord was now languishing in brutal exile, and this woman beside him was no more than a mere shadow of herself.

"Does he write regularly?" he asked out of politeness, because he was aware that only one postcard was allowed every two weeks, and the text for that was prescribed.

"He is dead," said Eva. And as she spoke these words, she

herself was so shocked by them that the nurse, who was busying herself clearing the dishes away from his little table, became alarmed and held smelling salts under her nose.

"He has died," she repeated. And then she fell silent again and once more stared into space, a lump visible in her throat.

"He died quite alone." Then she remained silent for some time; her emotions seemed exhausted.

In Buchenwald, they had regarded him as an agitator. Right on the very first day, he was assigned to a quarry where he had to haul rocks. If it had only been a matter of hauling rocks! But no, the guards had to have their cruel pleasures and, if it came into some thug's head, the rocks had to be carried at the double, at a run or to whatever beat he fancied. The food was bad and their strength waned rapidly. One day, Werner, exhausted by a heavy rock, fell down and lay there in a faint, with the rock by his side.

However, the masters' method of reviving unconscious men was to pour cold water over them, even in winter. That never failed to bring them round.

Werner, also, came to, but with pneumonia, and from that he never came round again.

The forlorn tone in which she related this, as if it was of no concern to her, was so moving that Felberbaum was unable to control himself and began to weep. She looked down at him the way that an animal watches the movements of a human being it cannot comprehend.

And then she looked towards the door and, without a word, stood up and went over to it. In the doorway stood a lady, who came hesitantly closer. She was wearing a dark blue suit and a blue hat, from under which her fair hair seemed to tumble in confusion, she was tall and shapely, she was very young, and even though she remained grave, her youth had something cheering about it. Eva led her to the chair, the only one available at each bed for visitors, and then stepped out on to the glassed-in veranda to take a breath of fresh air, leaving the patient alone with his new visitor.

And so Felberbaum had this sweet girl sitting by his bed; here they were, coming to visit him, first the lady, then the girl, and if it hadn't been for the fact that things were so bad for them, he would have been extremely delighted at such an honor. What an austerely beautiful girl! There was nothing doll-like about her, far less anything appropriate to the movies, her nose was tilted, her mouth full, and yet she radiated a bright light, like an angel. She asked after his health, as if it were a matter of world-shaking importance, how things were for him, she read off the chart at the head of his bed and seemed to understand it, because she said the diagnosis was brilliant and he would soon be fit again and running around happily. Whereupon he told her that he had already done his share of leaping about that day, but not of his own volition; in short, he embarked on the story of the morning's events, but not, this time, in order to complain, but firmly intending to bring out the funny side of it and make the girl laugh.

But something had changed in Felberbaum, in this man who always looked so kindly on the world. Something really had changed: as he started on his story and on making it all sound comical, his sense of humor deserted him, his speech became disjointed, coming in scraps, he himself was horrified at what he was saying, it sounded like one long complaint, so that he broke off and fell completely silent. His nerves wanted nothing to do with him, he said. We have to endure too much. So, how was that outstanding genius of a man taking it, the business with his brother?

How he was taking it was not altogether the right question, said Hilde. He was not bearing up at all. He did not even bear up to the news, back then, of the arrest. His temperature shot up; both brothers reacted to any great excitement in the same way, with a high fever and neuritis. He raved for quite some time, which was no bad thing, because only the fever and confusion of such a condition prevented him from going to the police to give himself up. Those were his words, "to give himself up," he was already talking of himself like a criminal, he could no longer see himself as anything else. When he was able to get up, he dragged himself away, still intent on "giving himself up" and setting his brother free. But he collapsed on the front steps and the janitor—an individual who at the start had strongly supported the regime, one of the most vociferous in its favor, but after a short time had broken with it and did not mince words about the corruption, the looting gone wild and the rationing of food—helped to carry him back into the house and urged him finally to leave this country and not to wait and suffer the same fate as his brother.

Even before he was strong enough to get on his feet again, the dreadful news arrived of Werner's death and cremation. Werner, who had died among rocks, in a quarry, killed by a rock.

The news of his death sent Kain's temperature soaring again and aroused a great sense of rebellion against life. And then followed—and this was the most awful thing in such a generous spirit—a state of apathy, which intensified to such an extent that they could only fear for his reason. He was still in this passive state, yet he nevertheless had enough strength of purpose when it came to searching back for memories of the departed, reading his notes, gathering together the little rock samples which he had left scattered about in drawers and pockets, and he was carrying his ashes around with him. Eva had managed him well enough so that he was no longer resisting the idea of making their departure, although she herself, of course, was practically at the end of her tether.

Felberbaum was tense as he listened to her, and the effort showed in his expression: what he was hearing at this moment went far beyond his powers of comprehension. He was incapable of visualizing these monstrous events; he could only imagine figures before him, now that cranky, warm-hearted researcher, now his brother, distraught, mourning over his death; in addition, for no real reason, he could see a doctor lending his support to the dying man, a doctor with a stern face and a white coat, making notes in swirls of Latin on the blackboard above the patient's head. That it would not be a sympathetic doctor standing by the dying man, if one were there at all, was something he could not conceive, and that was a good thing. Because the black shadows under his eyes had now spread right up to his eyebrows, and the girl's tale was undoubtedly not the most suitable story for an old man suffering from a head wound.

But Hilde's kindly mission had been to conceal so much, day in, day out, to show things in the best light, that now she was letting everything spill out.

"Just to imagine Werner," she said, "staring fixedly with his clear, blue eyes into the harsh light—until his eyes were like open wounds—it surpasses anything from the Inquisition." Staring wide-eyed at her, he was unable to understand a single word. "That's one of the usual punishments in the concentration camp. But you mustn't say anything to anyone else, in case the other two find out about it. There she stands, quite forlorn, she just can't go on."

Only the young have the gift of swinging from sorrow to joy—suddenly she laughed so happily that the patients in the surrounding beds raised their heads and were amazed that there could be so much merriment, so much shining beauty. Enviously, they took in the rosy cheeks, the burnished-gold hair, and Felberbaum couldn't help laughing, even though he didn't know why or what there could be to laugh about, but this radiant face before him was so captivating. Yes, something had happened to her which she wanted to confide in him, something uplifting to think about, and every time it comes to mind she is so terribly happy. Even though she had had to turn it down, on her parents' account, they needed her now; her place was now at her parents' side. She was so eager that she quite forgot to tell him what it was she had been asked and what she had turned down; he could not understand her, and asked some questions. She in turn was unable to understand his questions, indulging herself as she was in her memories. But then everything became clear and both of them laughed heartily, even if he was not altogether sure whether he had correctly grasped her meaning. The noble lady had asked her to come with her, with the two of them. But her father *was* in prison, and she couldn't leave, however happy that would have made her. She had to look out for her father's welfare, even if that only amounted to going the rounds of various offices; there was no more she could do.

At this, Felberbaum found himself in something of a quandary. The father was bound to be the sore point of this young girl's life, and his conscience was troubling him: he had done nothing, and had promised everything; he was lying here, pathetic and helpless, in this hospital gown, a dish with a spout on the bedside table and a urine bottle under the bed.

But she did not seem to hold this against him. She threw off her jacket, because she was too warm, the jacket which hung on her tall frame, inconsequential, completely dwarfed by her powerful build; she straightened the collar of her blouse and went on with her story: her father was sick, injured in the course of his arrest, and on top of that his gall-bladder ailment had been aggravated by the turmoil and the cold in the gymnasium, where he had had to sleep on the floor. It was best if he remained sick for a good long time; things had gotten to the point that they were wishing for that. At least he was now lying in a bed, in the prison hospital, among criminals—her father, that universally respected and thoroughly pampered man, yet the criminals in their beds were undoubtedly better than the agents of justice who had put him there.

She seemed to be getting even hotter; now she seemed about to slip off her blouse: she groaned and tugged again at her collar and was opening the neck of her blouse when she stopped, having noticed the nurse handing round thermometers. She insisted on him being given one too and having his temperature taken. She straightened his pillow, poured water into his glass and was so caring that, despite all the hardships, the world no longer seemed to him so gloomy a place, being, as it was, full of wonderful people among his fellow believers, and even the others were good, the Christians, because if they had all been bent on acting according to their Führer's speeches and the daily exhortations printed in the newspapers, then he would no longer be alive, nor this young girl here either. Yes, people are good, he now repeated out loud to Hilde, who fully agreed with him that the Führer's rabid machine-gun utterances could not corrupt devout souls.

The conversation subsided. The nurse came over to the bed, checked the thermometer, made a note of his temperature, changed the position of his pillow, tugged the blanket straight and scolded him because he had a religious pamphlet lying next to his pillow and he must surely have been holding his head too high while reading it. Then she moved on to the next bed.

Hilde had risen to her feet. Over on the other side, the door to the veranda opened and then closed again quietly, her friend approached the bed, having obviously fought a victorious struggle with herself, because she stepped close to the patient, seeming to have completely regained her composure. Bending over him, she apologized for the state she had been in.

"There is a certain kind of grief that never passes. Anyone burdened by it is at his wits' end. Too much is demanded of us," she said. And in saying so, she was including him in that grief— one more gesture by this highly respected lady to embrace him, lying there in bed, lazy and almost restored, within the circle of her own suffering. He felt thoroughly ashamed of himself.

And all at once, that simple man understood her. He realized that some guilt was weighing her down, that she was accusing herself.

"We're living here in a jungle," he said. "People are dragged away and murdered without any reason. In the end, we ourselves corrupt everything and we don't really know why."

"We have to go now," said Hilde. "Visiting hour is over and the nurse has already been looking this way. She just can't wait to get everything spick-and-span for the chief consultant to see. They work only for the senior doctor, these straitlaced creatures. The air is stuffy, things are poorly maintained, but they don't think about that sort of thing."

Eva took her leave with a firm handshake. He sat up in bed, despite that being forbidden, and as a result, the religious pamphlet lying next to his pillow fell to the floor.

"You'll see just what your husband, that brilliant man, is still capable of," he reassured her as he returned her handshake.

Her thoughts went to Kain and his careworn, so world-weary face, and she gave a quiet sob. In an effort to hide her face, she held up the pamphlet. It had fallen open, and her eye fell on a passage that had been marked with a small cross:

"*A beggar sits by the wayside, waiting. He is the Messiah. A stranger passes by and asks: For whom art thou waiting? The beggar replies: For thee.*"

XVI. HOW WERNER TRAVELED

In the station concourse stood three knots of people. The first group was made up of the quietly fearful. These were the particular friends in this city who had been classified by the new order as Aryans. They had come in order to demonstrate their respect for a very well-loved and honored man. Tiny farewell notes were smuggled into his compartment, concealed in bunches of flowers; it was farewell for a long time, of that they were aware. Noticeable about them was a hint of resignation, a hopelessness to which even pain is preferable. Because pain wears off.

To the second group belonged those in the city branded non-Aryan. They were behaving as if they had nothing to fear, for they had already lost everything. In their wan faces a shimmer of hope could be detected, and a quiet pleasure, because a man of repute was heading for freedom and would draw them with him. They made a point of keeping their eyes discreetly away from the first group, friends with whom, less than a year before, they would have been sitting in one room enjoying lively conversation together.

The third and last gathering was small. Yet they seemed closest to those departing. The man was wearing a cap on his head, the way a cardinal covers his tonsure. The whole time, he was laughing, openly and sincerely, so happy was he that this friend of his was leaving, that this universally respected man and his lady wife were going away to a country with a better outlook and better customs. The young girl next to him was beaming. Was she putting on this smile in order to conceal her dread of parting with them? It was impossible to tell. She urged her friends into their compartment much too soon, even though there was still plenty of time, and the couple were constantly being surrounded and embraced by the first and second groups.

Those marked by resignation were the first to take their leave, with many sincere words, and yet almost a trace of envy in their eyes. Slowly, they made for the exit.

The second group made emotional farewells, each of them burning with the desire to escape from a land in which murder earned the murderer a higher rank. They dispersed in pairs; an official demanded this, he would not tolerate any kind of assembly. With jangling nerves and heightened emotions, they slunk back into the hostile city.

The travelers were by this time standing at the corridor window outside their compartment, but Hilde had disappeared. She had crept away to avoid a despairing outburst; she had left quietly and left a gap where she had been standing. By the car stood only Felberbaum, who, when the bell rang the first time, unashamedly pulled out an enormous handkerchief and started sobbing in a quite heartrending manner. He apologized, saying that he was weeping for joy, mixed with sorrow, he was sixty after all, had been through a fair amount, was now watching his dear friends leave, watching a whole people disappear, would have to emigrate himself, at sixty, and try to seek a new life.

The bell sounded one final time.

He hurriedly dried his tears, shook the revered gentleman by the hand and pressed a small package into the lady's palm. It was a tiny star on a slim chain, which had accompanied him everywhere for many years and which she was to carry safely across the border.

A second handkerchief now appeared, no doubt having been pocketed with forethought. And that was just as well, because the first one was dripping with his tears and it would have been impossible to wave such wet material, to wave it vigorously until the train had moved round the curve.

Thank heaven, Herr Felberbaum, too, was soon to leave for

the country in which the same laws applied to everyone. Once more with a broad smile on his face, he stepped out of the station into the open air.

Dry-eyed, Eva gazed at the tiny star and, rather at a loss, hung it round her neck. The train lurched forward. And now she felt the way someone does who thinks he is standing on the pier, but the pier starts moving, it is no pier, it is a ship. This is astonishing, yet has she not yearned for this over many days, weeks, months, and yearned for it every hour? Are her senses dead then, that nothing comes to her mind other than a quiet amazement because the ground is moving as she leans against the window and watches the tracks, the tracks . . .

Kain drew himself into his window seat, as if trying to hide.

When the survivor mourns for his beloved departed, the loss is not the whole pain: his memory plays a cruel game with him. He sees the dead man only in the precious moments of their life together, he sees only the tender, beautiful occasions, he sees the joys, he sees the loved one's capabilities and strengths alone, sees his own inadequacies compared to the other, his failings, he sees himself in the wrong and the other transfigured. He sees him transfigured in his dreams, and sees dreams when he is awake. He sees the powerful life he has lost because his friend is dead.

And it can turn out even worse. It can happen that you are living on borrowed time. In the place of the other, completely innocent one, and that other is now dead. And it can be your own brother whose life you are borrowing. And you cannot forget this, you repeat it to yourself every hour, and every hour repeats it.

And you fear these hours, you are in fear of this life. You seek salvation on earth, but the earth breaks poisonously open, morbid vapors pollute it. Now it is the murderer who preaches in place of the redeemer. He transforms suffering into hatred, faith into vindictiveness, goodness is poisoned, poisoned by the morbid vapors.

You look to heaven. But in the ether, machines are flying in flames and plunging to the burning earth.

Perhaps life's little setbacks serve the purpose of keeping the mourner awake, like stabs and blows they prevent him from sinking into eternal sleep. It was perhaps for the best that other travelers came on board. Three of them, making free use of their elbows when they want to get through.

It was a woman with two men. She took possession of the seat in the corner by the window, opposite Kain. She was broadly built with heavy features, like so many of the women from the suburbs here. And her manner was loud; she was someone whom no hardship can ever subdue. She was wearing jewelry, most noticeably a diamond ring because, dangling loose and quite out of place, it had not been made for her finger. What had been made with her in mind was the floral-patterned calico dress which stretched tightly across her bosom, vulgarly highlighting her bulging contours.

She was obviously enjoying herself and her manner was offensive. In a quite mindless way, she laughed at anything and everything which, by comparison, showed her to advantage. She considered delicate limbs ridiculous, not to mention black hair, and the fact that the woman passenger opposite took up a book only provoked another salvo.

One of the men, the one next to her, was feeling in excellent form. In the course of her remarks, he kept running his hand over her shoulders and her arms. He was in favor with her, and she let him carry on.

The second companion was embarrassing. He could not settle down in the cramped compartment. Restlessly, he stepped out, only to return with a joke. He referred to the next compartment as containing the whole of Zion. The beauty laughed shrilly. He held her interest with similar *bons mots*. But the intended butt of these barbs remained absorbed in her novel, while the man next to her was altogether enigmatic.

A German soldier got in; they are taller than the local kind, and have broader shoulders. At a sign from the beauty, her two companions moved more closely together and he sat down in the fourth seat. He was only too happy to enter into conversation with his new compatriots, although he didn't seem to catch their drift. Nor, apparently, was he in the least interested in the nature and the character of the company and its racial composition, but talked of the beautiful country and the mild climate. He must have been an as yet unenlightened person, because, oblivious to "the matter in hand," he picked up a handkerchief belonging to the lady opposite him and handed it back to her with a smile. He soon got off the train again. But with the flow of her chatter somewhat diverted, the beauty went off to wash her hands.

She returned surprisingly quickly, threw the door open with a scream and was so agitated that all she could utter was the order to pull the emergency cord. The emergency cord was promptly pulled. After all, her two admirers could think of only one thing: that someone of inferior race had attempted, as was their way, to violate her charms. The train panted and slowed down, while the beauty panted and told the story of her misfortune. She had been washing her hands, oblivious to the fact that the car with the washroom in it was coupled directly behind the locomotive. The window was open. Then, all of a sudden, a huge cloud of smoke swirled in on her, covering her dress with soot. With wet hands, she went to close the window and her diamond ring slipped off her finger and fell out of the moving train on to the tracks.

When the object of her favors realized why he had pulled the emergency cord, he was incensed. The loss of a ring did not seem to him sufficient justification to offer the railroad officials, and he made no effort to conceal his annoyance. At that, she burst into a flood of deeply outraged tears, and so profound was her grief that it was some time before she came round to considering how much she begrudged the woman opposite any enjoyment of her predicament. With a glance full of malice, she dried her eyes and was embraced and comforted by her second companion, who thus quickly seized his advantage. The conductor appeared and asked what was going on—murder, robbery with violence, or threatening behavior? Since he was one of the old guard, he was furious at the irresponsible and trivial reason given and demanded payment of a fine, in cash, as laid down in the regulations.

At this, however, the dashing admirer went into action and achieved ultimate victory in the eyes of the woman from the suburbs. He flipped the lapel of his jacket to reveal his Party badge. Then he issued the order that the train would wait there until the ring had been found. Whereupon the three of them all got out, leaving the official speechless. He went away, came back after a while, looked with concern at their hand luggage, but the train moved off, poorer by one Party badge.

It seemed to the couple now left alone in the compartment as if they had evaded an enormous scandal. As if they themselves had had reason to be ashamed, and now their dignity was restored. They spread themselves comfortably in their compartment, gazed out of the window, dimmed the light and debated how best to make use of the small amount of money that the regulations allowed them for the journey. Should they take supper at a neatly-laid table in the dining car, or should they instead make the most of the peace and quiet of their little compartment and save their money for a rainy day?

They decided in favor of peace and quiet. That night was for them the way it is said to be for the condemned man, although of course that state was not ordained for these two. In that speeding train, what was certain was that images from the past would flash past them both, rocking their fevered brows from side to side and denying them sleep.

Nevertheless, darkness can be soothing. It relaxes tension in the nerves and wafts coolly over burning eyes. The regular jolts of the railroad are reminiscent of heartbeats, because man constructs everything after the patterns of the body, which play such a critical role in preventing him from detaching himself from the processes of the mind. Yes, even these two people rose in the morning, reached for toiletries and towels, washed themselves meticulously and, refreshed and at least somewhat rested, were served breakfast.

The countryside was changing. And the more foreign it became to her, the more secure Eva felt, even though they had not yet reached the border. That dreaded moment was still to come.

The train stopped. Other passengers came aboard. They, too, looked foreign, and their very foreignness was like a promise. One gentleman entered the compartment and had to lower his head as he came through the doorway. It was not necessary to glance at his newspaper to know that what they had here was someone from Britain; a certain practiced unassumingness identified him. Concealed behind his enormous paper, he occupied the second corner seat by the window and, with a glance towards the lady opposite him, he extinguished his cigarette in the ashtray. By the mere fact that three people were now sitting in the compartment, companionably and comfortably silent, the Briton's influence was clearly felt.

During a long stop later on, another gentleman opened the door, a man with lively features and black hair that stuck straight up from his head. He looked around the compartment, and seemed to like what he saw. He sat down in the seat next to the British gentleman and seemed determined to strike up an animated conversation with his fellow passengers. He asked Eva if he might have a look at her magazine, although he only leafed through it briefly, and then he inquired of Kain how long it would be before they reached the frontier and why the train was running so late. His soft, wheedling accents fell kindly on the ear and Kain felt moved to tell him the whole story about the delay, since indeed he knew all about it. The Englishman seemed to understand him, because he pricked up his ears, although his refined features barely betrayed a perceptible smile.

The lively gentleman expressed his thanks for the information and was about to address Eva, but she seemed not to notice. So he then turned to the Englishman, paying no heed to the huge curtain before him, and overcame his reluctance with the remark that military conscription was a good move and the Tommies would soon be joining up with the *poilus*, and under a general in whom even God trusted. The Briton lowered his newspaper and was no longer disinclined to join in a conversation which progressed with a scorn for all Germanisms and in two different accents.

Under different circumstances this meeting of foreign countries, with its halting conversation, would have held Eva spellbound. But she was in a state of profound turmoil. In a few minutes they would be arriving at the border. The dreaded, yet longed-for moment was looming closer and she sat paralyzed as the train drew to a halt.

The optimist took his case down ready for inspection, the Englishman pondered whether he should do likewise, but then remained calmly in his seat. The door was opened. The official stood framed in the doorway. He glanced fleetingly at the two foreigners' passports, and then it was Kain's turn. His travel papers were covered with a whole series of attestations required by the authorities, but he paid them no attention. He wanted to know whether he had any currency in his case, or gold or silver. Kain said he had not, and looked out of the window. The official turned his cold eyes on Eva and asked if she had any valuables in her case.

Her lips trembled. "We have one object of value. Yes. The ashes of our brother!"

The official pursed his lips. So they had allowed an enemy to escape. He handed back the passports and moved to the next compartment.

The four people remained silent.

The Englishman looked out at the bridge at Kehl, which separates two countries. He searched for a turn of phrase which might give solace to this tormented woman, but was unable to come up with anything.

His cheery fellow passenger lit a cigarette. He could not think of anything to say either.

"Is it still possible for the train to go back?" Eva asked at this point, and despite the terrible fear pervading the confined space, they all had to smile.

Kain traveled across the bridge at Kehl and looked back. Stared at the red earth of his homeland, as if nowhere else in the world was there such well-tilled, brown, warm soil; he looked for the mountains, for the veins in the rocks of his homeland, which glow as if from some inner fire warmed by the evening sun.

POSTSCRIPT

Included among Veza Canetti's unpublished works was the typescript of the novel, *Die Schildkröten* (*The Tortoises*), in the form of two versions, an original and a carbon copy (referred to here as Typescript A and Typescript B). Overall, there are no major differences between these two versions. Both have been corrected; Typescript A has a definite conclusion (Chapter XVI) and has been more heavily corrected, while Typescript B contains several different endings which have been crossed out. The chapter numbered VIIIa carries, in Typescript A, the handwritten note, in English, "Extra chapter intended," although without adding a title. For the present edition, the corrections—probably done by Veza Canetti's own hand—have been taken into account. Beyond that, only obvious errors and incomplete punctuation marks have been corrected and the orthography has been standardized. Typescript A carries a title page in Elias Canetti's handwriting: "VEZA MAGD; DIE SCHILDKRÖTEN, Copyright by Elias Canetti, London 1963" as well as—also in his hand—a table of contents.

The novel was written in 1939, during the first months of exile in London, and was accepted by an English publisher in July of that year. The outbreak of the war prevented publication. This is recorded in the chronicle of Veza Canetti's life (below), which appeared in the program of the Schauspielhaus in Zurich, Switzerland, dated May 1992, on the occasion of the premiere performance of her play, *Der Oger* (*The Ogre*), on which Elias Canetti worked in an advisory capacity.

The novel has a discernible autobiographical and historical background. Thus, for instance, the villa which Veza Canetti describes resembles fairly closely the large building in the Himmelstrasse in Grinzing, Vienna, in which Veza and Elias Canetti lived from 1935. It is described in *Das Augenspiel* (*The Play of the Eyes*).* In the Himmelstrasse, too, is the "*Hausfrau*," the "landlady," a Tyrolean woman who rented the apartment out to them, and there, in the extensive garden, stand several statues. The assassination attempt by the "little Jew" (in Chapter XI) is the attack carried out on November 7, 1938, by Herschel Grynspan on the Secretary to the Legation at the German Embassy in Paris, Ernst von Rath, who died on November 9th as a result of his injuries. During the night of November 10th, Jewish shops and institutions were destroyed and looted by the SA, in what the Nazis themselves termed "*Kristallnacht*," the "Night of Broken Glass." A few days later, the Canettis were able to flee from Vienna to Paris.

The Tortoises is a novel, and intended to be read as such. The question as to which real people the characters are based on and which actual historical events are reflected in the action should not be allowed to become the center of interest. Elias Canetti's observation with regard to *Die Gelbe Strasse* (*Yellow Street*) most certainly applies equally to this novel: "She was concerned with real matters, as she said, with people she knew. She was not interested in invention." And later: "But something very remarkable happened: all her characters give the impression of having been invented."

The Tortoises is not only a remarkable work of literature, but also an authentic testimony to our history: the humiliations and the cruel exclusion of people who are accustomed to peaceable and respectful coexistence, and who are completely oblivious to what further desecrations are about to befall them, unaware that they are all supposed to be murdered. It also bears witness to their movingly dignified behavior in this situation and to the scandalous vileness by which they were surrounded.

---

*The third volume of Elias Canetti's autobigraphy, covering the years 1931 to 1937.

The style of the novel also bears this stamp. The terse, pithy style, with which we are familiar from *Yellow Street* and the short stories of Veza Canetti, the masterly narrative tone, which never passes judgment and avoids any expression of hatred, the humor with which people are portrayed, all these seem, occasionally, almost to go awry in this work, as if under pressure from the memory of personal experience. We have refrained from editing any apparently illogical or linguistically confusing turns of phrase. *The Tortoises* is a work of significance, not merely on account of its literary quality, but also because of the circumstances from which it originated—it is a legacy.

—Fritz Arnold, Hanser Verlag

VEZA CANETTI

A Chronicle of Her Life

1 8 9 7

November 21: Venetiana Taubner-Calderon is born in the 3rd District of Vienna. Her father, Hermann, a merchant, comes from a family of Hungarian Jews; the family of her mother, Rachel Calderon, are Jews of Hispanic origin from Zemun in Serbia, who had previously settled in Sarajevo in Bosnia.

Early death of her father. When about thirteen years old, Veza experiences her mother's remarriage. Her short story about life with her stepfather is handed down by Elias Canetti in his *Die Fackel im Ohr* (*The Torch in My Ear*).

School attendance up to university entrance level. Frequent visits to relatives in England, where, among other things, Veza perfects her English.

After the First World War, Veza finds employment as a teacher in a private high school:

"Every time I was late, the head teacher would pointedly pull out his watch, but without saying anything. Within four years, we had brought the school to the brink of financial ruin; after that, private tuition and translations."

In the twenties, Veza lives, with her mother and step-father, in a rented apartment on the Ferdinandstrasse in the 2nd District, the so-called Leopoldstadt, which Veza later used as a basis for the location of *Die Gelbe Strasse* (*Yellow Street*).

Veza takes an intensive interest in literature. She is a regular member of the audience at the lectures given by Karl Kraus.

A mutual acquaintance describes her to Elias Canetti as follows:

"A beautiful woman with a Spanish face. She's very fine and sensitive, and no one could ever say anything ugly in her presence. She's read more than all of us put together. She knows the longest English poems by heart, plus half of Shakespeare. And Molière and Flaubert and Tolstoy . . . But she reads intelligently. She knows why she likes it. She can explain it. You can't put anything over on her."

Elias Canetti, The Torch in My Ear

I 9 2 4

April 17: At a reading by Karl Kraus, Veza meets Elias Canetti for the first time.

"She looked very exotic, a precious object, a creature one would never have expected in Vienna, but rather on a Persian miniature. Her high, arched eyebrows, her long, black lashes, with which she played like a virtuoso, now quickly, now slowly—it all confused me. I kept looking at her lashes instead of into her eyes, and I was surprised at the small mouth."

Elias Canetti, The Torch in My Ear

I 9 3 0 / 3 I

Elias Canetti writes *Die Blendung* (*Auto da Fé*).

In the early thirties, Veza, too, begins to write. Her subjects are those helpless people, those losers in society, whom she constantly comes across during her daily walks through the Leopoldstadt. Above all, she writes about women who are destroyed in the service of others or in a bad marriage.

"There were two principal convictions which kept Veza alive in the conflict with her melancholy: one was a faith in poets, as if it were they alone who kept creating the world anew, as if the world must wither and die the moment there were no poets any more. The other was that inexhaustible admiration for all that a woman can represent, when she deserves the name of woman. Beauty and charm were no less a part of this than pride and a brand of wisdom quite different from the usual one, as represented by men, the one that had come to domination in the world. Her convictions were not far removed from those one comes across often, and in a militant form, among women today, but she held them in those days. Nor did she display them in that rebellious manner that gives rise to divisiveness and aggressive splinter-groups, for she sacrificed nothing of her admiration of beauty, seductiveness or devotion.

Elias Canetti, in the Foreword to
Veza Canetti's *Yellow Street*

1 9 3 2

June: The short story, "Der Sieger" ("The Victor"), by Veza Magd, appears in the *Arbeiter-Zeitung*, Vienna's best-written newspaper between the end of the First World War and 1934. The *Arbeiter-Zeitung* was the organ of the Socialist Party, which governed Vienna at that time. In the literature section, it introduced short stories by Maxim Gorki, Isaak Babel, Joseph Roth and many other modern writers. The editor of the *Feuilleton*, the features section, and the "News of the Day" was Ernst Fischer, and Otto König was responsible for the literature pages.

August: "Geduld bringt Rosen" ("Patience Brings Roses") by Veza Magd appears in the *Arbeiter-Zeitung*.

In 1932 and 1933, the stories which Veza later brought together as the novel *Die Gelbe Strasse* (*Yellow Street*) are written and appear at irregular intervals, along with other pieces. The pseudonyms she uses are: Veza Magd, Veronika Knecht and Martin Murner.

Autumn: the anthology *30 neue Erzähler des neuen Deutschland. Junge deutsche Prosa* (*30 new Writers from the New Germany: Young German Writing*), is published by the Malik Verlag, Berlin, in which "Geduld bringt Rosen" is reprinted. (Since 1929, Elias Canetti had been translating several novels by Upton Sinclair for Wieland Herzfelde and John Heartfield's Malik Verlag imprint.) In the appendix to this first— and, for some considerable period of time—last publication in book form, Veza Magd makes mention of her literary works hitherto:

"My first book was a novel about Kaspar Hauser, and, full of enthusiasm, I sent it to a great writer. He was wise enough to let me wait sufficiently long for a reply for me to be able to provide it for myself. Since then, I have been publishing short stories and the novel *Die Geniesser* (*The Epicures*) in the German and Austrian working-class press." (Neither novel is extant today.)

December: *Arbeiter-Zeitung* competition for "the best short story," in which Veza Magd takes part. Her story, "Ein Kind rollt Gold" ("A Child Rolls Gold"), one of 827 entries submitted, wins second prize; no first prize is awarded.

In the same year, Elias Canetti writes his play *Die Hochzeit* (*The Wedding*).

1 9 3 3

March: "Ein Kind rollt Gold" published in the *Arbeiter-Zeitung*.*

"I myself am a Socialist, and I write in Vienna for the *Arbeiter-Zeitung* under three pseudonyms, because the very kind Dr. König, who has been reappointed, made it clear to me, in his gruff way, that "in the present atmosphere of

---

*This short story later became the first part of the final chapter ("Der Zwinger," translated as "The Fixer") of *Die Gelbe Strasse*.

latent antisemitism, one cannot publish so many stories and novels by a Jewess, and yours are, unfortunately, the best."

Letter, dated March 5, 1950, to Rudolf Hartung,
editor of the Willi Weismann Verlag in Munich.

Elias Canetti moves from 47 Hagenberggasse (where he wrote *Die Blendung*) to live together with Veza at 29 Ferdinandstrasse.

Elias Canetti writes the *Komödie der Eitelkeit* (*Comedy of Vanity*).

1 9 3 4

February: In the course of fierce struggles, Austro-Marxism succumbs to the increasingly fascist corporate state of Chancellor Dollfuss, who had suspended the constitution in 1933 and subsequently ruled with the aid of an Enabling Act. During the lawless period of the uprising by the *Schutzbündler* (Social Democratic Republican Defense Corps) against the police and the military, Ernst Fischer, a Social Democrat and editor at the *Arbeiter-Zeitung*, is on the run and finds shelter, with his wife, at 29 Ferdinandstrasse.

"Veza was filled with consternation. Nevertheless, her warmth and sincerity, her joy at being in a position to help us enabled us to forget that first impression."

Ernst Fischer, *Erinnerungen und Reflexionen*
(*Memoirs and Reflections*)

After the defeat of the Socialists, Veza's opportunities for publication are increasingly closed off. The planned publication of her novel *Die Geniesser* in the *Arbeiter-Zeitung* does not materialize. The novel *Die Gelbe Strasse* also remains unpublished.

Marriage of Veza and Elias Canetti.

Summer: "Drei Helden und eine Frau" ("Three Heroes and a Woman") by Veronika Knecht, published in *Neue deutsche Blätter. Monatszeitschrift für Literatur und Kritik* (Prague—Vienna—Zurich—Paris—Amsterdam. March 1934 to September 1934) (a monthly periodical for literature and criticism)—presumably Veza's last published work before the Second World War.

Der Oger (*The Ogre*), a play, is written using the thematic material of a short story from *Die Gelbe Strasse*, after it had become obvious that no further possibility existed that the novel might achieve publication.

"She considered it the best thing she had ever written. It was the first time she showed me anything without declaring that she did not think much of it. I had encouraged her, in every way, to write. Whatever she showed me, I praised, with conviction, and had to defend it against her. She had for a long time been determined to set no store by her works. . . . But with *The Ogre*, she looked me proudly straight in the eye for the first time and said, 'You will really like this!'"

Elias Canetti, Postscript to *Der Oger*

Autumn: Death of Veza Canetti's mother.

1 9 3 5

September: Veza and Elias Canetti move to 30/8 Himmelstrasse, in Grinzing.

1 9 3 8

March 12: Invasion of Austria by the German National Socialists. *Anschluss*: annexation of Austria into the German Reich.

September: Under the Nazi despotism, the Canettis lose their apartment in the Himmelstrasse. They move into a boarding house in Döbling.

November 9: In Vienna, too, in the course of *Kristallnacht*, most of the synagogues and temples are set on fire; Jewish shops laid waste, apartments looted and destroyed; Jews persecuted, deported and killed.

November 19: The Canettis flee Vienna. Two months at Elias Canetti's brother's home in Paris.

1 9 3 9

From *January*, exile in London. Within three to four months, the novel *Die Schildkröten* is written about the events of the preceding six months, and is accepted by an English publisher in July. The outbreak of the war forestalls publication.

Under the most difficult circumstances, Veza continues to write, in English as well as German.

She keeps herself busy as a translator from English.

1 9 4 7

Her translation of Graham Greene's *The Power and the Glory* is published.

She tries to arouse publishers' interest in her prose writings and her play *Der Oger*, but without the slightest success.

1 9 4 8

A contact with the Schauspielhaus in Zurich (Kurt Hirschfeld) begins promisingly, but does not bring about the desired staging of the play.

1 9 5 6

A novel by Veza Canetti is rejected. In a fit of melancholy, she destroys many of her manuscripts, and from then on she writes nothing else.

1 9 6 3

May 1: Death of Veza Canetti in London.

1 9 9 0

Die Gelbe Strasse published, with a preface by Elias Canetti, by the Hanser Verlag, Munich. To date, the book has been translated into seven languages.

1 9 9 1

Publication of the play *Der Oger*.

1 9 9 2

"Geduld bringt Rosen," a short story by Veza Canetti, published by Hanser Verlag, Munich.

Premiere of the play *Der Oger* in the Schauspielhaus, Zurich. Director: Werner Düggelin.